MINUS 14:30 HOURS.
JULY 2, WASHINGTON.

Peggy was chatting with a handsome colonel who had brought her a cup of coffee. Williams felt a twinge of jealousy. He was convinced he had put his affair with Peggy behind him, but now that she was here—

Peggy saw his glance and came over to him. "I see green. You look good in that color."

Williams turned to General Maxwell. "Is there any chance of finding the bomb *after* it's planted?" he asked. But Maxwell shook his head.

Williams reminded Maxwell that one of the small two-man oceanographic subs had found the hydrogen bomb dropped by accident into the sea off Spain some years ago. The General shrugged. "That operation took weeks, not hours. And with just a few subs to cover the whole ocean all the way out to the horizon they don't have a chance. Science won't help us here, George. If that nuclear bomb has been planted, only the man himself can save us by telling us where it is. And I don't think that's part of his plan."

"TAUT ... EXCITING!"
—Hartford Courant

"A compelling, fast-paced thriller."
—Publishers Weekly

THE BENEDICT ARNOLD CONNECTION

Joseph DiMona

A DELL BOOK

This book is dedicated to my friend and editor,
Hillel Black, whose wisdom and insight shaped
the story from beginning to end . . .

. . . and to my wife, Barbara,
who lived the book with me, and was so
enthusiastic and helpful all the way.

Published by
DELL PUBLISHING CO., INC.
1 Dag Hammarskjold Plaza
New York, N.Y. 10017

ISBN: 0-440-10935-3

Reprinted by arrangement with
William Morrow and Co., Inc.

Printed in the United States of America.

First Dell printing—November 1978

BOOK I

For
Revenge
of
Nancy

1

JUNE 30, A SUNNY DAY IN MINOT, NORTH DAKOTA. George Williams, Deputy Assistant Attorney General, U. S. Justice Department, stood beside the cyclone fence, which bore a sign, "Restricted, U. S. Government property." Beyond the fence strange humps of green steel and concrete dotted the government reservation.

In one of these humps the blast-resistant doors were open. The Air Force major with the light blond moustache said to Williams, "A fly couldn't get by that fence. Look at the sensors." He was pointing to metallic objects on three steel poles in a triangle inside the government reservation. Williams knew the sensors could detect any movement at all near this Minute Man III launching area, even outside the fence, and relay the warning electronically to a central command post which would dispatch security teams armed with machine guns. In addition to the sensors around them, each silo was equipped with electronic guards of its own which flashed a warning to headquarters if anyone touched the doors. Absolutely secure, fail-safe, untouchable.

Until last night.

Williams had known it would happen, but had always comforted himself with the fact that the Air Force was just as aware as he. Sooner or later the terrorist groups that had sprouted in the post-Watergate era would realize that hijackings and kidnappings were small, unproductive acts. And across the U. S. and Europe forty thousand nuclear warheads were stored in warehouses, planted in lonely plains, shipped in trains and trucks, in one way or another accessible.

But not just to anyone, Williams thought. The Air Force had taken too many precautions. What you needed was a superb organizer with a brilliant mind. His eyes took in the sensors and the open doors. No way anyone could avoid those sensors. Yet someone had gotten by. Someone had somehow opened the eighty-ton silo doors and stripped three nuclear MIRVs from the missile. And no warning had sounded.

"They had to have inside help," Williams said.

"Even with inside help it's impossible!" the major replied. But Williams wasn't listening. He had turned and looked across the little dirt road that ran parallel to the fence and saw something glitter in the sun. He walked across the road and was immediately disappointed. A piece of clear plastic with a fragment of a map inside. No doubt a road map, left by the occasional tourist who came by.

Still, Williams was thorough, as always. He pried open the plastic and started to pull the map fragment loose, but it crumbled. An old map. That was odd. *Very* odd. His fingers brushed across the paper, and that was even more puzzling. It wasn't even paper. A thicker material.

Williams stopped trying to pry out the map and looked at it through the clear plastic. It seemed to be an old military campaign map, with notes written in faded ink in the margin that he could just barely make out. The major was at his side now. "What the hell have you found?"

"I don't know," Williams said.

The major took the plastic-enclosed map fragment and held it a few inches from his eyes. Then he turned to Williams with a strange look. He said, "Did you read it?"

"Yes."

The major handed the map back to Williams. "Now let's not get crazy, Mr. Williams. Let's just try to figure out quietly what this means."

"You figure it out," said Williams, who once again was looking at words on an ancient map fragment found next to an ICBM site in the twentieth century. The mind behind the crime had been good enough to leave a clue to his motive.

In faded ink, the words said:

"For revenge of Nancy, beloved of Benedict Arnold."

2

TO: All Army, Air Force, Navy, and Marine commanders U. S. and abroad.

FROM: Chairman, U. S. Joint Chiefs of Staff.

SUBJECT: Missing nuclear MIRVs in unknown hands.

REF: AEC dated June 30, Ser. No. 73586/1, addressee Joint Chiefs of Staff.

CLASSIFICATION: MAXIMUM SECRET. Commanders only. No staff distribution or clearance.

The Atomic Energy Commission informs all heads of agencies and commands on personal basis only (no staff) that missing MIRVs are equipped with internal electronic safeguards that prevent explosion when not attached to the missile electronic system. These safeguards were installed to thwart accidental or other explosion by terrorist groups who may obtain the nuclear devices.

However, AEC concedes the possibility that the nuclear devices can be disassembled, and the electronic safeguards removed. AEC claims such a feat would be near miraculous and beyond the means and comprehension of all but a few engineers known to them, and those few are employed and accounted for at AEC.

In this regard, AEC states that more than one person penetrated the base. The size and weight of the nose cone and silo doors indicates more than one man was required. And at least one of the thieves had high technical skill necessary to evade the electronic safeguards surrounding the base and penetrate the silo itself.

In this emergency the President has asked the Chairman of the Joint Chiefs of Staff to personally supervise the investigation. The FBI, CIA, and other investigatory agencies will coordinate under my office.

At the further suggestion of the President, I have appointed Mr. George Williams, on temporary leave from the Justice Department, as my aide in the field. Any information of any kind should be passed at once to my office in the Pentagon, or to Williams, who will maintain his office at the Justice Department.

Destroy this memo after reading.

ROBERT MAXWELL, *Gen. USA*
Chairman
U. S. Joint Chiefs of Staff

3

10:30 A.M., JUNE 30, WASHINGTON. THE PRESIDENT of the United States stood on the lawn of the White House with a twelve-year-old girl in a green dress and a sash that said, "Dayton, Ohio, Girl Scout Troop Ten." The girl had written an essay called, "What's Right about America."

It was a photo opportunity for television and newspaper photographers. The President was usually effective at these affairs, projecting a "down-home" image that went over well with the public.

Today the President was smiling and cordial as ever, but as soon as the session ended he turned to an aide and said, with irritation, "We have to cancel all appointments today. Put out a story that I've developed a cold."

One of his aides pointed out that the President of an African country was supposed to be received at eleven and the Secretary of Agriculture at twelve on an import bill that would be voted that afternoon in Congress. But the President merely muttered, "A cold. That's the story."

The aides understood, although they had been urging the President to carry on business as usual ever since the startling news came from a small North Dakota air base five hours ago that three nuclear weapons were in unknown hands. There was no use inciting the public to panic before a message was received from the thieves.

A soft breeze billowed the blue drapes of the Oval

Office as the President entered. Five men sat in chairs awaiting his return from the photo session. Two of them were hunched together over a computer read-out. The President had called in the head of the Secret Service, the Assistant Director of the FBI, the CIA Director, the Atomic Energy Commission Director, and the Chairman of the Joint Chiefs of Staff, as an impromptu staff to advise him on this unprecedented emergency. Already the Army had set up roadblocks in North Dakota, issued warnings to Canadian border patrols, begun x-raying all baggage at transportation centers throughout America.

The President sat down. "We can't hold the story long, gentlemen."

Gen. Robert Maxwell, Chairman of the Joint Chiefs, was a tall, chesty man. He said, "My MPs are instructed to tell drivers that one ounce of radioactive material is missing from a nuclear power plant. But I agree that cover won't hold up long."

The President turned to John Pierpont, head of the Secret Service, and Fred Jarvis, Assistant Director of the FBI. "What have you found?"

The two men had been examining all terrorist threats that had arrived at the White House or at other agencies of the government in the last few months. The list filled a computer read-out, single space, a foot and a half long. The actual letters and telephone transcripts were in three bulky files. Jarvis said, "There are bombings promised all over the place—and some of them actually occurred. But no nuclear threats."

The President said to General Maxwell, "I want you to turn the Army into one million domestic policemen to search for these criminals, along with the FBI. And I'm authorizing you to take whatever action needed in case these people threaten a particular target. To be blunt, General, shoot first and worry about the law later."

The words—"threaten a particular target"—hung in the room. In that phrase the President echoed the major worry of everyone in the White House since the first moment when the FBI TWX had streaked over wires from Minot, North Dakota. A terrorist gang had finally managed to steal nuclear bombs. They could plant them in New York, Washington, Boston, wherever they wished. Then they could allow the government a few hours to meet an outrageous political demand, or see great cities destroyed. Now General Maxwell reminded the President that the nuclear bombs were MINERVA I's, the newest and most miniaturized generation of MIRVs. "We only have one base equipped with MINERVAs. It's odd that they hit that one base."

Robert Winthrop, the CIA Director, said, "You're implying it was the Soviets? I can't see Russian agents climbing over a fence in the middle of America to steal nuclear weapons. And, besides, the MINERVAs aren't a *new* weapon. They're just an improvement on existing weaponry. I don't think it would be worth the risk to them."

General Maxwell said he agreed, but he thought it should be borne in mind anyway, considering past Soviet actions. "President Kennedy couldn't believe the Soviets would risk installing ICBMs in Cuba, right under our eyes. But they did."

But the President said, "It *can't* be the Soviets now. You're suggesting they'd steal nukes just when we're ready to sign the new SALT III agreement limiting nuclear weapons? That doesn't make sense."

None of them spoke for a moment, considering the President's words. His logic was sound. The nuclear arms limitation, sharply lowering the number of nuclear weapons in the U.S. and the Soviet Union, had caused bitter division among his advisers. But the President was committed to lessening the "nuclear terror" that hung over the world; to "reversing the arms race." And he had decided to sign SALT III next month.

Finally Winthrop, the CIA Director, asked, "So who else could it be?"

Fred Jarvis, the Assistant FBI Director, was tall, gray-haired, and wore an old tweed coat and unpressed trousers. He smoked a pipe, and, thought the President, had a casual manner that was as unlike the conventional FBI image as your could imagine. But he was said to possess the most astute brain in the agency. Now Jarvis said, "There are at least twelve Middle East and African nations who would love to have three working nukes, aren't there?" The President nodded, and Jarvis continued, "Maybe they were stolen for sale, and no American cities will ever be threatened."

"Like robbing a store?" the President asked. "For money?"

"It's good merchandise," Jarvis said.

The President's buzzer sounded. He said on the intercom, "Send him in." A man in a gray suit, white shirt, and bright red tie, entered the office. "I'm Joe Randall, Mr. President. I have the AEC analysis of the MINERVA I."

The President read the analysis aloud. "If the MINERVA I is detonated in a densely populated urban center, the explosion would kill or injure all residents within an area of twenty square miles.

"But this is not the most dangerous application of the nuclear bombs in the hands of the terrorists. If MINERVA I is exploded underwater offshore, it will create a tidal wave one hundred feet high, filled with radioactive water that would poison hundreds of thousands of square miles, in addition to the deaths and injuries sustained."

Silence as everyone in the President's office visualized a hundred-foot-high tidal wave bearing down on beaches. The President stopped reading and said urgently, "We just *have* to recover those bombs. We can't allow uncontrolled people to have such power in their hands." He turned to Jarvis, "Has George Williams turned up anything at Minot?"

Jarvis asked to see the President alone, and after the advisers filed out, said, "Williams has found a clue that may mean nothing. A piece of what appears to be an authentic two-hundred-year-old map was found near the silo. It has a note, 'For revenge of Nancy, beloved of Benedict Arnold.' Now just in case it's genuine, Williams wants you to keep that clue confidential."

The President stared at Jarvis. "But . . . why? It's so . . . silly. Surely he doesn't believe—"

"On the off-chance that the map is genuine, it's the kind of clue you want to save in secret, until you get a suspect. It's routine police procedure, Mr. President."

The President was so stunned he could hardly retain his composure. All the way to Minot to find clues to thieves who stole nuclear bombs, and that was Williams' only contribution? An ancient map that could be a page from a discarded Bicentennial program—and meanwhile live terrorists were somewhere in this country with live nuclear bombs!

That was the great George Williams, the President thought. Jarvis and his other advisers had insisted that the President place Williams in charge of the investigation under General Maxwell. The President now regretted it. Williams had had success assisting the FBI on certain Justice Department cases, including a famous one in 1973. But, for God's sake, he wasn't even a trained investigator. He was only a Justice Department lawyer. An amateur.

4

Wind blew across the North Datoka plains. George Williams climbed down a ladder into silo Baker. The interior of the silo was a shambles. A storm of bolts from the nose cone had smashed into black boxes and the interior silo walls. The major followed Williams, picking his way carefully past the debris. Both men stood on Level One, a circular stage that surrounded the base of the nose cone, which was six feet high. The cone had been tilted on its side against a wall by the thieves while they removed the MIRVs. "Incredible," the major said. "Those were explosive bolts that held the cone to the body. According to our engineers it was impossible to trigger them from outside the missile. But one of the people who came down here knew better."

Williams asked about the alarms and was told that the silo doors, the ladder they had just descended, and the stage they were standing on were all wired. Move the silo door one inch or step on the ladder, and sirens would sound in command central underground.

A man who could calculate how to trigger explosive bolts from outside could also figure ways to bypass those interior alarms, Williams thought. But he would still need-keys to open the silo doors. Where had he gotten them? Williams and the major went outside and stood in the sun beside the silo. This break-in had been perfectly planned. Nothing left to chance. FBI agents examining the ground for footprints reported that the terrorists had worn Army boots precisely like those of the military personnel who swarmed over the grounds after the theft was discovered.

And the sensors had been defeated by the thieves' knowledge that they were vulnerable. Rain was motion and the sensors detected motion, so their screens were blurred and made useless in a storm. The thieves had waited patiently until rain struck the base, and made their move.

But they still needed those silo door keys. Williams went to see the Commanding General, a scrawny, cigar-waving man. "Come in, come in, Mr. Williams. I'm a career corpse right now. Sent my resignation to the Air Force as soon as this happened. I guess they've been too busy to accept it."

Williams said, "Anything unusual occur on the base in the last few months?"

"Such as?"

"One of your men seen around that silo when he shouldn't have been there?" He paused. "The thieves had to have keys to open the silo doors. Someone could have gotten wax impressions, then made duplicates."

But the General said that was absolutely impossible. "The sensors would have picked up anyone who moved a step near those silos when he shouldn't have been there."

Except in the rain, Williams thought. He asked the General who had access to the silos. "Maintenance," the General said. "The rest of us only get a peep in them when VIPs come to get their picture taken." But Williams' next question surprised him.

"When was the last time it rained before last night?"

"Oh, not for a couple of weeks. You want the precise date?" Williams said yes, and the General called an aide, who in turn had to consult with his secretary. The date of the last rainfall was June 12. Williams asked who was on maintenance duty that night, and this time the aide checked the records and came through with the answer quickly. "Sergeants Peterson and Colbert, sir. They had the night shift, and that's when it rained."

Peterson was on the base, Colbert was home with a cold, but both men said they would come to the General's office. The first to arrive was Peterson. A bulky man, he nervously shifted his feet as he answered questions. The General began by asking him whether anything exceptional happened on their shift that night. The sergeant hesitated, then said, "Well—"

He stopped. The General was irritated. "Sergeant, nuclear bombs have been stolen from this base. I won't have any of my men—"

But the sergeant interrupted his commanding general. "I think Colbert should answer for himself, sir."

"You tell us what you know first," the General said, and the sergeant finally answered, "Sir, Colbert's a happily married man. I know that. I've been to his house, met his wife. He has a baby."

"What in God's name has that got to do with anything," the General said angrily.

Peterson said, "Well, this one night when it rained, Colbert told me he had something going on the side. Another woman, sir. So he asked me to cover for him while he slipped out for a few hours."

5

SERGEANT COLBERT PRESSED THE ACCELERATOR TO the floor. His Volkswagen careened around a curve on Route 28, heading out of town. When the Commanding General had called and asked him about the night of June 12 he knew he was finished. He called Washington and was told to go immediately to a previously undisclosed "friend" of the organization who lived fifty miles away in Sawyer, North Dakota. The "friend" would give him shelter and a place to hide.

His wife had stared at him while he made the call. "What's happening, Bill? Why are you so upset?"

And what could he tell her? He said it was Air Force business. "Secret. Don't worry, honey. I'll have to drop out of sight for a few days but I'll contact you." But then he let her know that something was horribly wrong when he said to her at the door, "Whatever anyone says, I've been faithful to you."

Brown treeless plains of North Dakota stretched on either side of the asphalt road. Nowhere to hide along this route if they came after him! What a place this was. In New York he could have vanished into thousands of buildings.

The MP roadblock didn't surprise Colbert. He braked to a stop, made a hasty U-turn, and started back. Army cars roared in pursuit, then helicopters showed in the distance, beating their way across the sky toward the moving dot on the highway, and Colbert was done, a traitor for $50,000 cash.

He couldn't face a trial. People spitting at him. His family disgraced, and no money coming in while he was in prison. If he wasn't shot. But if he did what he was supposed to do in this emergency his wife and daughter would receive $200,000 cash from the organization in Washington that hired him. And the organization was very good about money. He was crying as he slowed the car, reached into his coat for a small packet, and contemplated a pill the organization had issued to him.

Williams arrived to find MPs standing beside a parked Volkswagen. Colbert's body was slumped over the wheel. Later a toxicologist told Williams it was cyanide. They stood in an Army hospital with Colbert's body on a white clothed table, his chest cavity opened. The dead Army sergeant named Colbert couldn't tell Williams who had stolen the bombs. He couldn't even tell him why a map had been left at the missile site. But the cyanide pill was a clue in itself that worried Williams.

Cyanide pills meant a very special kind of organization was involved in this nuclear theft. The pills were standard issue among espionage agencies around the world.

Not excluding the CIA.

6

THE NUCLEAR BOMBS WERE STILL MISSING AND NO threat had yet arrived as Williams interviewed Colbert's young wife, who was holding a baby in a red wool blanket and crying. No, she had never seen her husband with any civilian or stranger of any sort in Minot. Williams didn't want to do it, but he pressed the distraught wife. "Any unusual telephone calls? Unexplained absences? Odd letters?"

The wife hesitated. She was in blue jeans and black blouse. "Not here," she said, finally.

"What do you mean?"

"He had what you call unexplained absences in the Middle East. We were with the Army weapons program in Lebanon. Bill was always on the go then. If he got mixed up with something funny, it was there. Ever since he's been in Minot, he's been a saint."

She started to cry again, rubbing a fist across her eyes like a child, and Williams told her he was finished with the interrogation. He wouldn't be getting much more from her now. The local FBI agents would grill her later, when she was more calm, to see if a nugget of information surfaced. He stood up to leave and the woman looked at him, reproachfully, tears streaming down a reddened face. "Vultures, you are. All of you. How do you know my Bill had anything to do with this?" She stopped, then said bitterly, "You may have *frightened* him to death."

But where did he get the cyanide pill? Williams thought. However, he remained silent. The woman patted the baby's back through the blanket. She said, "But if he was mixed up with bad people I want you to get *them*." She stood up, walked to an old maple bureau, and took out a folded note. "I used to go through his wallet because he had a habit of writing down girls' names and telephone numbers in those bars he always went to. Now this one didn't mean anything to me, so I kept it to ask him about. But I forgot about it."

She unfolded the note and handed it to Williams. It read "D.M. June 29."

"Just the initials D.M. and the date," the woman said. "I don't know whether they mean anything."

Williams didn't know either, but June 29 was the date of the theft. He placed the note in his wallet, thanked the widow, and left for the nearby air base, where a military jet was waiting to fly him back to Washington. Fred Jarvis of the FBI had been on the phone. Washington was apparently going crazy with fear about the missing nuclear weapons, and Jarvis said the President wanted him back.

"Your inside man is dead," Jarvis told Williams. "And the only clue you've found is an old map that the President is convinced is a fake and waste of time. So come back here and hold his hand."

Williams flew to Washington, the bizarre features surrounding the break-in keeping him awake all the way. Paramount in his mind was that cyanide pill, and its inference of an espionage agency. Was it possible the KGB was involved? The Soviets had never in thirty years of the cold war made such an overt move.

Williams didn't want to think of the other espionage agency that just might be implicated. He had been accused only last night at dinner of turning soft on the CIA.

At the time he thought the accusation was all that he needed. The dinner was in honor of his birthday, perhaps the most wracking birthday he had ever experienced. And at the end of it he had to listen to an intense, pretty brunette from New York attack him on the one subject that made him angry, the same subject that worried him now, his failure to cope with the people in Langley.

7

EARLY THIS MORNING WHEN THE THEFT OF THE nuclear bombs had been discovered at Minot, George Williams had awakened in Washington with a hangover, only the third he could remember in the last five years. He also woke with the pretty young brunette in his bed.

She was a reporter for *New York* magazine, in Washington to do a story on the Justice Department. Apparently she had confessed to Williams' hostess at his birthday dinner that she had a "weakness" for one lawyer, Williams. Ever since 1973.

In that year Williams tracked down a young assassin who, on the tenth anniversary of President Kennedy's death, intended to slay six people who had worked for John Kennedy in 1963. His motive was to gain nationwide attention for his exposure of a hard-line group of CIA agents who were committing various domestic crimes. Williams, one of the six intended victims, had managed to trace the killer, beginning with no clue. And in the process he had found himself locked in a struggle with CIA.

Williams had lost that fight. But still young people like the reporter remembered him because he had tried so hard.

Now, the morning of the nuclear theft, the phone had rung for the sixth time. Williams glanced at his watch and saw it was 7 A.M. He answered quietly so as not to disturb the brunette, who now lay on her back in his bed, breathing gently.

Fred Jarvis told him there was a major threat to the
national security, and the President wanted Williams to
head the investigation under General Maxwell. "Nuclear bombs, George. Three of them. Broke through a
whole set of electronic barriers to do it, and now the
nukes are gone and the President's sweating blood."

Williams said he would be right in and hung up. The
theft of the bombs seemed almost appropriate. A perfect punctuation point to the last twenty-four hours in
which Williams had faced his life and found it wanting.

His birthday had begun peacefully enough. He had
gone to his office in the Justice Department at Fifteenth
and Pennsylvania, where he worked on a legal brief.
But lunch was with a disturbing visitor from a New
York law firm. A former U. S. attorney, Peter Gordon
had joined a Wall Street firm and was now reputed to
be earning $100,000 a year.

Gordon's message to Williams was simple. "You're
thirty-eight. You've been with Justice fifteen years.
You've paid your dues, and you're not going higher in
the department. It's time you made your move to private practice if you're ever going to do it."

Williams said that he enjoyed working at the Justice
Department, that he still felt there were things he could
do, and Gordon smiled tolerantly. "I felt that way once
myself. I really believed I could do something for the
country by remaining in government service starving on
a civil servant's pay. It isn't worth it, George."

Williams had disagreed, but thanked Gordon for his
advice. His mind, however, kept reverting to that conversation all day. His birthday made it so relevant. He
was indeed thirty-eight. He was never going to be Attorney General; his actions in the past had been too
controversial, and he had many enemies throughout the

government because he didn't compromise—and compromise was what Washington was all about.

And in this uncertain mood brought on by his birthday, he went to the glittering little dinner given in his honor by Washington's most glamorous hostess. The hostess, Sylvia Conrad, was a friend of his former wife, Sarah.

Williams' social life had undergone a dramatic change since two events had occurred: his divorce from Sarah, which made him "eligible," and a two-month affair with a beautiful New York woman named Peggy DuPont, which apparently gave him an enduring cachet in social circles.

Williams had always been regarded as handsome by women, even sexy. His aloofness seemed to intrigue rather than discourage them. And Peggy DuPont had passed the word that he wasn't as aloof as he appeared. Now hardly a week went by without his telephone ringing, and a hopeful hostess babbling about a lovely new girl who had just arrived in town. Williams turned down most of the invitations, but—lonely in the Georgetown house that his wife had abandoned—accepted some. In the period after Sarah had left him and before he met Peggy DuPont he had gone through a "hermit" phase, which he realized was not healthy for him.

He found people he knew at the dinner, a Washington *Post* editor and his wife, a Democratic Senator and his mistress, a *New York Times* correspondent and his date, and the Secretary of State and his wife. Sylvia Conrad had arranged a "birthday present" for Williams. The "present" turned out to be the *New York* magazine reporter. Sylvia called Williams aside and explained with a smile. "She asked me if I had any contacts in the Justice Department to help her story, and when I mentioned your name I swear she started to shudder. I didn't know you inspired such passion."

The dinner proceeded with quiet elegance, white-jacketed servants moving into the room with antique silver serving trays; wine poured from behind your shoulder as soon as your glass became half empty; political conversation revolving around the Secretary of State. The obligatory humorous remarks were made about Williams' advancing age, and a cane was promised by the *Times* man, to go with the necessary wheelchair.

Williams enjoyed himself because he liked the Secretary of State, but it was after dinner that he experienced his second disturbing conversation. Gail Matson, the reporter for *New York* magazine, turned out to have some reservations about him after all. "You sold out, didn't you?"

Williams didn't answer. He knew what she was talking about. It had been mentioned in a publication called the *Village Voice* a few weeks earlier, a copy of which had come to his desk. Gail Matson, who was sitting next to him, said, "In 1973 you promised to resign from the Justice Department if you didn't have success rooting out those monsters at CIA. But nothing happened. You stayed right on your job, as tame as a pussycat."

Williams said his personal investigation was continuing, a comment that brought a spark to her eyes. "Can I quote you on that?"

"Quote whatever you like," Williams said. "It won't make any difference with me—*or* CIA." The reporter wanted to know more. All this time when he was supposedly doing routine legal work had he secretly carried on his investigation? What about the Senate investigation of CIA assassinations? Was he involved in that, too?

Williams said it was his birthday, and the interview was over, but apparently he now had a committed devotee. The servants steadily poured the wine, and late that night Gail Matson, George Williams, and the rest of the party decided to go to Clyde's—a Georgetown saloon—because it was so "campy," and ended up in the Omelette Room with another Senator and his wife. Williams drank considerably more than usual the evening of his birthday, wondering about a move to a private job, Gordon's remark that he was getting nowhere, and the conversation about his failure with CIA, which still wounded him. He had lost that war long ago. Gail Matson was right, and if the struggle did continue, as he had said, it did so only in his mind. He had given up.

Williams did not want to think of his failures on his birthday. He had made a decision that a one-man war on CIA was absurd, could not work, would collapse as the Senate investigation eventually failed—in a cloud of cover, cutouts, shredded documents, and the insistence of the American people that they needed CIA. And Williams had turned his attention to other matters that concerned the country, ranging from organized crime to antitrust cases, and pursued his legal work at Justice like any other lawyer.

Suddenly Williams decided he wanted to leave. He paid his respects to his hostess, thanked the others, and went out into the street with the brunette clinging to his arm. It was going to be one of those nights. But different, too, because Williams, who rarely drank, realized he was high.

It was 2 A.M. when the reporter and Williams arrived at his Georgetown house. He was more than two hours into his thirty-eighth year and time was slipping by. Had he achieved anything at all with his life? His wife, Sarah, had left him because of his absorption in his Justice Department job. Did his career at Justice matter, anyway? All the effort, the drive, the urge to "contrib-

ute," Bobby Kennedy's favorite word? Right now all
that should concern him on his birthday was an eager
young brunette who had told him she was living with a
"really nice guy" in New York, but that he, George
Williams, was "adorable," that he really turned her on.
So they made love passionately, and in their frenzy Williams abandoned himself to physical pleasure and the
release it brought him.

But sex was only a momentary answer for Williams,
who awoke the next morning in a mental and alcoholic
haze, feeling uncertain about the life he had chosen, to
hear that nuclear bombs were stolen. And the FBI was
convinced that incredibly powerful nuclear weapons
were in the hands of terrorists who could destroy American cities. And he, George Williams, was needed again.

8

FRED JARVIS WAS WAITING FOR HIM AT 4 A.M. JULY 1
at Andrews Air Force Base in Washington.

Williams showed Jarvis the note that read "D.M.
June 29" that he had found in Sergeant Colbert's effects, but Jarvis was unimpressed. "We can't do much
with just initials."

He took Williams to his house in Georgetown. Williams said he would sleep until eight unless a communication arrived from the terrorists. Before Williams
opened the car door Jarvis said, "One of the nuclear
experts cheered all of us up today. He said that there
was no way you could stop the terrorists from transport-
ing and planting those MIRVs in any city they want.

The MIRVs are only eighteen inches long; and if you shield them with lead the Geiger counters won't detect them."

Williams said, "Then this is more 'cheerful' news. There must be a brilliant scientist on the team that went in there. The sergeant on the base helped them break into the silo. But once they were inside they had to remove a six-foot nose cone to get at the bombs. It should have taken hours."

"How did they do it?" Jarvis asked.

"Even the engineers can't tell. The bolts that held the warhead are all over the place." He paused. "They say at least one of the terrorists may be a genius."

"That good?"

"That bad," Williams said.

He exited from the car, and Jarvis saw the tall Justice Department man walk up the steps to his little red brick Georgetown house with the white shutters, and the brass lamp by the door. He wondered again what a strange man Williams was. So serene and composed on the surface. Always in control. Yet that affair with Peggy DuPont had hurt George, Jarvis knew that.

Jarvis drove off as it began to rain. The water pouring down his windshield reminded him of that tidal wave the AEC expert had mentioned. Was that really one of the possibilities? A catastrophe like that! Could any scientist, with his unique knowledge of the terrible power of those weapons, create such a wanton destructive force?

The scientist would have to be insane.

Peggy DuPont, daughter of the Duchess D'Ur-
bahn and Charles DuPont, an investment banker,
was intrigued when she heard that descendents of Benedict Arnold in America, Canada, and England were
gathering at Lake Champlain. She telephoned a cousin,
Ted Otis, and talked him into flying there with her. Otis
also had the Arnold brand but didn't even know it until
she told him a cousin of a cousin had passed on treason-
ous blood to him.

"They think Benedict was mistreated in the Bicentennial," Peggy said. "The party line is that he won the
Revolutionary War singlehanded *before* he sold out to
the British. But they gave Arnold no credit at all in the
pageant. So we gallant descendents are going to recreate
one of his victories and send the message right up
Washington's monument."

Otis laughed, and on June 30 they had flown north
across the forests, mountains, and pine-bordered rivers
of upper New York State and landed near a crystal blue
finger of Lake Champlain.

They took rooms that night at a Holiday Inn twenty
miles south of Plattsburg near Valcour Island, the site
of a Revolutionary War battle where Arnold's men had
built wooden gunboats out of the forest and turned back
a superior fleet of large British men-of-war.

They found the Inn crowded with Arnold descendents, most of them young, and many of them staring at

Peggy, whose photographs had often adorned the society pages of newspapers and magazines. Soft auburn hair that tumbled loosely around her shoulders, deep-set blue eyes beneath a wide lovely forehead, a fine up-curving nose; Peggy's fragile beauty was a legend in her set. But so was her sense of humor, which kept her suitors off balance. At least one wounded admirer had described Peggy, ruefully: "Body by Rubens, tongue by Gillette."

July 1 dawned clear and lovely on Lake Champlain. An eighteenth-century British warship armed with ancient stout cannon floated on the water, surrounded by wooden gunboats and rafts representing Arnold's ragtag fleet. As Peggy and Otis parked their car on a hill overlooking the lake that morning a cannon boomed from the British ship, and white smoke drifted in wisps from its muzzle. Peggy half expected an iron ball to fall among the occupants of an American raft.

None did, and at 9:30 A.M. Peggy sat lazily in the sun watching a short, muscular young man perform acrobatics on the beach. He had one rather clever trick. He would run toward a friend on the beach and leap at him, feet first. His friend would catch one foot and propel the acrobat into a soaring pinwheel high above the heads of the onlookers.

While Peggy watched, the acrobatic little man landed gracefully, and a buxom redhead in a white bikini rushed to congratulate him.

Peggy said to Otis, "We have talent with us."

"Yes. Illegitimate."

Peggy asked him what that meant and was informed that the acrobatic young man had told everyone he was a descendent of Arnold's mistress. Arnold started a shipping business in England after the war and sailed to

Canada on business ventures. He would remain there for months, and that's why "eight generations later we have an acrobat on the beach."

Peggy was fascinated. "All the history books I ever read say Arnold was hopelessly in love with his wife, Peggy Shippen. What was the mistress's name?"

"I didn't catch it," Otis said. "Who could be interested in a woman who's been dead two hundred years?"

BOOK II

The Strange
Behavior
of
Leonard Chew

1

9 A.M., JULY 1, A SAFE HOUSE IN BRYN MAWR, PENN-sylvania. Leonard Chew, a quiet man in a blue suit and vest, sipped a cup of coffee with the two associates who had accompanied him to Minot.

Yesterday morning, after the break-in, they had flown in a small private plane to Detroit, changed to a Lear jet for the trip across the country to a private field near Philadelphia, arriving before dawn. All day yesterday, as instructed, they had remained in the safe house in suburban Bryn Mawr to make certain they were not being pursued. Today they would make the nuclear bombs operational and deliver them to the organization. Mike Jensen asked Chew, "How long will it take to arm the MIRVs?"

Chew placed his cup in its saucer. He was wearing thin brown leather gloves. "An hour—unless we run into surprises."

The two men in the kitchen with Chew looked at each other. Jim Allworth, a slim young mustachioed man in jeans, asked tensely, "What surprises? You mean they might have boobytrapped the bombs?"

"They'll have a few devices inside to prevent premature explosion," Chew said.

The three men hired to steal nuclear bombs were a disparate group. Leonard Chew, at forty, was by far the oldest. He had been employed by the people in Washington to be the strategist and technician for the operation. Mike Jensen, twenty-seven, was a pilot who had conducted a profitable drug trade between Mexico and the States. Jensen was notoriously short-tempered, and quick with a gun.

Jim Allworth, only twenty-two, had four years' experience planting and exploding bombs in San Francisco and Los Angeles for radical causes. He was intelligent—disliked Jensen—was frightened of Chew, and wished he had never accepted this job, even with the kind of money they had promised him. The nuclear theft was too heavy, too awesome, completely out of his sphere. His little plastique operations were child's play compared to the world Chew knew.

And the complications! Jensen told Allworth the word from up top was to "watch Chew," that he was "unstable," with a history of mental illness. *Mental illness*—and he was going to be trusted to handle nuclear bombs? When Allworth heard that, he wanted to quit. Why did they hire someone like that? he asked Jensen. But Jensen didn't know. "He must have been the only one available," he said.

But that was not the real reason Chew was hired, Allworth thought. During the MIRV theft Allworth had recognized genius when he saw it. A team of maintenance men would have taken hours in that silo to remove the towering nose cone that hid the nuclear MIRVs; Chew had done it in minutes. He was a master, this chunky man who seemed so diffident and detached, a consummate pro who never hurried even under the most critical pressure.

Still, Jensen's words about Chew haunted Allworth as they walked down the stairway to a game room. There he saw thick green carpeting, gleaming aluminum exercise equipment, a mahogany bar with stools, and a pool table in the center of the room. But the men's attention was riveted to the area where the stolen MIRVs stood. Enough power in a few feet of space to level every building within twenty miles.

2

LEONARD CHEW PICKED UP ONE MIRV AND PLACED IT gently on the pool table. A green-shaded overhead light cast a cone of brilliance on the missile. Chew hoisted an old leather tool bag onto the table beside the MIRV.

The MINERVA I missile was three feet in length, finned, with USAF 91354 stenciled on it. Wires trailed out of holes, which had been connected to the mother rocket. Jensen and Allworth held their breath as Chew prepared to open the missile. He lighted a small acetylene torch. "Hey, no fire," Jensen said.

Chew said nothing. He aimed the flame at the missile shell and started cutting. Acrid smoke from the torch mingled with the odor of melting metal. "You know what you're doing?" Allworth asked.

Again Chew didn't answer.

Ten minutes later the MIRV was cut in two halves as Chew examined its interior. The bomb snuggled in the tip of the MIRV was eighteen inches long. Behind it was a gyroscope affair wired to fins, able to navigate the missile across hundreds of miles. Nothing new there, thought Chew, who had helped correct a flaw in its design when engineers from Sperry-Rand came out to Los

Alamos in 1961. They were close to panic because the vertical alignment with the star Arcturus would not stabilize. Chew showed them how to stabilize it. He was twenty-four years old at the time.

But it was the nuclear bomb in front of the missile that fascinated Chew. More miniaturized than he had ever thought possible. He looked across the table at the two men. "If you're going to remain in the room, you'll have to wear gas masks."

Jensen and Allworth were surprised. The gas masks hadn't been in Jensen's special instructions about guarding Chew. Jensen asked Chew where the gas was coming from.

Chew said that plutonium was the most toxic material in the world. One speck inhaled meant certain death. He reached into his tool kit and threw three gas masks onto the table, then pulled one over his head and bent over the missile.

The sight of Chew with a gas mask leaning over an atomic missile frightened Allworth. He quickly donned one of the masks himself and turned to see that Jensen had done the same.

Chew's precise moves on technical devices were executed with an elegance that fascinated Allworth. As seen through goggles, his hands appeared to be performers on a tiny round stage. Two fingers rotated a tiny steel screwdriver, then moved abruptly to a new position and operated the tool again.

After a series of these moves, Chew's fingers engaged the top shell of the bomb and lifted it.

The hands stopped, rested on the rim of the lower half of the bomb. Allworth saw that Chew was studying the interior of the weapon.

Allworth's curosity would not allow him to remain where he was. He walked to the pool table on the opposite side from Chew and peered inside the nuclear bomb. At one end of the bomb a gelatinlike compound surrounded a small core of a substance similar to white putty. An aluminum tube connected the core to a larger ball of the same compound in the other end.

Chew's hands came onstage again, rotating the horizontal aluminum tube until it loosened. The tube moved up slightly, and wires were seen to protrude from its bottom and descend into a maze of other wires below.

A tiny knife sliced some of the wires, other wires were reconnected, then the hands tilted the tube vertically. Metal components tumbled out.

The hands replaced the tube in its horizontal position, then the shell went back on top of the bomb and the little steel screwdriver began its work again.

Allworth was staring at the reassembled bomb when he heard a voice. "He says you can take it off." He turned to see Jensen without his mask and removed his own.

Jensen said to Chew, "Is it armed?"

Chew said, "Little deceit on the part of the AEC security experts. Two of the wires appear to be part of the security system, but are really in the detonation circuit. If you cut those two wires, the bomb will never explode. I've left those wires intact."

"So that bomb is armed?"

"Yes," said Chew.

Jensen was impressed. "I have to hand it to you, Chew." The telephone rang upstairs. All three men froze. Jensen said, "That's funny. No one is supposed to call."

Chew's voice was soft. "Our employers might be checking on us."

The ringing continued. Jensen's nerves were taut. He

went upstairs and found the telephone in the living room. The voice he heard was angry.

"Who is this?"

"Who wants to know?" Jensen said.

"Washington end."

Jensen knew he was supposed to report in code to the people in Washington as soon as Chew had armed the MIRVs and made them ready. But here was a call in the clear. "This is Jensen."

"You fool!"

The words were so filled with loathing that Jensen caught his breath. He said, "What's wrong?"

"He left a clue on his own at the site. A map. Right there under your eyes. We told you to watch him."

"He didn't do a *thing* we didn't see."

"Kill him," said the voice. "There's no other solution. Kill him as soon as he finishes arming the bombs. And don't fail."

"But he couldn't have—"

"He did. We just found out in Washington. And that means he has plans of his own. Whatever happens, don't let him leave that house alive." The connection broke off.

Jensen's hands were trembling. Chew had double-crossed them. He must have done it when they were loading the MIRVs into the truck; left a clue by the fence. A map—of what?

He went into the kitchen and poured himself a large drink of Scotch. The glass he drank from had a label— "God Bless America." Then he went downstairs to the basement and saw the scientist about to open the second MIRV, his gas mask in his hands. "Who was that?" Chew asked.

Jensen shrugged. "Our people wanted to make certain we were here."

"The procedure was to send a message *after* the bombs are armed."

"They were too worried to wait."

"I'm sure," Chew answered. Jensen watched as Chew placed the gas mask over his head and began to disassemble the second MIRV.

Allworth started to pull the mask over his own head when he felt someone nudge his elbow. Jensen gestured to him to leave the room. A few minutes later, standing in a room down the hall, Jensen told him they were ordered to kill the man who left a clue on his own. The man who was unstable.

3

ALLWORTH WAS WORRIED. "COUNT ME OUT WITH THE guns. I don't even know how to use the one they gave me."

Jensen screwed a tubular silencer on a .38 pistol. "Just back me up and try to look as if you know what you're doing."

"He'll take us both. We're amateurs compared to him. They told us he killed more than fifty people in the Middle East."

Jensen indicated his gun. "I'm the expert with guns. He's the big man with bombs and gask masks. No problem."

But Allworth was unsatisfied. "A man with brains like that is trouble any time."

Jensen grunted. Allworth was still reliving that theft. In fact Jensen didn't blame Allworth for being a little frightened of Chew. What Chew had done last night during that rainstorm had left them both awestruck.

Deep in the silo, the wind howling above them, Jensen and Allworth had watched as Chew led a wire around the base of the nose cone where it joined the missile body. Rain splattered the catwalk on which they were standing. Allworth had been stunned when he saw the six-foot-high nose cone, not only because of its size but because of the thirty-six bolts that fixed it to the rocket, each one embedded solidly in steel. It would take hours to free those bolts.

Chew wrapped gleaming copper wire around each bolt head before passing it on to the next. Neither Jensen nor Allworth knew what Chew was doing. Each detail of the theft from the rubber ladders to the smooth-wheeled truck had been Chew's strategic plan.

But now he was going so *slowly!* Jensen urged him along. "Whatever you're doing, hurry."

Chew wore coveralls, gloves, and rubber overshoes. He didn't look up from his work when Jensen spoke. He concentrated on placing tiny dabs of plastique on the wire around each bolt head. When he finished, he examined each bolt carefully, then glanced up and said quietly, "Out." They climbed the metal ladder, Chew playing out wire from a spool. Under a tarpaulin on the ground was a gray box with a red button and a fail-safe switch. "Stand clear," Chew commanded, and the two men moved back. Chew crouched over the box and attached the wire around a terminal. Then, without waiting, he pressed the red button, and a sound like that of a machine gun burst was heard inside the silo.

Silence. Chew sloshed across the grass to the silo and looked down. "OK," he said.

Two minutes later the three men were inside the silo again, lifting off the cone and placing it on the catwalk.

The interior walls of the silo were pockmarked everywhere, electronic black boxes smashed in the hail of explosive bolts Chew had triggered from outside the cone.

Three MIRVs nestled inside the missile. Allworth touched the point of one and shivered. My God, he had done it! What his Berkeley friends had *talked* about for years, he had achieved. He had actually helped steal three nuclear bombs!

Jensen had been standing beside the door of the game room. Now he turned to Allworth and said quietly, "He's finished. If you're out, I'll take care of him." He turned and walked back up the hall toward the game room. Allworth finally followed, pulling his gun out of his shoulder holster.

Inside the room the three MIRVs were standing on the floor by the wall once again. Chew was playing pool. Allworth almost had to smile. Chew must have known something was wrong ever since that phone call, but he certainly hadn't panicked.

Chew had set up three balls in a triangle about two feet apart from each other. From the corner he drove the white ball toward the nearest target. The ball that it hit caromed off a second, then rolled into the side pocket. The second ball hit a cushion and raced back to propel the third ball into a side pocket, then spun and rolled slowly into the far corner hole. Jensen watched, with his gun out, as if paralyzed.

Chew placed some more balls on the table and said to Jensen without turning his head, "The wires are crossed."

"What?"

"I reassembled each of the bombs with crossed wires. The MIRVs can't be used until I fix them."

Jensen and Allworth looked at each other. Jensen

held up the pistol and said, "You'll fix them right now."

Chew adjusted the balls for a new shot. "Do you realize how unintelligent that is? How will you know whether I assemble the wires correctly, especially since I know that you'll kill me when I finish?" He turned and stared Jensen in the eyes. "You have to admit, that's not much of an incentive." He picked up his cue and said, "If you intend to kill me, I'll make certain the MIRVs blow up in your face."

"Maybe I'll take a chance you're bluffing," Jensen said.

Chew said quietly, "Go ahead," and struck a ball that hopped over its target, smacked the cushion, came back on an angle and crisply drove the target ball into a side pocket across the table. He was some pool player.

Jensen said to Allworth at the door, "Hold the gun on him. I'm going to call Washington."

When he left, Chew said, "Allworth, you have intelligence."

He reached into his tool bag and withdrew a small snub-nosed pistol. Allworth said nervously, "You just stay here till we figure this out."

They didn't have long to wait. As Jensen ran down the stairs, Allworth called out over his shoulder, "He has a gun."

"Where is he?"

"Behind the pool table."

Allworth couldn't understand why Chew didn't attempt to duck behind the table for cover. It was two guns against one. He told Jensen, "He's not moving," and that was all Jensen needed. He was a man with five notches on his .38 earned in brutal street battles in Mexican border towns. Chew was a cinch. He ducked inside the door, pulled the trigger at point-blank range, and an explosion ripped Jensen's hand. He screamed as the fragmented gun dropped to the floor. "Holy Christ!"

Allworth tilted the muzzle of his own gun. There was soldering lead inside. Chew must have jammed their guns! The scientist came around the table with his gun in one hand and briefcase in the other. He drew handcuffs from his briefcase, and five minutes later the two men were inside a walk-in meat freezer behind the game room, handcuffed to an iron rail, Jensen's hand bleeding from a dozen shrapnel cuts.

A minute later the door clanged behind him. Car wheels scraped gravel outside. Chew was away. The two men looked at each other in their frosty prison. Great haunches of iced beef hung on hooks all around them.

For Jensen, Allworth had a bitter epitaph. "Thanks."

The cold was already seeping into their bones. Jensen said through chattering teeth, "Who the hell is he? If he was undercover, he would have taken us in."

"He's not a Fed, for Christ's sake," Allworth said. "The organization was supposed to use *him* to steal the bombs—he used *us* to steal them for himself."

"But why did he leave a clue?" Jensen said, and Allworth couldn't answer that. And what did it matter? They were dying right here. Already Allworth's hands and feet were turning numb.

Leonard Chew drove to a safe house he had rented in Chestnut Hill, Pennsylvania. He would then have to ditch the organization's car, disguise himself, and transfer the bombs to another vehicle he had prepared.

But one thought burned into his mind. The Arnold map had been found. Jensen's attempt to kill him proved that the organization already knew about it.

Which meant his plan was working.

Of course, there was a risk to himself, but that risk had to be taken if he left the map at the missile site.

There was one man who could identify Chew through that map. An Arnold descendent in Canada named Malcolm Bennett.

But Chew knew Bennett would be too afraid to talk.

4

11:30 A.M., JULY 1, WASHINGTON.

"Forget the map," the President told George Williams. "You're going to find it's a fake. That sergeant committing suicide with cyanide pills shows we're dealing with real pros." He paused. "And speaking of pros, I keep thinking about those people who broke into Watergate. Every last one of them was ex-CIA, only the 'ex' was doubtful. Do you think that could be the case here? Maybe even some 'rogue' agents acting on their own?"

"I don't know," Williams said, "but I want to find out what this map means. If it's authentic, it's an important clue because the thieves left it for us to find. I don't think a priceless historical map would be lying loose on a North Dakota plain."

The President tensed, as if trying to restrain himself, then said, "Go chase your crazy map, George. Find out it's a forgery and get this . . . *obsession* off your mind. It's ridiculous."

And with that doleful charge George Williams went to the Archives Building on Pennsylvania Avenue and within minutes learned that the map left near a missile silo was genuine. The man who told him was a Revolutionary War specialist in Archives named John McNamara, a wiry little man who wore a green eyeshade and a permanently indignant expression. His fellow archivists called him Angry John, partly because he kept a sword cane by his desk to terrify college students and DAR types who dared bother him for information. But McNamara liked Williams. He had worked with Williams once before on a case, appreciated the Justice Department lawyer's quick mind. He took one look at the signature and said, "That's Arnold. No question."

"How can you be so sure?" Williams asked.

In answer Angry John wearily, and contemptuously, inserted a reel of microfilm on a viewer. Williams saw letter after letter written by Arnold, the signatures magnified. There was no question it was authentic unless it was written by a master forger. The signature on the map was identical to that on the letters.

Still, Williams said, "If that signature was written by a ballpoint pen, we're nowhere," but his attention was diverted as Angry John suddenly took his blade out of his cane and slashed at the ceiling. "Goddam fly, Williams!" And, indeed, a sliced fly was on the cutting edge of the blade when he brought it down. He flicked the fly's corpse off with his index finger, gazed malevolently at the ceiling for other intruders, then reluctantly sheathed the sword in its cane. "Clears my mind, Williams. Action. Nothing like it."

Williams placed the map in his legal briefcase. McNamara said, "It's authentic, Williams. Go to the FBI lab if you want to waste your time, but the signature's right, and the paper's right. You know how many Revolutionary War maps I've seen and catalogued? More than a thousand. You have a fantastic find, and you don't even appreciate what you have."

"What do you mean?"

"Nobody's ever heard of a woman named Nancy in

Arnold's life. So who was she, and why did he want revenge for her? I mean, there's your real story."

The real story for Williams were professional terrorists with nuclear bombs to whom the map might be one clue. He went to the FBI lab, where an intense, swarthy-complected young technician named Joe Greenberg placed the paper under a microscope. "The paper's right for the time," Greenberg said. Williams asked him what he meant and Greenberg said, "It's cotton. Wood wasn't used for paper until after the Civil War." He delicately handled a sharp forceps to lift a tiny dot of ink off the signature and place it on a glass slide. Then he slid a glass shield above the dot and inserted the double wafer into an electroscope.

Graph paper moved, and colored lines indicating chemical spectrums rose and fell. Greenberg grunted, then peeled off a foot of the graph. "Well, *this* is unusual."

"What?"

"This ink has the chemical properties of the ink used in the Revolutionary War era, all right—but it was very rare, even then." The FBI technician looked at Williams. "It's *invisible* ink, George."

Williams called the Archives to get Angry John's reaction to that news and was greeted with satisfaction. "Now that makes sense, Williams. It shows why no biographies ever mentioned a woman named Nancy. The goddam note was invisible."

Williams said, "So how does that help me find terrorists who left the map at a missile site?"

But Angry John was unswayed in his enthusiasm. "It gives you a lead to find the map, Williams. The invisible ink meant that the map looked routine to everyone for years. Follow me? The collectors and libraries didn't know the note was there."

He paused. "I don't know who left the map at the site or why. That's your department, Williams. If it turns out to be an Ay-rab or a Russian or one of those Cuban killers that keep popping up every time there's a gunshot or an explosion, it don't make any difference. What makes the difference is this invisible note. Because whoever left the map couldn't even know there was such a note on it *unless somebody told them!* Got it? It was invisible. So who told the nuclear thieves about an invisible note?"

He paused again. "So old John here will save you. I got me a hunch. Somewhere there has to be a lead to a descendent of that woman Nancy, and that descendent could be involved."

"It could be an Arnold descendent—"

"Pound your own beat, Williams. I say it's Nancy who's got a real live descendent kicking around."

Williams smiled—but he felt the archivist was making sense. Any clue to where the terrorists obtained the map or where they learned about the invisible note could be helpful. And a descendent of Nancy, if there was one alive, was the most likely person to know.

After he hung up, Williams went to Fred Jarvis' office, on the fifth floor, and the FBI man said, "Surprise." He tossed Williams a copy of the Washington *Post,* folded to the Style section. Williams saw a picture of Peggy DuPont, arriving at an airport, smiling. The caption under the photograph said, "Society's Peggy DuPont visits Lake Champlain to join other descendents of Benedict Arnold in recreating Revolutionary War battle."

Jarvis said, "You're in luck. You have a contact right in the middle of the people who might know what that map is about." Jarvis was looking at Williams closely. He doesn't want to call her, he thought. After all, it *was*

embarrassing to telephone a woman who had once
walked out on you.

But Williams picked up the telephone immediately.
He called the Lake Champlain operator in Plattsburg,
New York, and listened while she traced Peggy DuPont
to a Holiday Inn at Lake Champlain. On the sixth ring
a voice Williams remembered too well answered breath-
lessly, "Hi. I broke my ass diving for the phone. Hold
on."

That was Peggy.

5

PEGGY DUPONT, IN A PURPLE BIKINI TOP AND SKIN-
tight jeans, lighted a cigarette, inhaled luxuriously,
then watched smoke swirl toward the ceiling. Only then
did she place the cigarette gently in a glass ashtray and
pick up the telephone. "Sorry to swear, but I really did
equal the Olympic sidesplit record with the help of a
loose rug."

The voice on the other end of the phone said,
"George Williams, Peggy," a name that startled her so
much she knocked the ashtray onto the floor. She
reached down to rescue the cigarette from the carpet
while telling herself to relax. Williams was now history
as far as she was concerned, a bit performer in the cav-
alcade of her romantic sex life—different from her
other lovers, perhaps. Well, more than *perhaps. Defi-
nitely* different. Honest, hard-working, sincere, dedicated. Which of the other men in her life boasted those

qualities, especially the one that contained the seven letters W O R K I N G? None.

But he was so serious it was a crime against women. A man so handsome and a mind that just couldn't concentrate on pleasures, niceties, good wine, good food, good fun. When she left him she had gone on what she called "a trivia binge" just to get her head straight again.

Still, there was no doubt the sound of his voice bothered her. She said, "What a surprise. Is this a long-distance carnal impulse?" And she smiled to herself as Williams said, "Business, Peggy. We need your help."

Two years since her dramatic walkout, two years without a word from Williams asking for the reason, and now she knew why. He had never noticed she was gone. She said, "I'm up here with a lot of people running around in Revolutionary War costumes, George. I don't see how I can help the Justice Department."

Williams said that nuclear bombs had been stolen and a genuine Revolutionary War map had been left at the missile site. The map had a note on its margin, "For revenge of Nancy, beloved of Benedict Arnold."

"George, have you been drinking?"

"Unfortunately not," Williams said. "This is serious business, Peggy, and I'm convinced that note is an important clue. Now Archives says that none of the history books mention a woman named Nancy in Arnold's life. So I thought you might ask the descendents up there if they ever heard of a Nancy."

Peggy said, "As far as I know, Arnold's only woman was my namesake, Peggy Shippen——" she stopped. "Well, I *did* hear something at the lake yesterday."

"What?"

"There's some fellow up here who's telling everyone he's an *illegitimate* descendent, and that means there was a mistress involved. Unless he's making up a little fantasy for some reason."

"His name?" Williams asked.

"I didn't get it—but I could find out."

"Check it and call me back, Peggy."

Peggy said, "What do I do if he says his ancestor's named Nancy? Shout stick-'em-up, and hold him against a wall?"

"Call this number," Williams replied. He gave her the telephone number of the White House and an extension. She said, "I thought you might be calling . . . for some other reasons."

Williams asked, "What other reasons?" and she paused before saying, "Baseball scores, new seafood restaurants in Dubuque, you know, general information."

But in reply Williams only frightened her to death. "One more thing, Peggy. Watch yourself. If you do find the man and he shows any reluctance to talk for any reason, drop it and call me at once. He could be dangerous."

And with that, and a request to check on the man immediately, he hung up. So much for a call from George Williams after two years' time. Until now she thought she had rejected *him*.

Peggy replaced the phone on its hook, rolled over on her back, and stretched one shapely leg toward the ceiling. She imagined the leg encircling Williams' back. It was nice imagining.

She and Williams had had such great times in bed. The man who was so cool and reserved in public could be surprisingly warm and affectionate in private. Of course he wasn't a sophisticate, a fact she had once revealed to him in typical fashion. "You'll never be known as the King of Foreplay." But he was accomplished enough in the main event. Even somewhat sensational, Peggy remembered.

Sweet memories. She realized she had been smiling ever since Williams had announced his name and she had recovered from the surprise. She was glad to hear from him. He was a challenge so difficult it was amusing. She had met him just after his wife, Sarah, had split for reasons unknown—Williams, of course, would never tell. He didn't talk of private matters to anyone. Peggy had come to Washington on a weekend and found herself charmed by the old brick houses of Georgetown, the small but elite French restaurants, the bustle of Capitol Hill, and the liveliness of the nighttime bars on Wisconsin Avenue. She had seen Williams at a Bicentennial affair, looked into clear blue eyes beneath slightly bushy eyebrows, noticed with interest his wide shoulders, and decided she wanted to know more about the Justice Department. And that was how she came to live with a Deputy Assistant Attorney General. It was a mistake. They were so different from each other in every way that they could not become lovers on a permanent basis, no matter how passionate in bed. Once Williams told her she reminded him of a woman named Stephanie Spaulding, now married to a baron in Madrid. In his words, "You both *try* so hard to be shallow." Only Williams would have meant that as a compliment. She never told Williams that the implication was false— that she was not profound and just *"trying"* to be shallow. In the All-Star Shallow League, Peggy knew she would be a starter and had long ago resigned herself to the fact.

She sat up on the bed. What had Williams said on the phone that had frightened her? Oh yes, danger. But there was no danger. The man she had seen on the beach—that stocky little acrobat turning flips in the sun while a redhead clapped—seemed so innocent. The whole idea of checking him was really a farce. How could he be involved with nuclear bombs?

Nevertheless, for George Williams, she would make a few telephone calls. On the second call she discovered that the acrobat's name was Malcolm Bennett, registered at the Helmsman Motel. She dialed his number. There was no answer.

6

LEONARD CHEW STOOD IN FRONT OF A MIRROR IN A safe house in Chestnut Hill, Pennsylvania, applying a disguise that would help him explode a nuclear bomb in his own country. A red hairpiece, moustache, and beard. Blue contact lenses for his brown eyes. Then Chew took a towel in his left hand and a razor blade in his right, and lightly dug the shaped point of the blade above his right jawline. A tiny drop of blood appeared. He cut a jagged line for three inches, shallow, but deep enough to draw blood. He held the towel to the cut, then absorbed the remaining flow with Kleenex from a wall dispenser. When the bleeding stopped completely he went over the cut with a stinging styptic pencil.

The jagged scar was not to fool people but computers. Every eyewitness interrogation card carried a line for "Any identifying marks." A mention of a scar would immediately sort his card in the wrong group, and once the card was missorted, the computer would not cause him harm.

Of course, if events went as he planned, his description would never reach the computers. But Chew took no chances. A few extra moments of preparation had saved his life in the past. And at this moment he was the most hunted man in the country.

He was glad his father wasn't alive to see him now. But in a way it was his father's hero who had put him here. Harry Truman, the man from Missouri—and Hiroshima.

7

ON JANUARY 20, 1949, THE OLD WASHINGTON *Post* Building on Pennsylvania Avenue flaunted a one-hundred-foot banner across its front. Written in letters five feet high were the words: MR. PRESIDENT, WE'RE EATING CROW.

Beneath the sign cold winds whipped an avenue flanked by tens of thousands of citizens who still could not believe Harry Truman had defeated Tom Dewey. Now marching bands high-stepped along between the crowds, and the first of the open limousines appeared with the District of Columbia chief of police, a bull-necked, fierce-looking man sitting in lonely grandeur in the back.

Then two cars behind, twelve-year-old Leonard Chew saw the little man with the glinting glasses, smiling and acknowledging the cheers with a waving hand. He passed right in front of them. Bess Truman, formidable as ever, smiled mechanically beside her husband. John Chew, Leonard Chew's father, heard later that at a dinner for the President's old Battery D Troops the night before, Harry had lapsed into some salty language and Bess was still angry.

John Chew had taken his wife and son to Washington to see the parade for a simple reason. "I don't like his politics but I admire the little SOB," he said. "Without his guts I wouldn't be here."

He was referring to Truman's decision to drop nuclear bombs on Japan. Many now regretted that decision but not Chew. John Chew had been a lieutenant in the First Marine Division on Okinawa at the time that happened, decorated twice for bravery in action. But the orders were already issued for the invasion of Japan, and no Marine who fought on the blood-soaked island chain from Guadalcanal to Peleliu to Iwo Jima doubted what kind of invasion that would be.

If John Chew did not get the kind of son he wanted, he never showed his dismay. Indeed, he seemed to be almost excessively fond of the little boy who wore glasses from the age of six. Neighbors who saw him walking with his son never tired of his introduction. "This is little Lenny, God bless him. Keep your eyes on this boy."

He did try to teach Leonard sports but was not successful—and once, when Leonard came home with his nose bloodied after a game of touch football, Mary Chew chastised her husband. Leonard never forgot his shame at that moment. His father wasn't guilty; he was—because he was so *weak*.

After the Inaugural Parade his parents went to the Ball, and he and some other children were left in a hotel suite in the care of a governess employed by a very rich Democrat.

One of the children, a girl of fifteen, was bored. "Let's escape," she said to the others.

They looked at her numbly. "My God," she said to

the governess. "Where do they get these small-town types?" Leonard asked her where she came from, and she said, "Places you only read about. Who are you, anyway? What does your father do?"

"He sells insurance," Leonard said, and for some reason this made her laugh. Leonard was embarrassed.

Later that night when his father came to pick him up in his rented tuxedo, along with his mother in her cheap Lit Brothers gown, Leonard told his father what had happened. John Chew smiled. "Hell, Lenny, they're rich, little fella. Old man Morrison owns half of Pennsylvania, the half with iron under it, and banks over it."

But when he saw the shame in Leonard's eyes he sat down on a brown and green chair in their room and stood his son before him. "Leonard, your old man isn't ever going to be loaded like that little girl's daddy. But while old man Morrison was counting pennies in a bank I was running eighty-seven yards for a touchdown that won a big game against Princeton. Now he couldn't run five yards to a nurse if he was constipated."

Leonard laughed and never thought much about money again because he knew that, to his father, life itself was rich, and America—in his father's words— had room enough for everyone to get himself "a piece of the action." It was "one super country." And then, a year later in 1950, half a million North Koreans broke across the 38th parallel, Harry Truman made his desperate commitment to the UN, and John Chew was called back to his beloved Marines as a lieutenant; and in the infamous "bowling alley" above Chosin, he was killed by a bullet that exploded in his heart.

Now Leonard Chew, son of an American hero, went into the attic, where he had stored a tape recorder and other electronic equipment. Ten minutes later he crouched on the back lawn of the house, listening tensely for any strange sounds. High hedges surrounded the property on each side—the nearest houses were hundreds of yards away. But still he felt vulnerable as he knelt on the grass with a tape recorder that contained a threat to the President of the United States. If a child ran by or a neighbor walked out to inspect his grounds, he could be compromised.

Quiet. No one came. Chew used a knife to saw at the insulation on a wire that led to the ground from a telephone pole—the last in a line of poles that ran behind the property. He cleared an area of wire six inches long, then clamped his transmitter onto it.

A car drove down the street outside of Chew's rented house. He stopped and waited, kneeling on the ground, until the sound of the engine lessened.

Then he pressed a button on his transmitter and the reel of tape whirled. A series of clicks was heard. The clicks dialed a sixteen-digit number at the North America Air Defense Command in Colorado Springs.

After he sent the threat he went back into the house. He had kept a diary ever since he began this one-man mission: a book not only to record the events but to reflect his state of mind at various junctures. Now he wrote:

"The plan has commenced. The threat is on its way. It's customary in these moments to call on God's help, while you do the devil's work. But I'm no hypocrite. I know just what nuclear weapons mean, and what will result when I explode them, and no prayers will help or stop me . . ."

2 P.M., JULY 1, WASHINGTON.

Limousines rolled up the curving driveway of the White House, discharging worried men with briefcases. A line of tourists stared at the government leaders, nudging each other as they recognized a face they had seen on television. Oliver Taylor, the Secretary of State, stout and urbane, drew murmurs from the crowd, as did Arthur Flanders, Secretary of Defense, with his thin black moustache and perfectly tailored gray suit. Other members of the National Security Council called to this emergency session were unknown by sight to the tourists: the Director of the Central Intelligence Agency, and the Director of the Atomic Energy Commission.

The fifth member of the Council, General Maxwell, was already inside the building, conferring with the President in the Oval Office.

George Williams entered the White House through the back door and met General Maxwell coming out of the President's office. Maxwell appeared tense. "We have it," he told Williams quietly.

"The threat?"

"Came into the Oval Office from Colorado Springs. Colorado told the President they had received it on the classified military-alert circuit out there."

"What did the threat say?"

Maxwell hesitated, then said only, "Bad, George. Worse than we anticipated."

The President entered the Cabinet room and stood at the end of the table, his fingers resting lightly on its varnished surface.

"Gentlemen, the threat has arrived."

9

THE THREAT RECEIVED AT THE WHITE HOUSE, JULY 1:

> Mr. President,
>
> To confirm my identity, the serial number of one of the stolen MIRVs is AF 9-70351.
>
> I have the stolen nuclear MIRVs in my possession. I intend to explode them. This threat relates to Weapon One.
>
> A tidal wave will be created at 6 P.M. July 2 by an underwater explosion in the Atlantic Ocean off New Jersey. When the wave reaches the shore it will be 100 feet high, filled with radioactive poison.
>
> One man can stop this catastrophe.
>
> He knows who he is.
>
> I don't.
>
> 949 747 833 944 578 847 364 999 697

SILENCE IN THE ROOM. EVERYONE WAS STUNNED. BOB Winthrop, the CIA Director, said, "If one deranged man has the bombs, we're in the worst trouble of all." And Arthur Flanders, the Secretary of Defense, pointed out an even greater problem. "He's only giving us twenty-eight hours to evacuate all those resorts and cities along the coast."

The President turned to General Maxwell and said, "That question is the most important. Can we evacuate those areas in time to save the lives of the people there?"

The Chairman of the Joint Chiefs replied, "Most of the shore communities in that area are resorts, so there'll be less problems. Asbury Park, Atlantic City, Hoboken, and Jersey City are larger cities, but I think we can handle them. At least the people aren't trapped on an island like New York."

"Will a tidal wave that size strike New York?" one of them asked, but Maxwell said no. The city was tucked in behind islands in the bay. "The tidal waves caused by hurricanes always roll straight to Long Island."

The President looked at his watch. It was 2:05 P.M. Twenty-eight hours? Less. Five minutes had passed! He said to Maxwell, "I want you to fly every one of your transportation, military police, and medical battalions to that coastal area at once and start evacuating all communities immediately. Don't waste a second." Then he turned to George Williams and asked what he thought.

Williams said he was interested in the "one man" mentioned in the threat. "If one man can *stop* the catastrophe, maybe we ought to concentrate on finding *him*."

But Flanders said angrily, "That's why that threat is so intolerable! It's uncivilized! No demand. No offer to negotiate. Nothing but an allusion to one man who can stop the catastrophe. But why so *vague*, for God's sake? Why not tell us who the man is, or give us some clue, or *something?*"

The Defense Secretary's angry monologue made him perspire. He sank back in his chair, patting his face with a white silk handkerchief.

Williams said, "Maybe he *does* tell us."

"How?"

"The numbers on the bottom of the threat. They look like a code."

Silence. The President said, "If you're right, George, we have an edge. NSA has a building full of people who do nothing but break the most advanced codes. This should be simple." He turned to Flanders. "Call the NSA Director."

Flanders did, but the NSA Director surprised him. "It most likely *is* a simple code, Mr. Flanders. A three-digit code usually means a page, line, and word code. That is, first digit for the page, second for the line, third for the word in the line. But if you don't know the book on which the code is based you can't possibly break it with all the modern computers in the world."

When he heard this information the President showed his tension for the first time. He threw a pencil on the conference table so sharply it was still rolling as he said, "The greatest, most modern army in the world and we can't stop terrorists from stealing nuclear bombs. The most sophisticated computers in the world and we can't break a simple three-digit code that looks like it's a child's puzzle." He stopped, then said, "Meeting adjourned, gentlemen!" To Maxwell he said, "Come with me," and left the room.

The National Security Council members were left in his wake, silent, staring at the walls. Williams went to the Situation Room in the basement, which Maxwell had told him would be their headquarters in this crisis. He glanced at technicians installing additional TV monitors, and the military men who supervised communication equipment. Williams then telephoned the Archives. Angry John told him at once what the code could be. "Benedict Arnold used a three-digit code when he corresponded with the British. He used the name Gustavus." Angry John continued, "The code's based on a book, *Blackstone's Commentaries*, Second Edition. Three digits, page, line, and word. Let me get old Blackstone and try to decode it for you, Williams."

Williams read him the numbers from the threat, and Angry John hung up. Less than ten minutes later he was back on the phone with the words, "Here's your decode, Williams."

He read it out:

"WHAT YOU DID IN THE MIDDLE EAST IS KNOWN."

The words were eerie, chilling. In the context of a threat from a terrorist who was determined to explode nuclear bombs they seemed incomprehensible. Instead of issuing the normal political or financial demand, the terrorist apparently addressed a personal message to one unknown man—and did it in a two-hundred-year-old code.

Williams was absolutely baffled. First an Arnold map at the site—now a message in Arnold's code. Who was this terrorist—and what did he want? And, most important of all, why the Arnold connection, which had been deliberately employed to keep government investigators harking back to a man two centuries dead?

There was a reason, Williams knew that. And his thoughts went to Peggy DuPont among those Arnold descendents in Lake Champlain. He decided to send FBI agents there, too. If a lead could be found to the Arnold connection, it might be more important than all the efforts General Maxwell was making from this room to stop the terrorist; roadblocks with inspectors armed with Geiger counters; special reinforcements at bridges leading into coastal resorts; regional Army commands set up along the coast of New Jersey, four in all, from Hoboken to Cape May, complete with helicopters and jeep patrols.

All to find one man who must be the strangest terrorist any nation had ever confronted. And, with the nuclear bombs, the most dangerous.

11

MINUS 27:00 HOURS. ON THE ROAD WITH CHEW.

The window of the shop on Chestnut Street in Philadelphia had a red sign, "Sporting Goods." In the bottom right corner of the window a smaller sign read: "Licensed Firearms Dealer." Leonard Chew went into the shop with fishing rods on the wall, a tennis counter, a yachtsman's corner. The goods sold here were expensive, but the shop was crowded with customers. Mohammed Yaffi, the owner, was busy showing a prospective buyer a shotgun. He paid no attention to Chew, who stood there patiently. Finally, when the customer walked off, Chew leaned over the counter and said, "Mohammed."

Yaffi saw a man he didn't recognize, with a red beard, red hair, and blue eyes. Then he looked closer. "Robert?"

Chew nodded. Yaffi had known him as Robert Patterson in the Middle East. Now Yaffi said, "Your goods have arrived. Come with me."

Chew went around the counter, past a girl ringing up a sale at a cash register, and found himself in a packaging room. Yaffi walked through that room and Chew followed him to another cubicle, with a twin silex of coffee bubbling on a wooden table. From there a cement stairway led downstairs to a basement.

Yaffi was in a suede coat, brown pants, and Gucci loafers. He sniffed at the dirt when he turned on an overhanging light in the basement. "Wouldn't come down here in a million years execpt for you."

Chew had once done a favor for Yaffi in Beirut; he killed a rival arms dealer who was intruding on Yaffi's Middle East trade. Yaffi gave Chew credit, because he didn't know the organization had ordered the assassination for reasons of their own. After the revolution in Beirut, Yaffi had come to America and now was legitimate. Except for "Patterson," for whom he had always said he would do anything.

Chew had needed special weapons for his mission and had asked Yaffi to procure them. Now Yaffi produced a gray metal footlocker and opened it. Inside was an odd-looking pistol with a large shotgun muzzle, some small grenades for the gun, a box of coat buttons that were actually 100 percent explosive, and an automatic PK Walther handgun.

"I got them through our friends in the 'company,' " Yaffi said. "Edgewood." He hefted the pistol with the weird shotgun muzzle. "But this gun I don't understand. You use it with the grenades?"

"Magnetic grenades," Chew said. He volunteered no further explanation as he opened his briefcase and placed the weapons inside. Yaffi smiled. "What are you up to in the disguse, Robert?"

"A bank job," Chew said.

Yaffi smiled. "You're too good for that, and you wouldn't need all those weapons, either."

"No questions," Chew said, and Yaffi understood immediately. "I paid three thousand dollars, and that's all I'm asking. No cut for me. Friends. OK?"

Chew handed him three one-thousand-dollar bills. Yaffi folded them casually and stuffed them into his side pocket. They went back upstairs. Yaffi said goodbye, and Chew walked around the counter into the crowded store with shoppers buying equipment for fishing, hunting, tennis, golf; eager customers unaware that he carried a briefcase filled with weapons that would ensure the explosion of nuclear bombs on this continent.

Chew silently pushed open the back door of Yaffi's shop. No one there. He passed through an empty freight room and saw a closed door on the side with the sign OFFICE. He listened outside that door.

He heard nothing. No voice. No telephone call alerting someone that Chew had picked up his weapons. Chew opened the door. A man in a red tartan jacket pointed a shotgun at him. A mannequin. Chew looked around the small office that contained no more than a desk and a phone, one straight-backed chair, a box of tennis rackets, and three fishing poles on the floor. No Yaffi. Chew went down to the basement and there, on a wall phone, was Yaffi. His eyes bulged in surprise when he saw Chew. He said into the phone, "I don't have that type of fishing tackle," which left the organization man on the other end of the line surprised. But not so surprised he didn't realize what was happening when he heard a small crack, then a groan, then silence.

Chew had shot Yaffi with a sugar flechette gun, his own invention, a weapon not among those which Yaffi had supplied him. The flechette pierced the heart, then dissolved. If the first people who arrived missed the tiny puncture in the skin, they would believe Yaffi died of a heart attack. Even if they discovered the microscopic wound, the flechette had another advantage for the killer. It left absolutely nothing to trace except a raised level of sugar in congealing blood.

12

MINUS 26:45 HOURS. JULY 1, PHILADELPHIA.

Two men from the organization drove toward Yaffi's shop in a blue Chrysler. Police cars were outside. They parked and saw a white ambulance arrive and a man brought out on a stretcher. One of the two men left the car and mingled with the crowd outside of the sporting goods store. He was told that the owner of the shop had suffered "a heart attack."

The man knew better. Chew was gone. Yaffi had had enough time to tell them on the telephone that Chew was disguised in a red beard but that his appearance would be changed. The organization knew that Chew was a master of deception.

Nevertheless, their report to headquarters in Washington resulted in orders to send motorcyclists along the road to the seashore, inspecting every driver closely in hopes of identifying Chew.

13.

MINUS 26:05 HOURS. ON THE ROAD TO OCEAN CITY.

Black goggles stared at Chew; a motorcyclist hovered beside his car at fifty miles an hour. Chew turned and looked at the cyclist.

The cyclist saw a driver with a gray wispy beard, a white T-shirt that revealed muscular shoulders. The shoulder nearest the cyclist was decorated with a tattooed Navy ship and a legend under it: "The Enterprise." A Navy veteran? The cyclist couldn't tell unless he reached inside and scratched at that tattoo. But the guy sure looked authentic. A retired bos'n's mate. The cyclist had been in the Navy himself, for three years.

Chew smiled and waved at the motorcyclist, who saw a blue stone ring on his hand with a gold anchor. The rider had almost bought one of those rings himself, in Norfolk. He moved to the car in front of Chew and stared at that driver, and Chew took his hand off the gun beside him.

Leonard Chew drove on toward Ocean City and was halfway there when newscasters started announcing an emergency address by the President. The President told the American people about the nuclear theft, the threat, and the government's program to deal with it.

"A national emergency is declared.

"All citizens of coastal communities in New Jersey and Long Island must evacuate their homes at once.

"The U.S. Army will assist the evacuation. Elements of the Army will be deployed in designated areas along the coast to provide police and transportation services.

"Special buses and trains will be sent into cities along the coast to assist the evacuation.

"The Army will establish evacuation areas inland with food, shelter, and medical facilities for those who require them.

"Special telephone numbers for those requiring emergency assistance will be designated in each area and manned around the clock."

Then the President mentioned that a fragment of an authentic Benedict Arnold map had been found at the site of the missile theft with a note, "For revenge of Nancy, beloved of Benedict Arnold," and urged anyone with information to contact the FBI. Chew found himself thinking again of Malcolm Bennett, the Arnold descendent who could identify him. Bennett was a former member of the organization. The map had been in his family's possession for many years until three months ago when Chew and an organization man named Kurt Edwards went up to Bennett's home in Montreal and forced him to sell it. If Bennett responded to the President's appeal, he would be able to describe Chew as well as Edwards and tell why the organization wanted the map.

But that was the safety valve in Chew's plan. The organization would make sure Bennett wasn't allowed to respond. The truth was that Bennett, wherever he was, would have to disappear if he wanted to live. In fact, he might already be dead.

14

In a motel room rented by a young lady on the Lake Champlain shore the news bulletins about the nuclear theft had gone unheard by Malcolm Bennett. He was otherwise occupied with a voluptuous redhead named Valerie Bentley. If their sexual act had been a wrestling match the authorities would never have allowed it to begin; Valerie was almost twice his size. Indeed, the small but doughty Bennett had spent the whole day wondering why he was so appealing to this beautiful giantess with the long flaming hair.

After hours of lovemaking Malcolm had dozed off, and now, when he awoke, he heard the shower running and his predatory woman singing. Jesus, he thought, talk about biting off more than you can chew. The words made him smile. He looked at his watch. Almost five o'clock. The whole day had been blown. And he smiled again.

The television screen remained blank. Two half-filled glasses of vodka stood on top of the set. Bennett stretched, stood up, and turned the set on. He wanted no more sex for a while—if only he could talk Valerie into cooling it. Perhaps television would divert her attention, at least long enough for him to regain his strength.

He went back to the bed, only dimly hearing the chatter of a news announcer. He lay back on the mattress naked and found himself dozing off again.

Valerie Bentley emerged from the shower and toweled her body dry. Feeling clean and refreshed, she entered the room where Malcolm Bennett lay asleep and shook him. "Time to raise the flag," she said. Malcolm Bennett opened his eyes and saw a profusion of curves above him. Valerie smiled, "Any last request?" she asked.

"Why last?"

"Because one more effort might kill you. Poor darling." She tossed the wet towel onto his face. "A blindfold for your execution," she murmured. "The condemned man was eaten."

Lips trailed down Malcolm's stomach, causing him to shudder. Suddenly, there was absence. Nothing. Then the weight of Valerie's body settled on him, and that was enough of the towel. He threw it off in time to watch Valerie straddle him exuberantly, her breasts jouncing, and she was too much. His hands reached forward and cupped her breasts. Valerie groaned, and increased the tempo, head to the side, lips open, red hair swinging. . . .

The voice from the television screen said, "The only clue, a fragment of a map bearing Benedict Arnold's handwriting, has so far led nowhere. Government sources are collating reports of missing maps from libraries throughout the country, attempting to match the fragment against photocopies sent to them. And in Lake Champlain, Arnold descendents attending a festival told reporters they were mystified about the note on the map, which reads, 'For revenge of Nancy, beloved of Benedict Arnold.' "

"Oh brother!" Valerie Bentley said. She had been pitched aside as Bennett sat up straight, staring at the television set. "What's wrong?" she asked. "What did he say?"

Bennett seemed stunned as Valerie said, "You look like you saw a ghost."

"I *heard* about a ghost," Bennett said. He started dressing hurriedly as Valerie watched in astonishment. She asked him where he was going.

"You want to live," Bennett said, "don't even say you know me, if anyone asks."

"There is no need to panic," the announcer said. "This is the word from the Pentagon, which is certain it can evacuate all endangered areas in the next twenty-four hours . . ."

Bennett stopped at the door. "Remember, if anyone asks, you haven't been with me. I'm telling you for your own sake, it may be dangerous."

"But you didn't steal any bombs. You've been right here at the lake."

Bennett didn't even answer her. He went out of the door, slamming it behind him. Valerie Bentley reached for the phone, then stopped. If the FBI picked up Bennett, reporters would track her down, and her name and address might be printed in every newspaper in the nation. And what had Bennett said? "You want to live, don't even say you know me."

Valerie's hand trailed away from the receiver.

Bennett drove back to his motel. He would throw his clothes into his car, and then drive as far as he could into the Canadian woods. He was thinking of the organization and most particularly of a man named Kurt Edwards, who had visited him once with the mild little scientist. And now they were into stealing nuclear bombs? Christ! The organization must be going crazy.

15

MINUS 25:15 HOURS. JULY 1, SARATOGA, NEW YORK.

The device looked like a telescope but with a wire grid on its end above the lens. Ten men in fatigues watched another man point it toward a window.

They were crouching in the woods in this training camp a hundred yards from a large four-story brick building on the Hudson River, thirty miles north of Saratoga. Behind them the Adirondack Mountains raised blue peaks toward the sky. A bright red cardinal swooped from a tree limb and strutted importantly around on the ground. The men paid no attention. They were watching the man with the teleprobe punch a button on a large video recorder.

Then they walked toward the building. They were led by Kurt Edwards, a tall, muscular, handsome man, with the high cheekbones of an Indian, and coal-black hair. Edwards wore combat boots with his fatigues. He was assigned as a temporary instructor in the training camp, and it was one large pain in the ass to him. The organization had shunted him here last month. At the time he was told, "We decided to keep you on ice while the MIRVs are lifted." Now he was training new recruits in counterintelligence and communications interception. It was no picnic. Three of the recruits were French, two German, and two Japanese. None spoke English, and Edwards had to rely on a multilingual Australian who was one of the translators in the camp.

They passed a steel dugout, which led underground.

A man in khakis standing outside nodded to Edwards. He was the plastique specialist, the "wizard of putty" as he was known at Saratoga. In a large underground cave beneath the dugout other recruits were learning plastique techniques on mockups of car engines, pipes, fixtures.

The training camp was used for an elite group of people who had political commitments to the idea of freedom. Or so Edwards had once been told. The flowery language held a hard kernel of truth, though. The men who came here for training were carefully screened because idealism was the drive the organization counted on. And there was never any shortage of recruits since the camp opened in 1962. An organization employee was paid richly, traveled all over the world, and spent much of his time waiting. The headquarters of the organization was in Switzerland; the Board that ran it consisted of five men who really knew what they were doing. And the company that provided the cover had its sign on a chain gate at the entrance to the camp. NAUGHTON AIRCRAFT DEFENSE CONSULTANTS, INC. NO TRESPASSING. THIS IS A FEDERAL SECURITY INSTALLATION.

The few people who inquired about the facilities were told that it was a "think tank," similar to Rand Corporation, and that explanation served as a cover for the foreign-speaking people who arrived and left at intervals. And it was secure, because Naughton Aircraft actually *had* a think tank contract with the Defense Department, but the "thinking" was done on the West Coast.

Leonard Chew had not trained here. He and Edwards had learned their trade in the old base, now closed, in North Carolina. But Chew had become a legend in a hurry and was still a legend in the organization.

Half of the devices shown to recruits in Saratoga were invented by him.

Now Chew was somewhere in a safe house with the nuclear bombs. Or so Edwards had heard. The news of Chew's betrayal had not yet reached him.

Edwards' recruits sat in fatigues in a screening room and saw and heard what the teleprobe had recorded through a window two hundred yards away. A closeup of the face of a man, talking, and every word he was saying, clear and loud in the screening room. And the window had been closed! The teleprobe was fantastic. The projectionist suddenly adjusted the lens, and they zoomed into the face so tightly that a small pimple rose like a soft mountain on the screen.

Edwards didn't need to tell these men what that new teleprobe meant as a blackmail device, as well as a conventional communications intercept tool. With a videotape recorder and a teleprobe, wiretapping would be absolutely unnecessary. Edwards called out to the projectionist, "Put on the Venetian."

The screen went white as the footage just recorded ended. Then the recruits watched a teleprobe film taken through a window shielded by Venetian blinds. The blinds were almost entirely closed, but an optical zoom to the slender opening between two slits revealed the face of a man in the room, while the words were heard. Edwards told the recruits, "Nothing stops the sound, not six-inch stone walls, not steel drapes. And with anything other than drapes, you get the picture, too." He waited while the Australian translated in three languages, and was happy when the door opened and someone called him out of the room. He told the Australian to take over and went through the corridor, following a brisk, short man with a choppy walk. The mes-

senger punched an elevator button, and they rode to the
fourth floor, where the executive offices were located.
Chauncey Harding, a small fragile man with a shiny
bald head, sat in a large leather chair behind a huge
desk. It was as if the large size of the furniture was
meant to deliberately emphasize his smallness—and, in
a way, provoke respect for his accomplishments, made
in spite of his size. Harding was the head of the training
camp, and the camp was growing as the organization
grew.

But now Chauncey took a daisy from a pink vase in
front of him and broke it with a snap. He tossed the
daisy onto the desk. "Chew's flown," he told Edwards.
"He took off with the bombs."

"Christ!"

"He left Jensen and Allworth in a freezer, and both
of them are dead. And Yaffi in Philadelphia is dead,
too."

Edwards sat down, his legs straight out, boots gash-
ing the carpet. He needed to be told nothing else. He
was the man who had personally recommended Chew
for the nuclear job. The others in the organization—
right up to Gustavus at the top—had felt Chew was still
too unstable after his Middle East trauma.

"So what are we doing?"

"We're trying to find Chew and we're sending a man
after our old friend Malcolm Bennett."

"What the hell has Bennett got to do with the nuclear
bombs?" Edwards asked Harding, who was regarding
him closely.

"That Arnold map you bought from Bennett, and
then so brilliantly lost. Chew left a fragment of it at the
missile site."

Edwards was absolutely stunned. *Chew* had stolen
the map from him?

His mind raced over the events that happened after he and Chew returned to Washington with the map. Edwards had told Chew he was taking the map to Gustavus. Mistake right there—but hell, Edwards was only taking it to a drop, not to the man himself. He didn't even know who Gustavus was. So what did it matter if Chew did tail him to the drop.

Not that he suspected Chew at that point. After an initial hostility Chew had been very cooperative, even enthusiastic about the missile theft. The technical aspects intrigued him. Three days afterward when Edwards went to pick up the Arnold map at the same drop, after Gustavus had seen it, he made no great effort to shake off a tail.

Of course Chew was a master of disguise and he probably could have followed Edwards anyway. But Jesus, now Edwards realized he should have suspected Chew at once when he was stopped by the Maryland State Police on suspicion of smuggling cocaine. While he was in State Police headquarters being stripped and searched, his briefcase had been stolen. And Edwards hadn't been suspicious of Chew because Edwards actually did use cocaine, although he had none on him when he was arrested. His cocaine habit was unknown to the Deep Men, so he didn't report the incident to them. Instead he told his superiors the map was stolen from his car by a street thief.

But it had been Chew all along. Chew! Harding continued, "And what's worse, Chew just sent a threat to the President and included a message for Gustavus. 'What you did in the Middle East is known.'"

"So Chew figured *that* out, too?" Edwards said. All was becoming clear to him. Somehow Chew had found out the truth about the accident to his family in the

Middle East—and all that "cooperative" bullshit had been a cover while he planned to betray them.

Harding said, "Gustavus isn't the most pleased man in the world. He's covering all tracks. How much did you tell Bennett about Gustavus?"

"I told him nothing. Just that the man who wanted to buy the map was respectable."

"Bennett has to be eliminated," Harding said. "He knows too much about us. He was with the organization in the Middle East. And he knows the organization bought the map from him. And if the FBI traces him, he'll talk. We can't take the chance."

"So what's it to me? Go after him."

Edwards was waiting for the kicker. Harding had not called Edwards just to tell him they were going to erase the little Canadian. Harding said, "They want you to fly to Towson today"—Harding paused, and consulted an elegant thin Cartier watch—"to be precise, in thirty minutes."

Edwards stood. "Do you know what's up?"

"We're hearing from all over the world. Great commotion, Kurt." He led Edwards to a room he hadn't visited before. A man sat at a switchboard ten feet high and twenty feet wide. It had green, red, and white lights. Edwards had heard of the board. The red lights were confidential calls being scrambled and relayed to Washington from all over the world. Green were calls in the clear. White were no calls. Now three-fourths of the board consisted of red lights.

Harding said, "There seems to be a consensus of opinion that Bennett is important, but a mere nuisance compared to George Williams."

Edwards knew of Williams, himself. Everyone in the business did. The CIA people walked in fear of him. "They want me to . . . handle Williams?"

"A nice word," Harding said, touching his lips as if in physical appreciation. "Yes. Handle. That's exactly what they're going to ask you to do."

16

MINUS 24:40 HOURS. JULY 1, LAKE CHAMPLAIN.

The desk clerk at the Helmsman Motel said to Peggy DuPont, "Malcolm Bennett checked out, ma'am. Ten minutes ago. Came charging in here, picked up his stuff, and ran. You're the second."

"Second what?"

"The second person who came looking for him. An hour ago an FBI man was here, but Bennett was still away. The FBI agent went out to check the beaches to see if Bennett was there." He paused. "Bennett sure acted funny when he heard the FBI was looking for him. He took off like a rabbit."

Peggy was thinking, what do I do now? She had expected to find Bennett, who would tell her that he was not the descendent Williams was looking for.

Now he was apparently running from the FBI. That was suspicious. She should call Williams at once, but by the time he contacted his men up here Bennett would be long gone. He had left only ten minutes earlier. She could catch him herself, in her rented Fiat. But she didn't even know Bennett's license number.

"Can I see the reservation book?" she asked.

The clerk said that was against regulations. Peggy was about to say she was from the FBI, also, and hope to God he didn't ask for identification when the man suddenly recognized her. She knew the signs immediately—a sort of stunned look, then anticipation, then stammering. "Say—I saw your picture in the newspapers," the clerk said. "Peggy DuPont, right? I'll be damned."

Peggy said, "I'm helping the FBI and he's running away. Could you show me the number of his license plate on the register?"

For this beautiful woman, the clerk apparently decided to forget every rule the motel had ever established. He turned the register toward her and pointed out Bennett's address: 135 King Street, Montreal, Canada. He had been driving a brown Ford Galaxie, license number NB 7–1876. She thanked him and ran to her car.

If Bennett lived in Canada, he was probably escaping in that direction. If he *was* "escaping." Perhaps the man had other reasons for leaving, having nothing to do with the FBI. But if he wasn't involved, he was certainly acting strangely.

Her Fiat raced north on a little road through stands of thick forest, the lake glimmering through the trees on her right. She wondered what she was doing. Not an hour ago she had been lying in a soft bed, scoffing at the thought that the little acrobatic man could be involved in Williams' investigation in any way.

And now she, of all people, was chasing him—as if it were the kind of thing she knew how to do. The fact was, Peggy had never chased anyone, but she knew how to handle a Fiat. At least one dividend from her background, Peggy thought. She imagined herself on the Grande Corniche, driving across the high blue mountains above the Mediterranean, full throttle out, wheel reacting gently to her touch, a party to be held on a Greek yacht later, and what would she wear, the red or the off-white? . . . and realized she was trying to divert her mind from a possible unpleasantness for which she had absolutely no experience at all. A man on the run who might turn on her with violence.

17

MINUS 23:50 HOURS. JULY 1, LAKE CHAMPLAIN.

KENTUCKY FRIED CHICKEN
LAST STOP

the sign on the diner said. Peggy DuPont slowed as she approached a gleaming white restaurant surrounded by cars, only ten miles south of the Canadian border.

Then she saw Bennett's brown Ford Galaxie, license number NB 7–1876. She parked her car behind his, blocking it off, then got out and surveyed the scene. She was hoping to find an outdoor telephone booth from which she could summon help from the FBI.

No phone. She would have to go in there alone. She pushed open the screen door of the diner and cautiously entered a wide room with booths along the windows and a long counter crowded with people. Her eyes went down the line of the people sitting on those stools—and then she froze. A face was staring in her direction from the end of the counter. Malcolm Bennett.

If she went to the telephone now, he would know something was wrong. Peggy decided to brazen it out. She walked down the counter toward the little man, who never stopped looking at her. A vacant stool rested beside him. She eased herself onto it and said, "The acrobat. How's tricks?"

Bennett apparently had seen her around the lake. He said, "What brings *you* here?"

Good question, Peggy thought. Brilliant, in fact. If she told the truth, she didn't know what he would do. If she lied, she wouldn't find out anything. "I'm racing you to the border. And right now we're even."

"I don't know what your action is, lady, but the race is about to start again. And you're going to lose." He stood up, but she put a hand lightly on his elbow. "Hey, acrobat. I'm on your side. Relax."

He was intrigued enough to sit down again. "Just what's up? Are you really trailing me?"

"Me—and the whole world," Peggy said. "I received my orders direct from the FBI, so if you think you can slide over the border and disappear into the woods, you're going to find a crowd around every tree."

"You're FBI? I don't believe it. Hell, I know you. The queen of the blue-bloods giving us a break just by showing up on the beach. Everybody just hoping you'll take one look at them." He paused. "Peggy DuPont isn't FBI. So what's up?"

Peggy said, "I'm not FBI, but a friend of mine is. He's looking for an illegitmate descendent of Arnold and you've been telling everyone all week that's what you are. So if you're mad at anyone, make a face in a mirror."

"But who told the FBI about me?"

"All I know is I'm to ask you one question. Are you descended from a woman named Nancy? Nobody wants to arrest you or anything. I'll tell them myself you've been right here at the lake, so you can't be involved in any bomb theft in North Dakota."

Bennett looked at her. "Nancy Bishop is my ancestor. OK? End of story."

"But why are you running away from the FBI?"

"I'm not running from the *FBI*," Bennett said, a statement that surprised Peggy. She said, "Look, no matter what you're doing, just talk to Mr. Williams and tell him on the phone about Nancy Bishop—and that you don't know anything else. That's all he wants." She saw him hesitate and added quickly, "I'll call him from here. It won't take a minute."

"Too risky," Bennett said.

"Too what?"

"You heard me." Bennett signaled for the check. Peggy put her hand on his wrist, but he shook it off.

"Please, Malcolm. There are some maniacs loose with nuclear bombs—and if you can help—"

"Don't tell me about the maniacs. Who do you think I'm worried about?"

That statement hung like a pall between them as Bennett took his check from the waitress. What should she do now? Call the FBI so they could barricade the road to the border? But they were too close and there wasn't enough time. She said, "I've blocked your car."

"What?"

"You can't move. I parked my car right behind you."

"You'll move it now."

Peggy said, "I'll tell you what I'm going to do. I'm walking into the ladies' room and dropping my car keys down the john. Now my car is locked, so if you want to call the police to tow it away—"

Malcolm was looking at her half smiling. "You've got balls, lady. Yessiree." There was sudden admiration in his voice. He paused. "Look, the minute I go you'll be on the phone to the FBI, right?" He thought a moment, then continued, "But lady, if I talk to the FBI, there are some characters I know who would slit you open just like you gut a fish. That means you're in trouble, too, just because you're with me."

Peggy could not believe him, so she said nothing. Who would kill her? She was just a messenger. Bennett went on, "What I mean is, if I go the other route I want protection."

"What's 'the other route' mean?"

"I'll tell your man Williams everything I know, but on one condition. I want FBI bodyguards all the way— until I say I'm safe. Can you arrange that?"

Peggy said she could, although the last thing she had arranged was a luncheon for twelve at Lutece.

She called George Williams from a pay phone in the diner, hearing the operator say, "The White House." An Army lieutenant picked up the extension, and then Williams was on the line. "I found him, George. His name is Malcolm Bennett. And he's agreed to talk to you."

"Does he admit he was running away? Does he admit that?"

"Yes, but not from the FBI. He's afraid of some other people. I'll put him on."

Bennett took the phone, and Williams told him neither the FBI nor the Canadian Mounties were going to let anyone disappear who might have knowledge of the nuclear thieves. He asked Bennett if he owned the map.

"No. But I used to—and I know who owns it now. They know I can describe them and they're killers."

"How do you know it's the same map we found?" Williams asked.

"Because there's a two-hundred-year-old letter that identifies the map—and mentions a message about revenge for Nancy. It's the map, all right."

"Where did you meet the people who own the map now?"

Bennett replied, "Middle East. I was an oil driller out there and ran into these characters. Biggest mistake of my life." He hesitated before saying, "Now that map is stirring up such a commotion, maybe I *am* safer with the FBI than on my own. If you fly me to Washington with a couple of six-foot-two guards, I'll tell you what I know."

Williams told Bennett to remain with Peggy, and he would send two FBI men to the diner. He asked Bennett to give him the names of the men he was worried about so he could start checking in Washington. But Bennett said, "Not on the telephone. I have news for you. You don't know what you're into. Your phone may be tapped."

"I'm using a White House phone."

"That's what I mean," Bennett said. "It's a rumor I heard once, but in this organization most of the rumors like that turn out to be true."

Which was a statement Williams was still pondering when he hung up and called Jarvis to make arrangements for FBI agents in Plattsburg to get Bennett and escort the Canadian to Washington.

Williams knew that U. S. Army technicians periodically swept the White House communication lines with sophisticated electronic equipment to detect any attempts at interception.

Nevertheless, Bennett's fear of talking to him bothered him for another reason. How would a Canadian oil driller from the Middle East have any information at all about a tap on the White House? From a rumor in an organization? Williams wanted to know more about that organization.

18

The "FBI agent" who had checked Bennett's motel before Peggy DuPont arrived sat in a green Buick sedan in the diner's parking lot. He was angry, although he didn't allow that emotion to disturb his professional poise.

His wrath was directed at himself because he had nearly missed Bennett altogether, driving off to the beach just when Bennett reappeared at the motel. When the "agent" returned, the clerk told him that Bennett had checked out, and a woman was pursuing him in a car.

That was the most unsettling development of all. Who was the woman who had appeared from nowhere to trail Bennett herself? When he saw her lead Bennett to a telephone in the diner, the "agent" was really alarmed. Did she know something about him?

Christ! He should cut out and call Washington, but they would take no excuses. Those were the very words that sent him in search of Bennett. No excuses! And now Bennett and the anonymous woman had returned from the phone to sit in the most dangerous location of all, the last booth down the line. If he employed his gun, even with a silencer, he ran the risk of being set upon by some local heroes at the counter before he could escape through the door.

No gun, not even a silencer, could be used. He drew thin rubber, flesh-colored gloves from a briefcase, and fitted his hands into them. Then he extracted a small gray tin from the case and removed the lid. The gray waxy substance inside resembled polish. The substance actually consisted of an oily compound known as Trichyclotiniline, a toxic chemical that acted upon its victim in minutes. He smeared the salve onto the palm of his right glove.

He went into the diner, approached Bennett's booth, and said, "Mr. Bennett?"

Bennett looked up at him suspiciously. The man said, "FBI." Then, as if surprised, he said, "Don't reach for a gun," and placed his gloved hand—the one containing the chemical—on the back of Bennett's hand. Bennett pushed it away, but the man knew it was already too late. He turned and walked out of the diner. Bennett stared at the back of his hand, then seized a napkin and rubbed the hand violently. "The son of a bitch," he said. "The son of a bitch!"

"What's wrong?" Peggy said.

"He put something on my hand, oh God," Bennett said. "Oh, my God! A doctor, Peggy, get a doctor!" He turned white as he slumped against the back of the booth.

Peggy ran to the counter. "Call a doctor, quick."

A car engine roared. Peggy did not look outside to check whether it belonged to the man who had come to their booth. The waitress she had approached shouted to the cook to call a doctor, another rushed to the booth with water. Peggy turned back to the booth and leaned over Bennett. "We're calling a doctor, Malcolm," she said. "Who was he?"

Bennett's lips were turning pale. He said, "Deep Men . . . did it . . . Edwards knows . . . Oh the . . . bastards . . . Help me, Peggy . . . Help . . ."

Peggy was living a nightmare. Tears welled in her

eyes as she stared at the little man, who was now beginning to shudder in a seizure and whose pleas for aid she could not answer. A woman who identified herself as a nurse shoved Peggy aside and felt Bennett's pulse.

Peggy remembered something. "Don't touch the back of his hand," she said, so sharply that the nurse dropped Bennett's wrist in surprise. When a doctor arrived, Peggy told him about the salve. He looked at her strangely but respected her warning. By the time FBI agents came, it was all over. Malcolm Bennett was dead.

19

MINUS 22:50 HOURS. JULY 1, WASHINGTON.

George Williams called the CIA Director at home. "You heard the news?"

"Yes—and I was expecting your call. I know what everyone in this town is thinking. First the cyanide pill, and now a poisonous salve."

Williams said that FBI analysts had identified the poisonous substance as Trichyclotiniline. "Does CIA stockpile that?"

Winthrop was irritated. "We stockpile *no* exotic chemicals. Congress put a stop to that sort of thing several years ago. We're out of the poison business."

Williams said, "Edgewood?" referring to the Army's Chemical Warfare base in Maryland, which CIA had once used. But Winthrop repeated his statement that the company was not storing exotic poisons *anywhere*. "Edgewood doesn't work for us anymore."

Williams paused before saying, "Could there be chemicals stored by agents in the company—and you don't know about it?"

"I won't lie to you, George. I had a private meeting with the President just a short time ago. I told him I don't have complete control over there. But I have made a special effort to ensure that we don't become identified with those chemicals again."

Williams told the Director that Bennett had mentioned a name, "Edwards," and an organization, "The Deep Men." And the inside man at the missile site had left a note that said "D.M. June 29." "D.M. could be the initials for the Deep Men. I want to have access to the Green Room."

The CIA Director protested, "Now, George, you know that no one—without direct orders from the President and only in the most extreme emergencies—"

Williams said, "I have the authorization from the President, and I need to check those names in the Green Room myself."

The CIA Director was irritated. He said good-bye curtly.

But twenty minutes later he was in his car waiting at the gate that guarded the entrance to a secret wooded enclave along the Potomac. Inside the enclave was a complex of buildings belonging to the CIA. What angered Winthrop was that Williams' presence in the Green Room would mark the end of what small influence he maintained over CIA department chiefs. Not even U. S. Senators—at the height of the well-publicized Congressional probe of the organization—had been allowed to enter there.

20

The Central Intelligence Agency's Green Room came into existence shortly after the formation of the agency in 1947. It was then housed in a small gray room in the old wooden CIA buildings along the Capitol Mall, not far from the Lincoln Memorial. Only one clerk was needed to supervise a modest array of file cabinets filled with cards.

Then the first computers were installed in a larger room. By 1961, when the CIA moved to Langley, Virginia, it already owned the largest, most comprehensive intelligence file in the U. S., quite possibly the world. And the records kept growing. In Senate testimony in 1975 its Director admitted that the file contained forty million "bits of information" on individuals and organizations.

Guards manned the entrance to the room. Even Winthrop had to insert his computerized security card into a slot beneath a screen, which then flashed the words "Valid. Title: CIA Director. Clearance: Unrestricted Access."

George Williams entered a room three stories high with dark seagreen walls against which banks of similarly colored computers seemed to be purposely camouflaged into invisibility. Black formica tables throughout the length of the high-ceilinged room supported television monitors about eighteen inches square, microfilm viewers with cranks on their sides, and typewriter panels in gray boxes. Winthrop guided Williams to one of the television monitors. "Most amazing computer in the world, George."

"Why?"

"Because it's something new, a subject computer. When you type in a request the computer will not only flash every bit of data it has on the subject, it will search out all relevant data, even though you may not *know* it's relevant. It thinks for you."

Williams said he wanted all information on an organization named the Deep Men, which Peggy had reported to Williams were among the last words Bennett uttered as he died.

"OK," Winthrop said. "Type it in. Here, I'll do it for you."

He sat down and typed, "SUBJECT: THE DEEP MEN."

Small electronic beeps sounded, and letters flashed across the screen:

"CONFIRM YOUR REQUEST."

"That's funny," Winthrop said. He seemed upset. Williams asked him what was wrong.

" 'Confirm your request' either means the computer has nothing or there is some special problem."

"Did you *expect* it to have something on the Deep Men?"

Winthrop's voice hardened. "I didn't *say that*. I'm just surprised the computer doesn't have it. I was certain every organization in the world was on these tapes."

He typed "CONFIRMING SUBJECT: THE DEEP MEN." Letters glowed on the screen:

"INFORMATION ON THE DEEP MEN ERASED FOR SECURITY REASONS DECEMBER 17, 1976, PER INSTRUCTIONS OF CIA DIRECTOR."

Erased! Winthrop looked at Williams, who was studying that electronic message intently. "I didn't give the computer those instructions, George. I never heard of the Deep Men."

Ten minutes later Williams had a print-out in his hands of no fewer than thirty men named Edwards, ranging from an IRS tax dodger in New Haven to an undercover agent in East Berlin. But if information on the Deep Men had been erased, the Edwards he was searching for would be nowhere on this list, either.

No luck at CIA. Never any luck at CIA. When Williams had tried to probe the agency before, he had faced a maze of blank walls, cutoffs, code names that had defeated him. Now he had hoped that by penetrating the Green Room itself, in a national emergency, he could somehow physically wrest the secret information he needed from the agency. But again he had been frustrated.

He was leaving the Green Room, wondering what his next move would be, when an idea occurred to him. Maybe there were other names erased. He asked Winthrop to return to the machine and type in a request for all the names that had been erased on instructions of the CIA Director.

The computer said:

"SUBJECT: THE DEEP MEN. ERASED."

"NAME: EDWARDS, KURT. ERASED."

"NAME: PATTERSON, ROBERT. ERASED."

Robert Patterson was a new name. Another Deep Man, and one so important that all information on him had been removed.

Williams needed to know more about Patterson, as well as Edwards and the Deep Men. But how could he get that information through a government whose files had been systematically rifled by an organization so powerful it could reach the ultrasecret tapes in the Green Room?

21

A FEW WEEKS AGO WHEN LEONARD CHEW, THE MAN who had been known as Robert Patterson in the Middle East, was in the midst of his torment, flying to different cities to scout targets, he had awakened one night in a lonely motel room shuddering from the most vivid nightmare he ever had.

He was with his two children and his wife swimming in surging ocean water, and orders had come to them that they must die, there was no escape, nothing they could do. Chew had tried to think, but waves battered and pulled at him, and his ten-year-old daughter, the one who was so bright, who "took after" her father and who loved him, said in her usual quiet way, "I might as well do it now," and she swam into the ocean and allowed herself to drown. He never saw his wife but sensed she was behind him, drowning too, and his nine-year-old son was swimming in the sea, but Chew couldn't find him in the waves, and a voice was saying to Chew, "There's no use waiting. It's all over." The body of his daughter drifted face up alongside him, brown hair surrounding her young face—and Chew woke with a feeling of nausea.

He couldn't banish the dream from his mind that

night. He smoked a cigarette, and thought of its symbolism. The tidal wave he would create? Yes. It burdened his conscience. He was not a mass murderer, no matter what they would say about him in generations to come.

But more frightening yet was the appearance of his family in that tidal-wave dream. They had died far from the ocean and were now buried in a grave in Lebanon. Wife, son, and daughter. His life was in that grave. And now they were dying again together in his tidal wave. Why? Their deaths had tortured him enough.

Driving on a road toward his first nuclear target, Chew forced that sick dream out of his mind. He had to.

What worried him most was that he might be experiencing a recurrence of the "nuclear fatigue" which had put him in a mental clinic for six months during his Los Alamos career, and from which he had never entirely recovered. He knew that. It was only the most urgent and overwhelming hatred that had seen him through this far with those bombs. And he would not fail. He would explode those bombs, and that would be the answer to all the agony that began so long ago in a little room in Los Alamos in 1962.

22

IN 1962 PRESIDENT KENNEDY ENTERED THE BROAD-cast room in the basement of the White House to make the most important speech of his life. A few minutes later, appearing tense and talking with great deliberation to control a possible quavering of his voice, he said:

". . . These are the photos of the nuclear missile bases which the Soviet Union is building in Cuba . . ."

23

IN LOS ALAMOS A TWENTY-FIVE-YEAR-OLD NUCLEAR scientist named Leonard Chew watched that speech on television and began to tremble violently. For the past few months his associates at the base had worried about him; he had appeared shaken and nervous, so much so that they took him off projects where he needed to do precise work with his hands. The phenomenon was familiar to everyone at the base; it was a recurring disease. Sooner or later the bright young technological men who came to them from universities began to understand just what nuclear weapons meant. Most of them adjusted, but the more sensitive sometimes cracked.

Chew had already shown symptoms of anxiety. For reasons Chew later could not understand it was the October missile crisis that brought on the final breakdown. A fellow scientist heard him groaning, rushed into his room, and found Chew in what he thought was an epileptic seizure.

Two weeks later Chew's mind came into focus. He was in a hospital bed, and the sweetest face he had ever seen was looking down at him, worriedly. The white dress and half-cap identified her as a nurse. Now, as she saw him open his eyes and look at her, she said, "Oh, good *morning, Mr. Chew.*"

He had been conscious during those two weeks but did not comprehend anything. Even now his mind felt sluggish and his eyes were not clear. The nurse turned out to have a lovely name, Hope Ryden. She informed him that he was in the "Special Patients" floor of the Los Alamos Neurological Hospital.

Chew didn't like the sound of the words "Special Patients," but in answer to his question about it she summoned a brisk young doctor. The doctor told him that "Special Patients" simply meant those people with undiagnosed psychiatric problems. "In your case," he said, "we're rather certain of the problem. Too much thinking about that devilish work of yours. But we've found this is just a symptomatic problem, nothing more. With luck, we'll have you out of here in a month."

"A month?"

"Oh, there are tests we have to take. You could use a bit of a rest anyway, don't you think? Your supervisor said you've been working ten hours a day."

He murmured something to the nurse about medication, then turned back to Chew. "Now, Miss Ryden will take special care of you, and I don't think we'll object to that."

But Chew wanted to know more. "What happened to me, Doctor? I remember I was watching television—"

"You had a seizure, Mr. Chew. That's why we must run tests. We don't want it to happen again."

When Chew heard that, he knew that his own world had come to an end. The years of study at MIT, those endless hours in the university Radiation Lab, the promise he had shown at Alamos, the designs, the plans, the life he had carved for himself were finished. He had become a mental cripple, perhaps even a hazard in this kind of work. The terrible thing was he started to cry.

The nurse said, "Now, Mr. Chew, there's nothing to get upset about. You'll be healthy as a horse in ten days, not a month. I'm going to make you my special project."

Chew looked into compassionate blue eyes and wavy blond hair and later would tell Hope that this was the moment he subconsciously fell in love with her. But at the time he saw her only as a nurse who knew how to comfort patients.

Mental clinics are the same the world over. Unseeing people with blank eyes shuffle down corridors, others sit in silence while a television set blares, and still others play Ping-Pong. No pool table, unfortunately for Chew. What he wanted to do was read in his room. But his wish to be alone went against psychiatric policy. He had to mingle with the other patients. And they were a strange group on this floor. One, the teen-age daughter of a colonel, walked the corridors quietly until, at regular intervals, she looked up at the ceiling and shouted "FUCK!" Chew at first thought it was a joke but then heard she had been here for six months. There was no medication that could prevent those agonized shrieks.

The colonel was tall, stiff, very worried. His wife was trim and youthful, in the style of Army wives everywhere. Only generals' wives could afford to be comfortably stout. During visiting hours the colonel and his wife walked their daughter up and down the hallway, talking quietly, and sanely, until suddenly the girl's face would convulse toward the ceiling and the word would ring out.

Chew suggested to Hope Ryden that the girl might not shout the word if she were outside in the normal world and was told that the reason they had confined her in this mental ward was that she kept screaming it in her college classes, on the streets, everywhere.

In the years that followed, Chew never forgot that girl and often yearned to have her disease, to feel what must be an orgasmic release in shouting his defiance in that one all-consuming word.

But in those days he was more worried about himself. It seemed he couldn't stop shaking. What made convalescence even slower was a shameful feeling that swept over him when he remembered the crisis, and he—a thousand miles away—had been overwhelmed with fear. Yet his terror made no sense. Chew's whole life— as that of all Americans his age—had been an unending series of wars and international crises. He was used to them.

One day, sitting in the sunlight on a porch surrounded by rubber plants, he spoke to Hope Ryden about it. She said, "I'm not a doctor, but I'd say you were fantasizing about your work on the bombs—and this Cuban crisis made it sound *real* for the first time."

Chew told her that his father had been a soldier in two wars, that he had died in battle in Korea, and that he, the son, must have some of his father's courage and stamina, so he couldn't understand why he had reacted in such a disturbed fashion. He had known from the first what nuclear bombs meant—they weren't just abstract mathematical formulas—so why did this mental breakdown happen in the first place?

The nurse told him it was not a "breakdown" and he shouldn't think it was. His problem was simply mental fatigue, nothing more.

But then she won Chew's affection by asking to hear more about his father, and Chew found himself telling her of John Chew's football exploits, and the battles he had fought, and even of the time in Washington when he had explained to his son the difference between rich and poor people. Hope liked that.

Chew said, "I wanted to be like him, but nature intervened. I applied for West Point when I finished high school, and I couldn't pass the physical. Weak eyes, and a body half an inch too short." He paused. "So I had a scholarship to MIT, and here I am."

"You mean you didn't want to be a scientist?"

"Oh, no, I enjoy it. I have a mind that likes to solve problems. I have no *quarrel* with my mental ability. It's my muscles I hold against God."

Hope Ryden laughed, and Chew grew to know her better, and when he was released in ninety days and faced the Los Alamos Director in his office he was neither surprised nor saddened when the Director said, "For your health, Leonard, we think you should take a good long holiday."

A holiday that meant forever. But Leonard Chew could not be depressed. He had found a wife, if she would have him. And a man from a large aircraft company had already offered him a well-paying job "in Beirut, which might be very interesting to you."

Chew took that "position" with Naughton Aircraft in 1963, the year he married Hope Ryden, and in the next two years a daughter and son were born, and those were the three people in a grave somewhere in Lebanon now while he was on the road to a place called Ocean City, New Jersey, where he would make this country pay one final price for its madness.

24

Leonard Chew arrived at the bridge that led to the island and the resort city off the Jersey coast. There he was stopped by a roadblock. MPs with white helmets and armbonds were checking cars, using Geiger counters. It was not a popular move with the many anxious drivers who were going into Ocean City to rescue their families and possessions. The wait seemed interminable. Finally, soldiers inspected Chew's car, turned up seats, poked Geiger counters everywhere.

Chew had packed the nuclear bombs in the rear axle of his car, where they were protected by lead. An MP, lying on his back on a flat rolling platform, slid under the car. When he approached the rear axle, Chew was lighting a cigarette and chatting with a guard. The Geiger counter passed under the axle, two inches away. No clicks.

The Cape Cod cottage at 2872 Central Avenue was white with green shutters, dormered windows, and a red stone terrace. Its attic had been carefully prepared by Chew. He drove the car into the garage, closed the door, and spent an hour removing one of the nuclear bombs from the axle of the car.

Then he went to the attic and donned his gas mask, to begin preparing the bomb for the explosion. This time he also put on heavy gloves, for he was going to handle the plutonium itself. He removed the lump of nuclear material and started to work. A thump on the roof startled him so much he froze. What was that? He waited for a minute—then—Thump!—it happened again. He replaced the plutonium in the bomb from which he had removed it, then walked to a trapdoor, lifted it, went part way down the ladder, and closed the door above him.

The thumping noise now sounded remote. Chew went out the front door. A tennis ball bounced over the roof and came down onto the lawn, rolling into the street.

Tommy Hill, the boy next door, ran around Chew's house, stopped short when he saw Chew. "Oh . . . Hi!" he said. "I was playing outfield."

Chew knew the game. Throw the ball on a sloping roof where it remained hidden from view until it rolled off and the player dived for it. He smiled at the boy. "In the dark?"

"It's more fun if it's hard to see," the boy said. He ran by Chew to retrieve the ball from the gutter. When he returned, he said, "Where you been, anyway? My father says it's funny your house has been empty."

"Why?"

"Every place in Ocean City has been full this summer. And yours was the only empty one."

Chew said he had been "up north on business" and was sorry he had missed part of the season.

The boy bounced the tennis ball on the pavement and caught it. Sometimes he missed. Now he stopped to pick up the ball. "My father wants to stay but we won't let him."

"With the bomb threat?"

"That's right. My father thinks it will never happen. That sooner or later the bad guys will call it off."

Chew said, "Well, I'm not taking any chances. I

came back to get my things. But if your father's right, I'll return in a few days."

An attractive woman came to the door of the house next to his. "Tommy, come in and have a peanut butter sandwich before we go."

"OK, Mom," Tommy said. "Mr. Monroe's back."

The woman opened the screen door and came out. She had a lovely smile. "My goodness," she said, "the legendary Mr. Monroe. Tommy's ready to trade his father for you. And his father isn't too happy about it."

Chew smiled. "I showed him how to spin a basketball once. Maybe I should teach his father, too."

"I'll tell him," she said. "Would you like to come over for a drink before we leave? I've finally convinced Joe that we should go."

Chew said, "Thanks, but I'll be busy packing."

"If you change your mind, we'll have a drink to the tidal wave, and the end of this town." She was smiling brightly. Chew couldn't tell whether there were tears in her eyes.

Chew said he would try to drop over and Tommy grinned and ran across the lawn to his own house. Chew went back upstairs with the gas mask and in five minutes was crouching beside the bomb again, preparing the plutonium which would explode tomorrow, destroying both these houses and killing everyone who remained inside.

My God, what was he doing? Suppose those people next door didn't actually leave. He must put them out of his mind. That mother with a smile. That boy who reminded him of his own son.

And they wanted him to have a drink with them!

He finished preparing the plutonium, turned to a radio transmitter, and started testing it with a meter he had stored in the attic. Power up. Breathe into mike. The needle jumps. Good.

Now he used a drill to bore through the roof beneath the screws that held the weather vane. A few minutes later he was threading wires from the radio transmitter through the roof.

When he finished his preparation the nuclear bomb was packaged with a radio receiver in a green plastic waterproof bag. A radio transmitter that would send the signal at 6 P.M. tomorrow from the attic was connected to the weather vane. Chew stored them in leadlined containers behind a false panel in the attic.

Built in a very special way, the panel was backed by a four-inch coating of rubber. An inspector tapping the wall to see if it was hollow would hear a thud that sounded solid.

Chew went downstairs. Through the windows he saw the Hills packing their car. Joe Hill was a heavy man in a flowered sport shirt. He came out of the house now with the basketball and threw it to Tommy.

Leonard turned on the television, which was running nonstop news, live, on all three networks, and heard, "George Williams of the Justice Department announced moments ago that the government has identified two men connected to the organization involved in the murder of Malcolm Bennett. Kurt Edwards and Robert Patterson."

Chew froze. The Justice Department had the name he had used with the Deep Men in the Middle East. Bennett must have told them before he died. What else had Bennett said? Had he given a description of Chew?

Chew had never used the name Robert Patterson in the States. Still, the disclosure of his Patterson name bothered him. It could lead to further information about him, if the government knew where to look.

25

George Williams was stymied. He called Mitchell Birch, an ex-Justice Department attorney who had moved to the Library of Congress to become head of its American Law Division. In this position Birch knew just about everything that passed through Congressional hearings, and he did not disappoint Williams now. "I already heard about your 'Deep Men' on television and I was thinking about them. Do you know Jim Parker?"

Parker was the Chief Counsel of the Senate Subcommittee on Multinational Corporations. Williams had followed the unfolding story of the Senate investigation, with its testimony of bribes amounting to millions of dollars that were passed to princes, premiers, and government leaders throughout Europe, Asia, and the Middle East. Birch said, "While that chicanery was going on, there were all kinds of secret organizations founded by the multinational corporations in Europe and the Middle East. The Deep Men might be one of them."

Williams told him he knew Parker, but one of the Senators or staffers would have called him if the Deep Men had been mentioned in a hearing. Birch didn't agree.

"Might be classified, so they're still getting clearance first. Or maybe someone's holding back. Or the Deep Men is not one of the organizations that were mentioned."

Williams called Jim Parker at home. A soft voice answered. Williams told the Senate Counsel he was looking for any information on a group known as the Deep Men.

Parker surprised him. "I have something on them. Can you meet me at my office? Alone?"

A small office on Capitol Hill, with a desk piled high with papers, briefs, and reports. Jim Parker sat back in his chair, a harsh overhead light glinting on his glasses. "I know you're wondering why I didn't call you as soon as I heard the name of the Deep Men on television." He was talking so quietly that Williams had to strain to hear him. "I can now tell you why. The Deep Men were mentioned in a hearing that was not mine. It was testified to in one of the CIA Assassination Hearings. I got a copy of the CIA hearing only by a fluke. The Committee Counsel sent me a copy because it had some dope on multinationals, and I never got around to returning it. Now I hear that all the other copies of that hearing have disappeared. When I offered to return my copy, the Counsel on the CIA Committee told me to hold onto it. He said it's more secure with me because no one knows I have it. And he doesn't trust his own staff. Can you beat that?" Parker went to a small green safe that squatted in a corner of the room. He spun a combination, opened the door, and pulled out two green-covered transcripts. The top one bore the title:

CIA ASSASSINATIONS OF FOREIGN LEADERS
Secret Executive Sessions

"That's the one that has testimony on the Deep Men," Parker said.

Williams said he still didn't understand why one of the Senators or staffers who attended the CIA hearing hadn't called the FBI with the name of the Deep Men. Parker told him, "They *have* called—each other. They have a problem, and that problem is sensitive. You'll realize what it is when you read the testimony. But, of course, with nuclear bombs on the loose, they finally decided that everything else goes out the window. My friend at the Committee called and told me he had obtained Senator Carson's authorization to let you see the transcript."

Williams was about to open the small green book when Parker stopped him. "You should read some testimony at this other hearing first. It will help you understand the background." He handed Williams a three-inch-thick transcript with the title:

Hearings
before the
SUBCOMMITTEE ON
MULTINATIONAL CORPORATIONS
of the
COMMITTEE ON FOREIGN RELATIONS
UNITED STATES SENATE

Parker said, "I'm sure you followed the multinational hearings."

Williams nodded. "American multinationals were accused of funneling money to foreign leaders."

"That's the public part," Parker said. Williams asked him what he meant, and the Counsel leaned forward in his seat, elbows on the desk. "The testimony we couldn't reveal, which is still secret, had to do with a sensitive intrigue that emerged, and that's relevant to the people you're looking for."

"What was that?"

Parker said. "You probably know that some of these

companies set up private organizations in Europe as blinds that were cut off from the companies that sponsored them. I think Naughton Aircraft's version, the so-called Economic Improvement Corporation, is the one that has meaning for you."

"Why?"

"Because from the way I read the record Naughton's company, EIC, is the germ from which the Deep Men grew."

Parker explained that EIC was incorporated in Switzerland, with a front man as the President whom the people at Naughton never met or saw. All the stockholders were completely unknown to Naughton.

"And that isn't all," Parker said. "EIC's contract with Naughton stated that it would never communicate or report in any fashion to the corporation that financed it. It would operate completely in the dark. Look what Senator Carson says about that. He can't believe it's real."

SENATOR CARSON: You had no idea who EIC hired as its agents. EIC just sold weapons using bribes or other methods, which you never knew, through agents you never saw?

MR. HALL (*Naughton President*): That's correct, Senator.

SENATOR CARSON: It's one thing to employ salesmen in a foreign country to inform you of local procurement practices. But this corporation is organized so that you couldn't even know what it was doing. You didn't even know who the agents were, or what they did. As far as you knew, they might have done nothing. But still, if F-20 aircraft were sold, you would pay them 1 percent of the contract as a fee. That is a strange setup, to say the least.

MR. HALL: But it was legal, Senator. Mr. Koenig is a lawyer who is an expert in this field. He advised us.

"Stop right there," Parker said. "Mr. Koenig is the key."

Parker told Williams that for many years Koenig had served as West Germany's legal counsel in the United States. "Koenig told Senate investigators that he had never before concerned himself personally with any business arrangement other than as a legal advisor. Suddenly, he not only involved himself in a business arrangement—but he did it with a curious combination of CIA agents and German military officials. How did EIC start? Very interesting. Koenig set up a meeting in Europe between Naughton's President and two high-level German military men. The Germans were accompanied by an American who was supposed to be with the U. S. State Department." Parker pointed to a page. "Here's Mr. Hall's testimony on that meeting."

Williams read:

"Mr. W. M. Reinhardt and Mr. Eric Yost of the German Ministry of Defense came to the meeting. An American arrived with them named John Collins. The Germans told me that Collins was a representative of the American State Department."

Parker was reading the paragraph over Williams' shoulder. He said, "Collins wasn't State. He was a CIA case officer in Berlin. We checked CIA. They admitted he was theirs. But we had some trouble confirming Collins' role in the incorporation of EIC. We were told that he had resigned from the agency in Europe and was unavailable for testimony." He looked at Williams. "And good luck on finding him now.

"So guess where the President of this outfit came from," Parker continued. "His name is Dr. Franz D'Albert. Mr. Hall told us he never met D'Albert in person, but he was recommended very highly by the Institute for Political Affairs in Princeton. Now I believe Mr. Hall was pulling our legs with that one because everyone in the room knew the Institute in Princeton was and is a CIA front. Do you get the picture? The facts are a German lawyer, two German military men, and an American CIA agent established a secret organization with another CIA agent as President. Why? For business?"

Williams waited, and Parker said, "For funny business. Where money is only a sideline."

"What do you mean?"

"That's where the CIA Assassination Hearings come in."

Williams opened the transcript of the second set of hearings; these were on the CIA. He turned to the pages Parker had marked:

SENATOR MARCH: I want it stated in the record that the witness is appearing before the executive committee in a black headdress that covers his face. For purposes of this hearing we will call him Mr. Rowe. Mr. Rowe, were you ever employed by the Central Intelligence Agency?

WITNESS: Not exactly, Senator.

MARCH: You mean you might have been so employed and might not know it?

WITNESS: Yes, sir. I was hired by the Deep Men. . . .

MARCH: Who, sir? Would you repeat that, please.

WITNESS: The Deep Men. That was the organization run by EIC in Switzerland. Unofficial name for us EIC people, sir.

MARCH: What is EIC?

WITNESS: Economic Improvement Corporation.

Supposed to be a sales organization for Naughton Aircraft, sir. But we weren't in sales.

MARCH: What did you do?

WITNESS: Whatever the people in Switzerland told us to do. EIC is really owned by ex-CIA agents, sir. The sales organization is just a cover. It's a way for them to get financial backing while they make their own hardline political moves.

MARCH: Does Naughton know this?

WITNESS: I don't know, sir. That part's above my head. Maybe the Deep Men are fooling Naughton; maybe the Naughton people know all along where their money's really going.

MARCH: But if not for sales, for what? What exactly do you do?

WITNESS: Political pressure, Senator. Make the world safe for democracy—and capitalism. Bribery, blackmail, sometimes assassinations are what we use.

MARCH: With all respect to you, sir, I find this testimony difficult to believe. I know the President of Naughton Aircraft. Can you give us one example of a *real* assassination attempt?

WITNESS: Yes, sir. In 1975 in Beirut we were going to mine the limousine belonging to the Lebanese Vice-President. It was in a repair station, and it would be simple to get in there and fix some plastique in a way it wouldn't be found unless they tore the car apart looking for it. So that's what we did.

MARCH: Who did? Be specific, please.

WITNESS: Mr. Robert Patterson. He was a scientist who worked with the Deep Men.

MARCH: What happened next?

WITNESS: The worst thing that ever happened to a man. At five P.M. every day the Vice-President was driven home to the suburbs in his limousine. We set the timer for five fifteen so he would be out of the city. But we didn't know about the Lebanese Art Gallery.

MARCH: What did that have to do with it?

WITNESS: On September 4, the art gallery opened and tourists were invited. Instead of going home the Vice-President went to that opening, and at five fifteen, when the bomb exploded, his limousine was parked beside cars belonging to tourists. Ten people were killed, including Patterson's own wife and two children. My God. (*Witness pauses.*) Poor Patterson went crazy when he heard his wife and two children died in the explosion.

MARCH: What happened to the Vice-President?

WITNESS: He was saved, but he got the message. He quit shortly after that.

MARCH: What happened to Patterson?

WITNESS: Nothing. The Deep Men got him out of the country. They took care of him. He's back in America now, and that's one reason I'm wearing this hood.

MARCH: I yield to the Senator from Minnesota.

SENATOR NORTH: Is this typical of the kind of actions you participated in there?

WITNESS: Yes, sir. And in America, too.

NORTH: You have Deep Men in America working to undercut the President? And assassination teams, too? Mr. Rowe, I'm afraid—

WITNESS: It's true, sir. Just to give you one example, the White House communication lines are all being intercepted right now.

(*Commotion in the panel. Several Senators interrupting.*)

NORTH: (*angrily*): Do you have any proof of these accusations that are taking up so much of the committee's valuable time?

WITNESS: No, sir. As I told your Counsel in executive

sessions, even if I did, I couldn't reveal it because that would enable the Deep Men to pinpoint who I am.

NORTH: And you can't give us your real name so we can check your credibility? You can't give us any proof at all. All you do is ask us to believe there's some sort of conspiracy complete with assassination teams—and all backed by legitimate American businessmen. I must say, speaking for myself, I am very, very skeptical.

SENATOR BRICKER: May I have the floor, Mr. Chairman?

NORTH: I'll yield.

SENATOR BRICKER: Unlike most of my colleagues on this panel, I'm inclined to believe you. But you must understand, Mr. Rowe. This panel has been subjected to the most bizarre witnesses over the past weeks. Mafia gangsters of every type have come to us with incredible stories about CIA, spreading important names all over the place. And other people, in disguise like you, claiming to be ex-CIA agents, have testified that CIA was behind every assassination and outrage that has ever happened in this country. And we find it very difficult to separate fact and fantasy. Now you come to us with an even more incredible story. Ex-CIA agents are operating out of Switzerland behind the cover of a corporation set up by a legitimate American business. If you could just bring one small item of proof—

WITNESS: I can't, Senator. I don't *have* one item of proof. (*Laughter.*)

BRICKER: Surely you have one piece of paper. One copy of an intercepted message.

WITNESS: Nothing, Senator. The Deep Men made certain of that. All I have is my knowledge, my experience—and I'm pleading with you Senators because you're the ones that can do something—

BRICKER: We can't run without the ball, Mr. Rowe.

What do you expect us to do? Go out to the press and announce there's some sort of evil conspiracy involving American businessmen, and we have no proof, but a man in a hood with a fake name told us?

The testimony trailed off into derisive comments at the witness's expense, and he was dismissed. Williams looked at Parker. "What was Naughton Aircraft's reply to Rowe's charges?"

"Flat-out denial. EIC was a sales organization. Period. Assassinations and violence? Never."

"Then what did CIA say?" Williams asked, adding, "Winthrop told me tonight that he never heard of the Deep Men, but they're accused in a Senate hearing that CIA must have been aware of."

"*Secret* hearing, George. CIA had liaison men on the Hill during the sessions but both of us know the 'company.' This particular testimony might have never circulated to the Director. I can find the names of those liaison men, and you can start checking in Langley."

But Williams told him not to bother. He had already tried to do that. He thanked Parker and went back to the White House, his mind on one name. Robert Patterson. According to the testimony Patterson was a scientist who belonged to the Deep Men who was in this country. And something terrible had happened to him in the Middle East, the loss of his entire family— something that could have driven him mad.

26

MINUS 20:00 HOURS. JULY 1, OCEAN CITY, NEW JERSEY.

Night in Ocean City. Leonard Chew backed his car out of the garage and turned south to drive along the ocean. A jeep approached with four soldiers, its headlights blinding him. One of the soldiers glanced at Chew as the jeep passed.

Chew was on his way to reconnoiter the beaches from which he would launch the nuclear bomb. The southern area of the island was his choice because it was heavily duned and had fewer houses from which a last-minute straggler might spot him.

Chew wanted to see for himself what security measures the government was taking to prevent him from launching the bomb.

He parked the car at Fifty-fourth Street in the front of a house on the beach. The house had been evacuated. He went inside, climbed to the second floor, then walked into a bedroom with chenille bedspreads, a sailing ship on a maple dresser, and a rocking chair with a blue cushion decorated with a Navy anchor. Chew went to the window, dropped to his knees, and looked out at the dark beaches.

A pale phosphorescent glow filtered through the thin white surf of the breakers. Then a helicopter swung south, searchlight bobbing across the waves. Almost at the same time a jeep moved slowly across the beach, its light sweeping the dunes.

Chew waited fifteen more minutes. Another helicopter came by, and the patrol jeep returned from its trip to the south end of the island.

Helicopters and jeeps, but widely spaced. The Army had the whole coastline of New Jersey and Long Island to patrol. He could handle that type of security. At 3 A.M. he would be crouching behind that dune right in front of his house with the craft that would propel the nuclear bomb to its resting place beneath the sea.

Nothing could stop him now.

27

MINUS 16:30 HOURS. JULY 2, WASHINGTON.

General Maxwell was angry. The Chairman of the Joint Chiefs stood alongside Williams in the Situation Room, a large map of the New Jersey shore suspended above them on a wall. Maxwell said, "A whole coast to cover. It's damned impossible."

He pointed to the magnetized symbols indicating helicopters and jeep patrols along the coast. "We've forbidden any boats in the ocean. Arrested some small boat crews today and scared a Russian freighter to death. But still—"

"A man like him will find a way, with or without a boat."

The General nodded. "It's so frustrating. If we only knew which town, which region, we could concentrate our forces—but he's too smart for that."

Williams was leaving the Situation Room for the airport to pick up Peggy DuPont. Peggy was flying from

Champlain with the description of the man who had killed Bennett. She had also spoken to Bennett's sister. He saw that huge map on the wall with its small symbols and didn't have any more hope than Maxwell that they could prevent that bomb from being planted. It could be happening right now, in the dark night off a quiet shore, away from prowling helicopters.

George Williams made one more check of the television monitors before he left. He had found the search a fascinating spectacle. Right now on one monitor he saw dark waves below a helicopter off Hoboken suddenly whitened by the chopper's searchlight, passing back and forth. On another a jeep rolled along a ghostly beach at Asbury Park. On a third monitor a Coast Guard sailor on a lookout tower gazed out to sea in Atlantic City, a frightened look on his face.

Other monitors showed scenes of the evacuation, which was going well. Only the hospitals in the larger cities had posed a real problem, and the Army had sent fleets of ambulances and medical personnel to aid the transfer of the ill.

General Maxwell pushed a button. A great tent city outside of Asbury Park appeared on the monitor. But Williams' attention was on another TV monitor. A man in a speedboat was racing out to sea. Helicopters closed in on him; searchlights showed a white face staring up in anger, shouting. A burst of gunfire crossed his bow— and the boat slowed, then stopped. A helicopter lowered a soldier toward him.

Maxwell said to Williams, "You think—"

"I don't know."

Maxwell shouted to a colonel, "Get me the helicopter frequency up there."

The colonel tuned in a far-off gabble of voices: "Baker Seven, we're holding."

The monitor showed the soldier now in the speedboat arguing with the boatsman. Then the radio crackled, "Hell, he's one of ours, Baker Seven."

"Hawk Three, identify speedboat owner."

"It's a Navy guy who owns a boat, Baker Seven. Came out to help the patrol, he says."

"Arrest him, anyway, Hawk Three."

Williams was turning away, "Not our man," he said.

"Why not?"

"If it was, the people in the helicopter would be dead."

But as Williams left the White House he felt one small hope for Maxwell's operation. The ban on boats made it difficult for the terrorist. And where it was difficult to operate there was always a chance of something going wrong.

28

MINUS 15:00 HOURS. JULY 2, OCEAN CITY.

Leonard Chew lay on the sand, peering over the edge of a dune. Quiet. To the north he saw the red and green running lights of helicopters on patrol with searchlights sweeping the water beneath them. To the south the headlights of a jeep that cruised slowly, fanning its searchlight across dunes like this one.

Chew ducked as the noise of the jeep grew louder. The jeep approached, bumping over sand. As the man in the jeep worked the searchlight back and forth, light swept over Chew's head, whitened an empty house behind him, then moved on. He heard the sound of the motor receding and looked over the edge of the dune again. The jeep rolled slowly north, its light playing across dunes and houses.

Now! He hoisted the heavy duffel bag onto his shoulder and walked through the sand to the water's edge. Breakers crashed. He put down the duffel bag, then stood up and looked north and south. Nothing but the jeep traveling farther away and the helicopters circling up ahead. He zipped open the duffel bag and drew out a dark blue rubber package. He opened two air compressors, and the rubber bloomed into a raft. He placed it on the sand, then took a waterproof plastic green bag out of the duffel bag. It contained the nuclear bomb and a radio receiver. The third and last item from the duffel bag was a small high-poweerd outboard motor. He fastened the motor onto the raft, then took off his clothes until he wore only his bathing trunks.

This was the most dangerous time in Chew's whole mission. If one of those helicopters swept south, he would be caught in the open.

He placed the bomb package on the raft, then shoved it into the water. The first breaker hit him, and he almost lost control. The raft swept back toward the beach, but he regained it and pushed ahead to the second swell of breakers. The water was up to his chest. Somehow when the next breaker hit, he had more control. He held the raft tightly, one hand on the package inside it, and then he was behind the breakers, treading water. He started the outboard engine, then took a long needle from a sheath on the raft and made a tiny puncture in the raft itself. The roar of the motor drowned the hissing sound. Then suddenly, disaster! He was being tugged out to sea by the bucking raft before he could let go. He pushed himself away, but he was farther from shore than he planned! The rubber raft headed toward deeper water as Chew turned and struck out for land. Ahead he saw the backs of breakers and plowed steadily toward them, hoping for the tide to give him a push. Then he was cresting on a breaker, and diving, bruising his knees when he hit the ground.

He was on the beach. He picked up the duffel bag and his clothes and ran across the sand to the safety of the dunes. Far behind him he heard the putt-putt of the outboard motor—the raft would go on until the slow leak caused a complete collapse, and then it would sink to the bottom with its nuclear package.

Chew was on his way to his house when he heard an engine. Between the houses on the beach he saw an Army helicopter flying south, its searchlight bobbing. The helicopter was still blocks away from where the raft had been launched, but Chew was worried. He looked at his watch. Allow five minutes so that he could return to his car—and another three minutes on the road. No way you could estimate the collapse time of the raft without knowing the precise diameter of the puncture he had made. Still, eight minutes should do it. The raft should have sunk by now, the nuclear bomb planted at the bottom of the bag.

29

MINUS 14:50 HOURS. JULY 2, WASHINGTON.

A security guard at Andrews Air Force Base escorted Williams to a private jet that had just arrived. Maintenance personnel rolled a mobile staircase to the aircraft, a door opened. An FBI agent appeared, his suit jacket rumpled in such a way that Williams could detect the outlines of his shoulder holster. The agent saw Williams on the tarmac, then turned to say something to a person behind him, and Peggy DuPont emerged, followed by another FBI man.

When Peggy DuPont had lived with Williams she had been a casual dresser, usually roaming around town in jeans, pullover cashmere sweaters or Indian blouses, and boots. Tonight she was more formal in a simple blue shirtwaist dress, white open-toed sandals, and no jewelry. But the leather bag slung carelessly from her shoulder looked expensive, as did the woman who wore it. Her eyes lighted warmly when she saw Williams.

She embraced him, her hands clutching his shoulders tightly before relaxing, then she looked up at him with the old mocking smile. "If you wanted to see me again, you didn't have to go to quite this much trouble, George."

"It's real trouble, though."

Peggy stopped smiling. "I know it, George. I've never seen a person killed before." She paused, "And it was so strange. I only knew that little man for a few minutes—he was cocky and arrogant—but I liked him. Then he was gone. I want you to find those men who killed him, George."

As they walked toward the terminal, Peggy's hand on Williams' elbow, George said they had to worry about *her* safety now. The two agents who had accompanied her from Plattsburg fell in step behind the couple. One of them said to his associate softly, "I'm going to transfer to the Justice Department if she goes with the job."

"Keep your voice low," the other agent replied, "or you'll be transferred to the Sanitation Department."

While the agents spoke, their eyes probed everywhere, most particularly toward the terminal, where a sniper might lurk. Both men had seen that dead body in the diner the previous night.

30

MINUS 14:30 HOURS. JULY 2, WASHINGTON.

In the FBI car heading back to Washington, Peggy told Williams what had happened up north following Bennett's murder. "We called Malcolm's sister in Montreal and had to tell her of the death of her brother. Then, on top of that, while she's still recovering from the shock, we had to ask her all kinds of questions about the map and the people who had gotten it from Malcolm."

Peggy said that the Royal Canadian Mounted Police had driven Sarah Bennett to Plattsburg to take care of Malcolm's body. Sarah Bennett had brought a copy of the Arnold map from which the fragment was taken and a letter of Arnold's. Peggy handed them to Williams, who saw first a Xerox copy of a British military map of New Jersey. In the Egg Harbor area was a caption: "Arnold's ship captured here, September 8, 1778."

"You want to know why it was a conspiracy against Arnold?" Peggy asked. Williams was more interested in hearing the descriptions of the Deep Men who had gotten the map from Bennett, but he had learned earlier in this case to pay attention to the seemingly innocuous historical details. So he listened as Peggy said the artist who drew the map died September 1, 1780—and the date of the capture of the ship was September 8, a week later. Obviously the artist—and the British—knew ahead of time that the ship was going to be captured. So, Peggy continued, it was part of a scheme. Capture Arnold's ship and when Arnold reacted—as he did—he would get into trouble. When Arnold saw the map after the war he suspected he had been framed, and most likely by Robert Shewall, the man who came to him with the business proposition about the boat.

"Fascinating, right?" Peggy said. "But it gets even more intriguing. Arnold wrote to Nancy and told her to contact Alexander Hamilton and tell him about the map, which proved the conspiracy—and Arnold's suspicions about Shewall. But Shewall was by then a respected businessman, and so were his associates. Nancy wrote Hamilton a letter, but in reply Hamilton sent word that Arnold was so blackened by his treason that nothing could resurrect his reputation. But news of Nancy's letter must have leaked to Shewall and his friends, because a few weeks later Nancy Bishop was killed in the woods near her home, and her attacker was never found.

"When Arnold heard of Nancy's death he suspected the worst. He returned to Canada, wrote the note on the map in invisible ink for Shewall, and left it with a letter for his son."

Williams asked, "Why did Arnold write the note to Shewall in invisible ink?"

"Arnold didn't want the note in plain ink because he didn't wish his son to be caught in America carrying a map that promised revenge from the hated Arnold. Shewall and Arnold used invisible ink for various correspondence about the boat—and the letter accompanying the map would tell Shewall that the note was in that type of correspondence."

"If Sarah Bennett or her ancestors knew all this, why didn't they develop the invisible ink long ago?" Williams asked. "This makes the map priceless. They could sell it for a fortune."

"Because neither she nor her ancestors knew what I just told you about the invisible ink. Sarah says she figured it out after she realized the map had a note on it, and she reread the letter Arnold had written two hundred years ago. Read the letter and you'll see why she didn't know."

Williams read the Xeroxed letter addressed to Arnold's illegitimate son.

Dear John,

I am leaving this map and letter in the care of your guardian. When you are old enough I wish you to take it to a Robert Shewall, a trader in Philadelphia. Tell him there is a message on its margin in the style of our business correspondence. That it relates to the death of your mother, Nancy, and that I know all, and will not rest until I have my revenge.

There will be enough land and moneys bequeathed to you in my estate to take care of you for a lifetime. I grieve that I can not remain at your side, but fate—and evil men—have ensured that I remain in exile, and forced to work and fight for whatever money I can obtain in England.

I want you always to know that you can write to me for any assistance you may need, and you have my abiding love and affection, as is natural.

Affectionately, Always,
B. ARNOLD.

Peggy said that Malcolm Bennett's sister told them
that their family believed the message on the margin of
the map had been erased long ago, and never dreamed
it was still there in invisible ink. But someone in the
Deep Men, smarter than they, had read the letter and
realized the note was there, after all.

Peggy and Williams entered the White House
through the secret gate in the back. When they reached
the Situation Room they could hear loudspeakers
broadcasting the voices of the helicopter pilots as they
talked back and forth. The monitors showed scenes of
the feverish patrol activity. Maxwell told Williams that
the terrorist might already have planted the bomb. "His
only chance to slip out in a boat is at night. And the
bomb is supposed to explode at six tomorrow evening.
If he needs darkness, it's tonight."

"Is there any chance of finding the bomb *after* it's
planted?" Williams asked. But Maxwell shook his head.

"Magnetometers on helicopters detect changes in
magnetic waves caused by a metal object," the General
said. "We use them to find submarines. But an
eighteen-inch bomb is so small, I don't think any magnetometer is going to pick it up."

"What about oceanographic subs with searchlights?"

"I've sent out a request to the Navy, and they're
flying in as many subs as they can get to the various
regional commands. There are not too many in existence, you know. Only ten on the East Coast. But we'll
have at least a few at every major headquarters up
there."

Williams remembered that one of the small two-man
oceanographic subs had found the hydrogen bomb
dropped by accident into the sea off Spain some years
ago. But when he reminded Maxwell, the General
shrugged. "That operation took weeks, not hours. The

problem is that down deep in the ocean those search-lights on the subs can only see four feet in front of them. And with just a few subs to cover the whole ocean all the way out to the horizon they don't have a chance."

He added, "Science won't help us here, George. If that nuclear bomb has been planted, only the man himself can save us by telling us where it is. And I don't think that's part of his plan."

Maxwell went to the phone while Williams turned to see that Peggy was chatting with a handsome colonel who had brought her a cup of coffee. He felt a twinge of jealousy. He was convinced he had put his affair with Peggy behind him, but now that she was here—

Peggy saw his glance and came over to him. "I see green. You look good in that color."

Williams said it was too many hours spent in the basement of the White House. The FBI agent from Plattsburg showed him composites of three men: Bennett's killer and the two Deep Men who had visited Malcolm Bennett months ago and bought the Arnold map from him. Bennett's murderer was a gaunt-faced man with protruding ears and a high forehead. The two Deep Men who bought the map from Bennett, Kurt Edwards and William Monroe, were an interesting contrast. Edwards' face had an Indian grandeur, but with small hard eyes. Monroe was a round-faced man with rimless glasses and seemed out of place beside the other two.

"Let's hear the tape," Williams said, and one of the FBI agents punched a button on a recorder on the conference table, and the interrogation of Malcolm Bennett's sister sounded sharp and loud in the room.

31

IN 1775 BENEDICT ARNOLD STORMED UP THE STEPS OF English-held Fortress Quebec at the head of a ragged line of American troops. A musketball shattered his leg. When he was carried to the Plains of Abraham below, the courageous attack failed.

Arnold didn't quit. The man the English feared as the most effective officer in Washington's army mounted a siege for months until his starving troops were driven off by the arrival of a large English fleet.

Almost a year had passed since Arnold asked Washington for permission to lead a force on foot from Massachusetts to Quebec through primitive forest and neck-deep swamps. Such a march was considered impossible, but Arnold somehow got enough of his men through to make an attack on powerful Quebec that nearly succeeded.

But now he had to fall back, and the English moved confidently to take advantage of his plight. If they could sail down the lake chain from Canada to the Hudson, they would cut off New England from the rest of the colonies and put an end to the American Revolution in its very first year.

Arnold surprised them. At Lake Champlain his troops hewed timber from new forest to build rudimentary ships, barges, and rafts. He hid this makeshift fleet behind Valcour Island in Lake Champlain. The British fleet, including a great man-of-war, sailed serenely down the lake believing no other ship was within a thousand miles. Arnold's "fleet," created out of the forest, swarmed around them when they passed Valcour Island. The surprise was total.

The British fleet sank all of Arnold's boats but in doing so sustained so much damage that it was forced to return to Canada, putting off the invasion for a whole year. That delay proved fatal. The next year the American land forces were better prepared. Even so, the critical battle of Saratoga was swinging in England's favor when a general on a black horse rode onto the battlefield, rallied the retreating Americans, and galloped straight into the enemy front lines. The general was Benedict Arnold. Because of a dispute with his superior, Gen. Horatio Gates, he was not even supposed to be on the battlefield. But now his horse led all the others, flying across a hedge to land in the midst of the startled enemy. A musketball splintered the same leg wounded in the Quebec fighting, leaving Arnold crippled for life. But the British forces broke and fled under the cavalry assault; the tide of battle turned; Saratoga was won. When the French heard of this victory they decided to join the American cause, and the British never recovered their advantage in the Revolution.

There are historians who believe that Arnold personally saved the Revolution in those first two years. And there are a growing number of Americans who believe that Arnold's heroism should be recognized at long last. These people call themselves the "Benedict Arnold cult" and year by year mount campaigns to clear Arnold's name and restore him to the honored place in American history that should be his. Many of their petitions state that Arnold was a patriot who was railroaded by politicians who practically forced him into treason. And those who can afford it among the Arnold cult compete for Arnold memorabilia. Now, on the tape of Sarah Bennett's interrogation, Williams heard of one of these collectors who worked through agents: "Two men Malcolm knew from the Middle East," Sarah Bennett was saying. "They showed up one day in our home in Canada and wanted to buy the Arnold map along with our letter. Kurt Edwards and William Monroe were the names they gave. I said no, but Malcolm sold it to them anyway. He told me later he had to."

FBI: Why did they want the map so badly, Miss Bennett? Was Edwards a collector?

BENNETT: Him? No. But it *was* Edwards that Malcolm told about the map in the Middle East. After Edwards got back from the Middle East he told some big shot who collects Arnold mementos. Edwards told us he was a very respectable man in Washington, but outside of that *I* wasn't told anything. They shooed me away. And Malcolm was mighty close-mouthed, too. But I just guessed the collector was a member of the Arnold cult.

FBI: The what?

BENNETT: The Arnold cult. That's what they call themselves, these people who don't have a drop of Arnold's blood in their veins. They go around getting publicity in the newspapers, trying to resurrect Arnold's reputation or something. Malcolm and I never paid any attention to those fakers. We knew whose blood was in *our* veins.

FBI: Miss Bennett, Peggy DuPont would like to ask you a few questions.

BENNETT: That's all right. Peggy's a fine girl. She's been—good to me tonight. (*Pause.*)

PEGGY: Are you all right?

BENNETT: Y—yes. (*Pause.*) Go ahead, Peggy.

PEGGY: The man who killed your brother wasn't Edwards. He was thin-faced, slim. You described Edwards, as we drove over here, as a big, muscular man who looked like an Indian.

BENNETT: Well, if Edwards didn't do it—he was involved in some way. Malcolm said his name, didn't he?

PEGGY: What I'm getting at is that it might have been the second man who came to your house to buy the map who was the killer. Was he tall, slim—?

BENNETT: No, no, he's short—but you're off there, anyway, Peggy, I'm sure Mr. Monroe had nothing to do with this. I could tell just by talking to him.

PEGGY: Talking? I thought you said they shooed you away.

BENNETT: Into the kitchen. When Malcolm and Edwards went upstairs to argue about the map, Mr. Monroe kept me company in the kitchen. He couldn't talk to me about the map or who really wanted it, but he seemed like a nice fellow to me, I'm sorry to say. I gave him a piece of peach pie I had baked. He was quite complimentary.

PEGGY: Still—

BENNETT: (*Continuing over Peggy's interruption.*) Mr. Monroe and I had something in common. He asked me what I did for a living, and I told him I was a registered nurse. He said his wife had been a nurse. I asked him if she worked in a hospital, and said no. She wasn't alive. Mr. Monroe's wife and two children had been killed in an accident in Beirut.

"Stop the tape!" Williams said. He looked at Peggy with surprise, and Jarvis patted her on the back, smiling.

"Good girl, Peggy." Apparently she had elicited something enormously significant because Jarvis went to the telephone immediately, without waiting to hear the end of the conversation with Sarah Bennett.

Peggy was surprised. "What did I say?"

Williams told her they had found a lead to a scientist associated with the Deep Men named Robert Patterson, who had lost his wife and two children in an accident in Lebanon. Peggy's interrogation showed that William Monroe was Robert Patterson. "And," said Williams, "we know at least one of the names he's using here in the United States. And that means we can start tracking William Monroe."

"How?"

"Blanket the country. Rental car agencies, hotels, motels, real estate agents, gun dealers, explosives manufacturers—wherever a terrorist using the name William Monroe might have appeared."

"You can do all that?"

"With a nuclear bomb about to go off we can do anything. We've got hundreds of FBI men assigned just to this case. If we get onto Mr. Monroe's trail, it's the biggest break so far. You did a good job, Peggy. You hung in there."

"Hung in? All I did was ask a few simple questions."

"Interrogation is an art," Williams said, "and you were an artist up there."

Peggy had made enough polite objections. In actual fact, she was thrilled with herself. She said, "What's my next assignment, chief?"

Williams smiled, and surprised her by saying, "To get some sleep. You've been up all night. We've rented a room for you in the Hay Adams Hotel right across from the White House, and we'll have the FBI guard it."

Peggy didn't want to leave. "I could use some sleep, but why not here? This house is for people, isn't it? I'm people."

Williams called the Chief White House Usher and was informed that a request would be made to the President. Apparently, the President was staying up all night; earlier he had called Williams to check on the progress Williams was making. Now he telephoned Peggy personally. "How would you like to sleep in the Lincoln Bedroom, Miss DuPont? It's available."

Peggy said she would love it. "I've never slept with a ghost," she said, a remark which amused the President.

"I won't pursue that," he answered, "but the room is yours. I'll send a butler to escort you."

Peggy was smiling when she hung up. To Williams she said, "I may trade you in for the President."

When Williams pointed out that the President was married, Peggy said, "A detail that never bothers me."

In two minutes a butler appeared at the door. Peggy took Williams aside. "Take me to bed. I deserve a reward."

"You pick a brilliant time for a proposition," Williams said.

"Tell me a dull time," Peggy replied.

Williams said, "I'll hold your hand later. But I have some business to attend to first."

Peggy smiled and said he would hold more than that. She badly wanted him now. Perhaps it was the shared danger, the crisis that had thrust them together, but Williams' passion for what he called "business" didn't bother her now as it had in the past. The butler was at the door. "We'll take you up, Miss DuPont."

Peggy heard Williams calling Los Alamos as she left and realized something about Sarah Bennett's interrogation was bothering her. But she couldn't figure out what it was.

32

Leonard Chew drove into the garage of his safe house at 2872 Central Avenue at 4 A.M. In fourteen hours the nuclear bomb would explode in the ocean, whose rhythmic lapping he could hear even now.

No one could prevent that explosion, not even the entire might of the Army, the Air Force, the Navy. There was no way they would ever find an eighteen-inch metal object buried under three hundred feet of water somewhere along a hundred-mile shore line.

In his living room Chew sipped a Scotch and water, then went to a bedroom where he kept his diary in a bureau. Slowly, he wrote:

"Oppenheimer said of the scientists who created nuclear bombs during World War II, 'All of us, no matter our motive, have known sin.'

"Tomorrow I will explode the first nuclear bomb in an open residential area in America. Many will die in the tidal wave. Others will be poisoned by the radiation, made to suffer long, lingering agony. It will be dreadful!

"But I swear before God it is right . . ."

BOOK III

The Day
of the
Tidal Wave

1

MINUS 11:00 HOURS. JULY 2, OCEAN CITY.

7 A.M. July 2, Ocean City, New Jersey. An Army bus rolled along Central Avenue, stopping at every corner. People clambered aboard with mattresses, suitcases, money boxes, clothes—whatever they most wanted to save. These were the latest evacuees. The traffic flowing out of town the previous night had been unceasing. The crisis posed special problems for boat owners. Some battened down their boats and hoped they would ride out the tidal wave, others had their boats lifted out of the water and placed on trailers. Still other owners just jumped in behind the wheel, and ran their boats across the bay to the Somers Point marina where a crane worked full speed taking them out of the water.

House owners boarded up windows. The great demand had caused a lumber shortage, and trucks with new supplies of wood had difficulty reaching everyone. Still, hammers swung, and nails were driven in, across the island.

The sun rose higher above the east coast of New Jersey. Military trucks with loudspeakers drove through quiet streets of resorts, jeeps careened along beaches, helicopters hovered over the seashore, as the great tide of civilians flowed out of the endangered resorts to the safety of inland spaces.

On NBC's "Today Show," television cameras brought the spectacle live to a dazed people. They could not believe it was happening! No one was actually going to explode a nuclear bomb. No one would create a hundred-foot tidal wave. The Army would stop it some way. They had to.

2

MINUS 10:50 HOURS. JULY 2, WASHINGTON.

But dawn in Washington brought a dread premonition of disaster to the Army. The night had passed; the terrorist had not been found. General Maxwell believed the nuclear bomb was planted. And if so, the explosion was inevitable.

The TWX in the White House Situation Room clattered all night with William Monroes found by FBI agents fanning out in the early morning hours and pounding on doors. Williams told the agents to concentrate on New York, New Jersey, and Pennsylvania because the threat had said the bomb would be planted off New Jersey.

And William Monroes started to emerge in those states. One had rented a house in Chestnut Hill, Pennsylvania, three months ago by mail. The real estate agent never met him. "Unusual—but the house was a dog," the agent said. In that same town Avis had rented a Buick sedan to a William Monroe, also three months ago. Williams took the license number, but he was certain the license plates had been replaced. That was basic procedure.

What Williams hoped for was a record of the rental of a house or hotel or motel room on the shore of the Atlantic, but no William Monroe had yet appeared. He was feeling disappointed, when the phone rang at 8 A.M. and Peggy DuPont told him from the Lincoln Bedroom that she had solved the case. She could find the man with the bombs herself.

Finding the terrorist was the only chance they had. The Army had helicopters and subs, but it was blindman's buff out there on the ocean. General Maxwell called it "a nuclear crapshoot." Williams would take any clue he could get.

3

MINUS 09:00 HOURS. JULY 2, WASHINGTON.

Peggy DuPont, in a see-through blue lace gown, sat against the cushions of a four-poster bed in the Lincoln Bedroom of the White House. If Mrs. Lincoln had looked as good as that, Williams thought, Abe would have found little time to run the Civil War. Peggy said they had both overlooked a clue.

He came to the side of the bed, and Peggy said, "A smattering of sex first," and pulled his head down to hers for a kiss. Her fingernails played with the back of his neck. When they parted, she said, "Just wanted to be sure my old magic still works." But she was breathing faster. She said, "Now for the reward. You missed the important clue in that interrogation of Sarah Bennett, George. Hate to put you down, but when criticism is deserved, criticism must be issued."

Williams watched her, waiting. She continued, "You heard something—and jumped right to the criminal factor. But you missed the really important clue."

"The criminal factor was the accident to Monroe's family."

"Correct. But where does that get you in identifying him? Nowhere. You need his *real* name, George." She paused. "And there—right in Sarah Bennett's interrogation—was the clue that will get you his real name. And that clue was"—she paused for effect—"that William Monroe's wife was a *nurse*."

She stopped, then went on, "You know the man is most likely a nuclear scientist. Why don't you call the *hospital* at Los Alamos and see *which nurse* there ever *married* a nuclear scientist. You might learn his real name through the marriage records."

There were objections that crossed Williams' mind. The man might have married a nurse elsewhere. Or there might be twenty nurses over the past fifteen years who had married scientists. These were the same objections he had overcome in his mind when he telephoned Los Alamos at four this morning. Alamos was checking and would call him back.

But he didn't tell Peggy that. In fact, he was impressed with her. He told her it was an excellent idea, and he would follow it up right away. But Peggy surprised him by pulling him to the side of the bed, looking up at him, and saying seriously, "You're not going to stop him anyway, you know."

"Why?"

"Because he's a scientist and you're a lawyer." She paused. "You'll never out-think him when it comes to planting nuclear bombs."

But he realized she was just stalling for time when she tugged him closer and pulled his face toward hers again.

Soft yielding lips opened—this time she guided his hand to her breasts. Then she gently pushed him away.

"Previews," she said, "of coming attractions."

After Williams left, Peggy started to dress. Her mind was absorbed by the drama she was living. What a change in her life in twenty-four hours! Yesterday she was floating on a lake with dilettantes, wondering only how to escape familiar ennui, and with which attractive man. Today she was a hunted woman, more frightened than she would admit, protected by FBI guards, living in the White House—and playing a role in a war with a scientist who was absolutely determined to explode a nuclear bomb.

She wondered if Williams would find that nuclear scientist who had married a nurse. If they could only discover who he was, they might have a chance to appeal to him from another direction. The man must be human, mustn't he?

4

MINUS 07:00 HOURS. JULY 2, NORTH OF OCEAN CITY.

Leonard Chew drove north. The entire east coast of New Jersey was being evacuated. Every road appeared to be clogged with cars packed to the roof and above with baby carriages, bicycles, mattresses, whatever the owners of houses hoped to save. The trip from Ocean City had taken hours, beginning with a two-hour wait at the bridge.

Chew passed a huge tent city with Army personnel riding around in jeeps and signs sprouting labels like

MEDICAL DIV., ADMINISTRATION DIV., even a FINANCE DIV.

The tent city behind him, Chew observed another characteristic of the evacuation: hitchhikers, mostly young people. Not owning cars, many of them were stranded without transportation. So they took to the road to thumb their way out of danger. Most of the cars were full; Chew's, though, was the exception. At an intersection where a long line of cars waited, a young blonde in jeans came to his window. Sixteen, Chew thought. Maybe seventeen. "Ride, mister? For me and my friends."

"I'm going to New York," Chew said. He knew most of the traffic was headed for Philadelphia and towns across New Jersey. The girl said, "Great," ran around the car, and jumped in.

Chew said, "You're going to New York, too?"

"Anywhere, pops," replied the girl. "And I don't have any friends. Just told you that because I thought you might be scared."

"Of what?"

"Of me. I'm the mad bomber," she turned and made a horror face at him. Chew laughed. He stopped laughing when the girl said, "I have another specialty. I yell rape and the cops come running. Unless I get some money."

"You plan to do that now?"

"No, I did it once. Poor old guy fell apart. Gave me three hundred dollars and I split." She leaned back, and Chew saw that she had shucked off her white sandals. Her tanned bare feet were propped on the dashboard. She turned to him. "What I am most is a liar. Don't listen to anything I say."

But Chew had decided it was a good idea to have a

young girl with him on the trip north. It was better than one lone man on the road.

He said, "What's your name?"

"Hope."

Chew said nothing. The girl looked at him. "Did I say something wrong?"

"That was my wife's name. She passed away."

"Hey," the blonde said, "I'm sorry, man." She paused, then pulled her right foot to her chest and examined the big toe with a critical eye and a probing thumb. "Hope is a great name. Do I remind you of your wife when she was young?"

"Not quite. But if you don't yell rape I'll be glad to take you to New York anyway."

"Nice man," Hope said, "but we have to have some music on the trip. Tidal wave music." She reached over and turned on the radio, but there was no music today. It was all news from the shore, where reporters were monitoring the Army's efforts to find the nuclear bomb. One reporter said, "There are helicopters with magnetometers flying low over the ocean—"

Chew smiled to himself. Magnetometers wouldn't do it. Scientific impossibility. The reporter went on to mention the oceanographic subs. Chew had computed the odds against one of them blundering its way through the pitch-black sea and coming across a small bomb. A million to one. The reporter said, "Bulletin—Bulletin—Bulletin. The nuclear terrorist has been tentatively identified as Leonard Chew of Haddonfield, New Jersey, the FBI announced moments ago. The identification was made by tracing the record of his marriage to Hope Ryden in Los Alamos."

The blond young girl named Hope was staring at him.

5

THE GIRL DID SOMETHING STUPID. SHE SAID, "OH MY God!"

The news reporter said, "Leonard Chew is described as in his forties, stocky, round face, brown eyes, brown hair, rimless glasses." Chew now wore a red wig and beard and blue contact lenses. He looked at her and said, "What's the matter?"

"The man with the nuclear bombs! He has a wife named *Hope*."

Chew smiled. "Now you're saying *I'm* the mad bomber?" But the girl had already lost interest. She went back to examining her big toe.

"You have blue eyes," she said. "Now that's something you can't change."

6

MINUS 06:45 HOURS. JULY 2, WASHINGTON.

Williams was on the telephone to Jim Ryden, Hope's father. "Do you know of any of Chew's relatives anywhere? We've checked his home town and his mother and father have passed away."

"He had an uncle who came to the wedding," Mr.

Ryden said, "but I'll be damned if I can remember his name." He paused, "Dago."

"What?"

"Excuse me, Mr. Williams. I used to be in the Navy. San Diego is what I meant, that's what we Navy fellows called it. Chew's uncle came from there."

"Can you remember what he did for a living?"

"Electrician, I think. Something not so . . . grand, if you know what I mean. Course Mrs. Ryden and I don't put any store by what the relatives do. I never did think Leonard had anything to do with that accident, Mr. Williams. I know character. That's what he had." He stopped, then went on, "But when he disappeared that way after the accident I had to think he was guilty. Maybe if I had looked harder for him at the time, put out a message somehow that we knew he wasn't to blame, this all might not have happened."

"Do you know why he is exploding nuclear bombs?"

Ryden hesitated. "Well, he has to be unbalanced right now, don't you think? Any man that's exploding one of those bombs, he can't be normal." The phone was silent, then, "And Leonard had a history of . . . mental illness. We thought it was nuclear fatigue."

Williams asked him what nuclear fatigue meant and Mr. Ryden told him it was really just a nervous breakdown, according to what their daughter had said. Brought on by too close contact with those bombs. "Isn't it funny that he's the one actually using those bombs with a mental history like that—Bobby."

"What?"

"Bobby Chew. That was the name of the uncle. I just remembered. Electrician in San Diego, Mr. Williams. You can find him."

Williams called the electricians' union in San Diego.

No Bobby Chew. "How long ago was that?" the labor rep asked.

"Fourteen years."

"Let me check with national. I'll get back to you." Williams waited, and when the phone rang he received the unwelcome news that Bobby Chew was dead. He had moved to Portland, Oregon, and passed away a year ago. But they had his address and Williams called the number to talk to the widow. A boy answered. "Mom's in church."

"This is the FBI calling from Washington—"

"I'm not surprised. Why do you think she went to church. She heard the news about Uncle Leonard."

Williams told the boy to find her immediately and bring her to the phone. They were trying to stop a nuclear explosion. "How are you going to do that?" asked the boy.

"Depends on what your mother says," Williams said.

The boy was excited. "I'll run right down to the church and get her." He took Williams' number, and hung up, and Williams had to wait; colonels and enlisted men in this room watching him, and time ticking by, twelve o'clock now, six hours to go, the helicopters had found nothing, the subs were having no luck—and what could Bobby Chew's widow tell him that would help find a bomb on the bottom of the ocean. The whole exercise was ridiculous. He was roaring along as if he was going to get somewhere. The telephone rang. Mrs. Bobby Chew said, "I only met the man once. At the wedding in Los Alamos."

"I'm hoping for anything you can tell us that we might use to appeal to Chew—or locate him somehow. We think he's already planted the bomb, and there's no way we can stop it from exploding unless he tells us where it is."

Silence. "Well, gosh, I don't know much at all like that. Hardly spoke to the man. But I did feel bad because he was a relative of my husband's—and here he goes and disgraces the family like that. They'll think we're all maniacs—"

Williams cut her off. "Mrs. Chew, the bomb is planted off the New Jersey shore, and we're trying—"

"Well, sure, that was where Leonard went in the summer."

"Where?"

"Ocean City, for heaven's sake. His parents had a house there, and Leonard spent his summers at the shore. I remember when he heard I grew up in a beach house in San Diego, he said he'd spent a lot of time on the beach, too—"

"Where, Mrs. Chew? Where on the beach?"

"What do you mean?"

"An address. Do you know the house in Ocean City?"

"Well, for heaven's sake no. I've never been near the place." She paused. "He told me"—she stopped—"but that's way out of date now, I'm afraid."

"What?"

"He said that Ocean City's only celebrity was Grace Kelly, and his house was two blocks away from hers."

Williams thanked Mrs. Chew, hung up, and called Jarvis at the FBI. In five minutes Jarvis was back with the news that Grace Kelly's family still lived at Twenty-sixth and Wesley Avenue in Ocean City, and Williams raced to a helicopter on the lawn of the White House, transferred to a jet at Andrews Air Force Base, and flew to nearby Atlantic City as Army MPs swept out around a two-block area surrounding 2600 Wesley Avenue, the childhood home of Grace Kelly.

7

Minus 04:30 hours. July 2, Ocean City.

The Army Command of the South Jersey region had set up headquarters at the Atlantic City airport. Ocean City was just to the south, ten miles away. Williams transferred to a helicopter and flew to the location of the MP patrols. He found a colonel, sweating. "Hell, Mr. Williams. We don't even know what we're looking for. I mean, if he packs those things in a suitcase, he left no traces."

Williams said, "I don't think he got through the road-blocks with the bombs in a suitcase. And if he had to cover them in lead, he might have left some evidence. Tools, discarded lead. Something."

But an hour later, nothing had been found. Every house and garage had been searched. It was 2:30 P.M. The nuclear bomb would explode in three and a half hours. The colonel gathered his men around him and looked at Williams. "What now?"

"We search again," Williams said. But now, for the first time, he saw fright on the faces of the MPs in front of him. The time of the nuclear deadline was approaching. Who knew if the terrorist would stick to that deadline to the minute? Nothing was certain. Williams said, "Forget what's lying around on this trip, and concentrate on the house itself."

No one knew what he meant. The colonel asked Williams, who said, "If he used a safe house, he might have made structural changes to the house, secret compartments to hide the bombs while he waited for nightfall."

"So we concentrate on the walls?" a sergeant asked.

"Concentrate on the attics," Williams replied, "unless the bottom floors seem to have room for a false compartment. But attics first." And the men fanned out in the streets with Geiger counters, leaving Williams and the colonel alone. Williams was standing on Wesley Avenue, a beachfront road. He turned and looked out to sea. Tall grass whipped in a breeze on the crests of dunes. Between two of the dunes Williams could see a stretch of gray-green ocean beyond curling breakers. A helicopter moved slowly along the oceanfront, trailing a magnetometer on a cable. The colonel stood beside Williams. His light sandy hair poked from the fringes of his field cap; he stuffed his hands into his back pockets and stood spread-legged, facing the sea as if it were enemy terrain. But the colonel was overwhelmed. He took off his cap and slapped it against his thigh to straighten it, then restored it to his head. "I just can't believe it's happening, Mr. Williams. I was sure Chew would call, make some demand. But nothing."

Williams said, "He won't call because he *wants* to explode that nuclear bomb."

"But that's . . . crazy, sir."

"It's a crazy world—but only to the people on the wrong end of the bombs," Williams said. A gull swept down toward the curve of a breaker. Williams continued, "We dropped the first nuclear bomb on civilians in World War Two. And the American military at the time said it was a sane military decision. We know what the people in Hiroshima thought."

The colonel shifted his feet. "Well, Mr. Williams, the Army didn't *invent* those bombs. But once they're there—"

Williams wanted to say, "You end up in a place like Ocean City wondering what went wrong," but he let it go. The colonel was melting right at his side.

An MP stood in front of them. "We've finished, sir. Nothing to report. We banged every wall in every attic."

The MPs had been separated into teams assigned to search various blocks. The MP in front of them was from Team A. Other teams reported. One of them had found what they thought was a false panel in an attic, and hammered through it. Nothing but empty space behind. Williams looked at his watch: 3:30 P.M. Two and a half hours to go. A red-haired sergeant was running across the street, arms outspread in jubilation. "We found the goddam thing, Colonel! We found it. We're smashing it."

"You found what?"

"A radio transmitter in an attic behind a false wall with a timer set for six o'clock. Hell, that's it, Colonel!"

Williams ran with them toward a small Cape Cod cottage with green shutters. 2872 Central Avenue. A discarded red and white striped basketball was on the lawn of the house next door.

8

MINUS 01:50 HOURS. JULY 2, OCEAN CITY.

Williams watched the three technicians finish demolishing the transmitter. One of them even kicked it, then looked shamefacedly at Williams. "Sorry, Mr. Williams. But the bastard who put this here almost did us in."

Williams asked how they had found the house and

was told, "We came to the attic, and found a wire leading from a weather vane that seems to go under a wall, only it isn't a wall."

Williams said, "What's with the weather vane?"

"Well, that we don't know, sir. It was connected to the transmitter. I think maybe he had the transmitter fixed so it wouldn't activate until the wind was blowing the right direction."

"Offshore?"

"If he doesn't want to kill a million people with a radioactive cloud inland."

"You shouldn't have smashed the transmitter before I got here," Williams said.

"Why not?"

"It will give us a fix on where the bomb is planted."

But the sergeant said they knew the direction. The antenna had been set at 130 degrees. Which meant the bomb was planted somewhere along that directional line off the coast. But the sergeant said, "What's the difference anyway? We knocked out the transmitter, so the bomb is inactive. We can take our sweet time finding it."

"You don't have any time," Williams said, "if he has a backup timer in there."

"A backup timer in the bomb that doesn't depend on the radio signal?"

"A secondary system in case some bright Army inspectors looked behind a fake wall in an attic and found a radio transmitter."

"You think he did that, sir?" The sergeant sounded indignant. It wasn't fair of Chew to build in a backup system when they had so cleverly found his transmitter. Williams said they had better proceed on the assumption he had installed a secondary system or they would be met by a monumental surprise at six o'clock. He flew back to the Atlantic City terminal and asked General Horton, in charge of Army operations, to round up every helicopter pilot and oceanographic crewman.

"We only have two subs in this area. But we have plenty of chopper pilots," General Horton said.

9

MINUS 01:25 HOURS. JULY 2, ATLANTIC CITY.

It was 4:35 P.M. General Horton, in command of the Atlantic operation, faced nervous helicopter pilots and civilian oceanographic crewmen. Their hopes had risen fifteen minutes ago, and now the General was telling them the nuclear bomb could still be live.

An Admiral had plotted the directional line from the transmitter. The General showed the line to them, and said, "We're not just groping blindly now. We know the bomb is planted off Ocean City, and we know the approximate area. If one of your subs crisscrosses the line of direction from the transmitter while the other cruises up and down the same line, we just might find the bomb. The helicopters will fly as low as possible with the magnetometers above the ocean. I know it's almost hopeless, but if we do it, we stop a tidal wave."

"How do we communicate?" one of the submen asked. "We can't use radio underwater."

The Admiral told him, "We're putting a black box in your subs. Electric Counter Measures equipment, which detects sonar waves. You'll hear pings from the chopper's sonar. If they find something, they'll cut the sonar off, and when the pings stop, you go to the surface fast and then communicate by radio."

Everyone murmured approval. General Horton took over again. "Men, we're told and told again that it's hopeless to find that nuclear bomb. It's too small. The ocean's too deep. The water's too dark down there. But I say it's up to you. If that bomb is still alive, it can turn the whole east coast into a poisoned lake. Now that's worth almost any risk to prevent. And I'm breaking what some of you boys call military tradition by going right out there with you in a chopper."

Williams didn't smile at the pep talk because he found it appropriate. The more he thought about it, the more he was convinced that nuclear bomb was still live. And there were only minutes to go, and the one chance of finding it rested in two egg-shaped oceanographic subs in a pitch-dark world. Other subs were being flown in, but they would arrive too late.

Two minutes later helicopters lifted off landing pads, and a few minutes after that the search was on in earnest, along a line 130 degrees true south from a Cape Cod cottage in Ocean City, New Jersey. Williams, though, had little hope they would find it. Even with the line of direction the area wasn't narrowed down enough.

And the magnetometers in the helicopters were worthless. All depended on those subs. If one of them could just take the precise path that led to a little metallic bomb on the ocean floor! But they were nearly blind down there.

10

The *Karen* groped through the black depths of the Atlantic Ocean off Ocean City, its searchlight splaying a beam ahead.

The *Karen* was a tiny egg-shaped white vessel just large enough for two men. Its glass bow curved from the deck to the overhead. Outside, a sophisticated grappling device nestled against its prow. Controls inside the sub could extend the grappler and open and close its claws to retrieve everything from small mineral rocks to large shipwreck salvage.

Two oceanographic men in electrically heated black divers' suits lay flat in the cockpit, peering ahead. Soft lights from the control panel lined their faces in a green glow.

Bob Robinson was at the steering controls. Jim Wentworth, beside him, operated the searchlight. As the sub moved forward Wentworth played the beam back and forth in an arc before them. Brightly colored fish darted through the beam; an eel slithered across the floor, pinpointed for an instant in its light, then was lost in darkness.

Every passing minute made Robinson more nervous. When he had accepted this gamble for his life, it was an act of bravado, a seemingly sensible thing to do in a room filled with Generals and helicopter pilots and other oceanographic scientists. But now, in these murky depths, he realized the futility of what they were attempting.

Lying in a black rubber suit, staring out of a thick plastic window at a beam lighting ocean depths with its fish, flora, and sharp-edged boulders, Robinson suddenly knew he might die. A nuclear bomb could explode right beside the little eggshell and disintegrate them in a tidal wave that would—

"Over there!" Wentworth said.

Robinson turned. His eyes traveled down the short length of the searchlight beam to a hill, green with slime. "That isn't any bomb," Robinson said.

"I think I see something on it. Let me poke around it a second," Wentworth said. Two rods in the cockpit controlled the grappler. Wentworth pushed one forward, and the grappler device unfolded into a rigid rod, six feet long, with two gaping claws. Wentworth gently turned a knob control on the second rod, and the claws closed around a small brown hump. "Got it," Wentworth said. He operated both rods to bring the package through the water toward the sub. The folding action of the grappler moved the package from a horizontal to a vertical position just as it reached the window.

"Jesus Christ!" Robinson said.

A skull with hollow eyes stared into the window! The skull was even more frightening because it seemed alive. The remains of a slime-covered military cap tilted rakishly on its head. Robinson recognized a rusty Nazi insignia. "A German officer. That hill is a Nazi sub."

"I think we're looking at the captain," Wentworth said. "Poor bastard." He was already opening the claws of the grappler. The skull fell to the ocean floor and rolled, losing its cap at last.

The two men resumed their search, feeling strangely

subdued. After a while Robinson said, "What would that Nazi think if he knew what we were doing now? Looking for a nuclear bomb an American planted in his own country."

11

MINUS 00:58 MINUTES. JULY 2, OFF OCEAN CITY.

Anti-sub helicopters droned above the sea's surface trailing long cables with football-size cylinders at their ends. This was the magnetic sensing equipment, played out aft of the helicopters to avoid magnetic interference caused by the aircraft structure. In one of these helicopters Williams and an Admiral watched a graph trace a wavy line.

Suddenly the stylus bumped high, made a large inverted V, and returned to its normal pattern. "What's that?" Williams asked.

"Too big for a bomb, too small for a sub. Might be one of our ocean boats."

The stylus then resumed its tracing with infinitesimal jiggles. The sailor saw Williams' expression.

"You see a jiggly line," the sailor said. "I see the pattern of the ocean floor. Don't worry."

But Williams worried. He went forward to the cockpit and looked out over the ocean expanse. To the north he saw the venerable resort, Atlantic City, now the new East Coast gambling paradise, with gleaming hotels and office buildings rising along its famous boardwalk. The Steel Pier extended far into the ocean, surmounted by a jumble of entertainment structures with huge signs.

The helicopter hovered directly off Ocean City, New Jersey, a quiet place, Williams had been told, which allowed no drinking and characterized itself as a wholesome family resort. Out of such a place had emerged a boy named Leonard Chew who had matured into a nuclear terrorist.

Williams looked down at great ocean waves, rolling toward shore, and toppling and disintegrating in great white frothy explosions that cannonaded along the length of the beach. Seen from the back, the waves surged with hidden power that was almost frightening as their momentum built to a shattering climax. And beneath those waves, on the ocean floor, was a tiny charge of plutonium that could dislodge microscopic atomic worlds and create an awesome wave that would tower a hundred feet above the waves Williams was peering at now.

Williams looked at the houses lining the beaches, so close to the ocean, so vulnerable. A wave like that would be—and was—unthinkable; the mind couldn't really grasp the image of a wall of water ten stories high racing toward those homes.

Time passed, the helicopters droned, the magnetometer crewman stared at his graph. But no sub broke the surface with a little bomb in its claws. Could Williams have really hoped that would happen? One eighteen-inch bomb at a three-hundred-foot depth, no doubt obscured by seaweed and fauna; perhaps even half buried in the silt of the ocean floor.

And all they had was a directional line that was not precise; the bomb could be buried on either side of the line hundreds of yards away; there was just no way they were going to find it.

A helicopter passed them; its pilot gave them the thumbs-up sign. A white scarf billowed from around his throat, his Army cap was tilted. The military fly-boys never changed. They had been nervous in the briefing room—searching for a live nuclear bomb was a dimension removed from reality—but once they were in the air the old optimism of fliers everywhere apparently returned. Williams gave the pilot the thumbs-up signal, and the pilot smiled and was gone, his chopper swerving in orbit, the useless magnetometer trailing behind on its cable. And Williams knew that man's life was being jeopardized by himself, as were those of all of the crewmen out here. The margin of time they had allowed for escape—fifteen minutes—was perilously slim. If something went wrong with a helicopter engine or a sub had trouble on the surface, the fireball would consume them in an instant.

Fireball. Williams had never seen one, live, would gladly have lived his entire life without the experience. But right here in this ocean off this shore a giant incredible nuclear explosion was about to take place. And they had to prevent it. He looked down at that tantalizing sea, above the brute waves pushing into shore, and wanted to dive into them himself, plunge straight down to the ocean floor, see that bomb sitting there, and destroy it.

It was maddening to know the bomb was there, yet impossible to find.

12

A CBS TV reporter in a helicopter whirling above Ocean City. "Walter, we're over Ocean City and right out there in front of us you can see the Army helicopters orbiting the ocean searching for the nuclear bomb . . . what's that? . . . Oh, right . . . the pilot just told me that the Army is insisting we move back another hundred yards."

WALTER:
What are those cables trailing from the helicopters?
REPORTER:
They're magnetometers, Walter . . . supposedly they can detect the bomb by the change in magnetic waves that metal cause . . . but what we can't see of course are the oceanographic subs that are way down deep looking for the bomb. Those men are brave, Walter. If something goes wrong with one of their boats down there, no one can save them.
WALTER:
Jim, what does the Army say are the chances of stopping this catastrophe that's about to happen? I'm sitting here in a television studio in New York and I really can't grasp the fact a tidal wave might erupt right in front of our eyes, on schedule, that would make all the science-fiction films I've ever seen look tame.
REPORTER:
Walter, the Army isn't hopeful. One officer told me

they're really depending on a miracle—that one of those little subs will float by accident right over the bomb and find it. Otherwise they only have a general line of direction from a radio transmitter and that includes too much space for a few subs to cover with only four feet visibility in their searchlights."

WALTER: (*To camera.*)

This reporter has covered the astronauts' flight to the moon, but I must say that until this moment I never sensed the reality of the great weapons race we've been talking about all these years. Because some scientists on a squash court in Chicago more than thirty years ago created a nuclear reaction, our civilization has now reached the point where one deranged person can single-handedly cause the greatest catastrophe this world has ever seen. I believe that whatever happens it would be fitting for politcial leaders of all countries to sit down after this happens and see what can be done to stop the spread of these terrible, terrible weapons.

13

MINUS 00:48 MINUTES. JULY 2, ATLANTIC CITY.

Tom O'Neal was angry. He had been up all night on helicopter patrol, then out again for another shift, and now he was trying to nap on a bunk in military command headquarters at the Atlantic City airport.

But sleep proved hopeless. People running back and forth, loudspeakers blaring, someone yelling. And at that point a dogface private came running by with a

Silex of coffee with a colonel screaming at him, and tripped. The scalding coffee flooded the thin sheet above O'Neal's chest; he jumped up shouting, "You goddam moron." The GI was only interested in how much coffee was left in the Silex to please the colonel. O'Neal looked at the soggy, steaming bunk. Jesus! He gave up on the idea of sleeping even a few minutes.

He dressed, went into the improvised mess, and ordered a hamburger from a sweating Army chef. The chef said, "Hear the excitement? They found the fucking bomb."

"They did? Where?"

The chef said, "I don't mean they *found* it. I mean they know where it is. Off Ocean City."

The chef told O'Neal that a radio transmitter had been discovered with its directional antenna pointing to the area off the southeast coast of Ocean City. The southeast coast of Ocean City! Christ, O'Neal thought.

The chef saw his expression. "What's wrong?"

"I thought I saw something right there last night. It looked like a raft or something. But it disappeared. I threw the light everywhere. Nothing. So I thought it must be a shadow from a cloud in front of the moon or something—"

14

MINUS 00:45 MINUTES. JULY 2, OCEAN CITY.

Green waves flecked with spume, the wind kicking up. Clouds formed in the sky as a storm approached. It was 5:15. Forty-five minutes from the explosion.

The radio on the helicopter crackled, "FIRESTORM ONE. THIS IS ACADEMY. OVER."

"FIRESTORM ONE, GO AHEAD."

"We have a helicopter crewman who thought he spotted something that looked like a raft in your area last night. He says the raft disappeared, so he believed it might just be a shadow of a cloud or something. Still, for your information, here are the approximate coordinates of the spot he saw the raft. About three hundred feet off the beach, and five blocks from the south end of the island."

Williams listened. A raft? That could account for the fact that no boat was seen last night. And the location was in line with the radio antenna! He said to the Admiral, "I think we should bring the subs to the surface fast. Go with it."

"Concentrate on the place where the helicopter might have spotted something?" asked the Admiral.

"You agree?"

After a few seconds' thought the Admiral said, "We've got nothing better." He gave the order, and it was more priceless time wasted, five minutes for the subs to get to the surface, then five minutes more before they were headed down, but this time they could concentrate on an exact location. If that helicopter crewman was right, they might make it yet. They might find Leonard Chew's bomb.

15

Peggy DuPont paced the Situation Room of the White House nervously. For two hours she had sat here, fascinated by television screens bringing them live pictures from the tidal-wave target while military men around her initiated and relayed orders. Peggy could actually see the helicopter in which Williams was flying. A colonel had pointed it out to her on the screen.

Then at 5:25 P.M. had come the electrifying news that they had narrowed the area even closer. The subs, which had been cruising widely, could now zero right in on a certain point off the coast!

5:35 P.M. No news. Bomb experts in scuba gear were on helicopters ready to plunge into the ocean the minute a sub appeared with the bomb in its grappler. But the time! Only minutes to go! And the helicopters and subs had to abandon the area at 5:45 at the latest, or they would all be killed.

God, Peggy had never been so nervous. Those subs had to find that nuclear bomb. But where were they? Why weren't they breaking to the surface with the bomb?

16

Minus 00:20 minutes. July 2, Ocean City.

It was all over, Williams thought. We've lost. The sun was just beginning to lower in the west; its light caused strange silhouettes to flit across waves like ghosts far removed from the helicopters that caused them. The chopper turned west and the sun momentarily blinded Williams. He turned to look down at the sea, which was flecked with spray caused by freshening winds. The Admiral beside him said, "Well, at least we have an off-shore wind."

Williams didn't answer. Someone shouted, "Over here!" An oceanographic sub broke the surface a hundred yards away, dripping water from its hull. Its hatch popped open, a crewman in a black skin diver's suit waved. Williams' helicopter raced to a position above the sub and lowered a bucket seat on a line.

Two minutes later the first oceanographic crewman was aboard Williams' chopper, splattering saltwater in the cabin.

But where was the other sub? Williams' watch said 5:45 P.M.; the sub should have surfaced by now.

17

Deep in the ocean Jim Wentworth looked forward with a strained expression. They were supposed to have started for the surface five minutes ago. But lighted in his searchlight beam was a *green plastic bag!* It sat on the ocean floor with something bulky inside. The black rubber of a deflated raft was all around it on the ocean floor. They had found it, and they still had fourteen minutes to go! The sub was jockeying into position while Wentworth unfolded the grappling device. Goddam, that was the bomb all right. Robinson could see the outline of a radio with an antenna inside the bag.

"Stabilize the boat," Wentworth said. "I'm having trouble."

They were so nervous that Robinson had overshot the spot for a minute. Now he threw the engine into reverse to stop its forward thrust. The tiny sub quivered throughout its length, then became stable. Wentworth carefully tried again with the grappler, moving it to a position behind the bag.

5:48 P.M. He thrust the grappler forward purposefully, and success! The bag was between its jaws. They had it! Then something happened. The bag started to *inflate!* "HURRY, GODDAMIT!" Robinson shouted, and Wentworth twisted the handles feverishly, closing the grappler, but too late. The claws moved shut just as the bag drifted upward and sideways above them. As if in a dream they watched the bag disappear up, up, up toward the light green surface.

18

Minus 00:10 minutes. July 2, off Ocean City.

Consternation in the helicopters. The timer in the transmitter had been set at six; evacuation ordered at 5:45 P.M. But one sub was missing. The two-man crew of the other sub was already aboard Williams' chopper, their diving suits streaming water. Anxiously, they peered out of helicopter windows toward the heaving surface of that ocean below. Where was Robinson's sub?

The radios in all of the search helicopters crackled insistently, "ABANDON THE AREA! ABANDON THE AREA! THIS IS AN ORDER!" At the airport General Horton was furious.

The pilot of Williams' helicopter turned to the Admiral. "What'll I do, sir? He's my boss."

Williams said, "We'll send all the other helicopters back in five minutes. That will give them time to clear." He was not sure it was enough time, but he wanted every possible minute on his side. He said to the pilot, "If everyone agrees, our own helicopter will stay a few minutes longer."

"I'm willing, sir," the pilot said, and the others nodded. But the Admiral was not certain. "If all those people are killed, and I disobeyed an order—" Then he stopped and said, "I won't be around to court-martial, will I? So we stay?"

5:52 P.M. A green plastic bag carrying a small nuclear bomb and a compact radio drifted slowly upward through the Atlantic depths. Because of the weight, its negative buoyancy was slight; its ascension rate slow. Toward the surface of the ocean the water became lighter, green, streaked with sunlight. Leonard Chew had computed ten minutes for its rise from three hundred feet to the surface. He was off by twenty-nine seconds. The green plastic package broke through at 6:00:29.

19

MINUS 00:05 MINUTES. JULY 2, OFF OCEAN CITY.

By 5:55 P.M. Williams had decided that something had happened to the sub below—a mechanical failure? an entrapment in old wreckage? It had happened before to those deep ocean subs. And the Admiral was firm on one point. "Courage is one thing; suicide another."

They were heading north toward Atlantic City when Williams and the Admiral, who had been watching with binoculars, saw a sub break surface far behind them. "Oh, Christ!" said the Admiral.

And now the radio from the sub could be heard for the first time. "We've found it! Green plastic bag!"

Williams clapped his hand on the pilot's shoulder. "We're going back."

But the Admiral, staring through the binoculars, said, "It's right in front of them, George. They'll have it before we can get near there!"

Williams looked through the glasses and saw the sub's white prow bobbing toward a green package not twenty feet away, and it was a miracle! They had *found* that nuclear bomb. But how much time did they have?

Jim Wentworth stood in the open hatch of an ocean sub on the surface, a kapok jacket on, and a sharp knife in his hand. He was trembling—but ready. Their orders were to cut away all wiring connected to the bomb.

6:08. He and Robinson should already be dead. 6 P.M. had passed and no explosion. What did that mean? The bomb must be inert. The destruction of the radio transmitter had rendered it harmless, unless there was an internal timer, too. Oh Jesus, there it was! The nose of the sub actually touched the little plastic bag, which bobbed beneath the surface for a minute, then popped up and now drifted along the hull.

6:09. He had the bag in his hands! He stood in the hatch of the little sub, tearing at the plastic bag with a knife, a great lifting in his heart, and there was the bomb in his bare hand with all kinds of electrical apparatus attached to it, and he swung his knife like an ax, and a timer so small he did not see its hands connected at 6:10.

A great fireball boiled up!

The sub vanished in a massive orange inferno . . .

The ocean beneath the explosion turned into an enormous subterranean well, while a churning mushroom climbed into the sky above the fire . . .

. . . and Williams' chopper careened upside-down, smashed by the giant blast, the pilot fighting the controls, everyone flung in disarray, the chopper falling . . .

. . . and on the shore a Coast Guard sailor in a tower watched in awe and fright as the greatest wave he had ever seen rose like an enormous wall and raced toward the beach where he stood.

20

THERE WERE PEOPLE ON THE BEACH THAT DAY AND others in houses fronting the ocean. The hasty evacuation had not been complete. There were young people and campers who hadn't gotten the word. And others who, for a variety of reasons, decided not to leave.

These stragglers were joined by some intrepid newsmen who had crept in by boat or car, one of them a TV news crew in a van with film cameras.

Pat McGrady and his girl, Lynn Lippincott, were on the beach, the resort behind them, when suddenly off to the left in the ocean, a fantastic fireball roared and ballooned upward, so bright it blinded them in daylight. Shock waves battered them viciously; Lynn fell backward as the sand turned into a storm of flying particles. Pat picked her up and saw the ocean in front of him retreating outward until the sand showed, far, far out to sea. It was incredible!

And then he saw the tidal wave forming, a mountainous trembling concave wall, furious white froth on its crest beginning to race toward the beach. Lynn screamed; they turned to run off that beach, but too late! A giant tide sucked them under water. McGrady was tumbled over and over, and then, breathtakingly, found himself out in the open, on the crest of the great wave, looking down from high above the beach as they raced forward.

A street ahead . . . the wave did not break! McGrady saw green-roofed houses directly in front of him, then felt a trembling and a roaring beneath him, and he was hurtled down, down toward the houses as the tidal wave broke in a thunderous roar, cracking timbers everywhere. And the two broken bodies of Pat McGrady and Lynn Lippincott were swept inland on the flood.

In Atlantic City the boardwalk was deserted. The Army had closed it off; no stragglers leaned against its iron railings to see the great bubble form in the ocean beneath the fireball. From the slopes of the huge bubble a tidal wave raced toward the famous resort. It uprooted first the Steel Pier. Thousands of tons of iron broke off from the boardwalk, turned sideways, and became a monstrous battering ram sweeping everything along its path. The wave rolled on, gathering momentum and height until it fell with an unearthly roar on boutiques, restaurants, hotels, amusement centers, custard palaces, taffy stores, drugstores, novelty shops. The most famous boardwalk in the world disintegrated into jagged timbers, plaster, and rusty iron, smashing toward the center of the city.

And on the Coast Guard tower, the frightened military guard watched helplessly as the tidal wave rolled toward his spindly outpost. It seemed as if it were about to break upon him, but instead it held, and suddenly he heard a cracking sound. His tower was afloat on the ocean crest, bobbing in white froth and green boiling water! Then, thank God! he was *behind* the crest, which broke with a thunderous sound, and the guard clung to his fragile wooden tower as it raced downhill in water over the city. Houses and roofs joined him in the flood. Beneath him, on the streets of Atlantic City, he heard a sound he would never forget. Auto horns and burglar alarms, short-circuited by the saltwater, shrieked in a lost cacophony beneath the deep water.

On the roof of a bank on the bay side of the city the tower jammed long enough for the guard to grab support and hold on till rescue.

And the TV news cameraman in a truck parked on a street beyond the boardwalk took film that would be shown around the world again and again the next day, of the most frightening tidal wave ever seen, a film that ran in horror up to the moment the monstrous wave towered like a skyscraper in front of them and then broke on the camera lens, the film swirling upside-down and going out of focus, and their truck lifted in the torrent and carried inland till it smashed against a stone building.

21

IN THE HAMPTONS ON LONG ISLAND IT WAS THE height of the season. At Asparagus Beach in Amagansett, a "singles" beach, the pretty girls stood up to be seen in their string bikinis, some of them topless. On more sedate beaches at East and Southampton mothers looked after their children who dashed into the water, while at Westhampton girls watched volleyball games.

On all beaches portable radios blared the warnings throughout the afternoon. "If the bomb explodes off South Jersey, the resulting wave will reach the shore of Long Island." But cynical New Yorkers felt that even if it did, how fast could a wave reach here from a hundred miles away? There would be plenty of time to flee if it came to that.

Then an electrifying radio bulletin flashed along the entire shore. From portable radio after radio came the excited voices of announcers: "The nuclear weapon has just been exploded off the shore of New Jersey. A tidal wave is spreading from the center of the blast. All residents of shore communities are warned to take cover at once. Do not let the water touch you! It is radioactive!"

And the girls of "Asparagus" were gathering lotions, towels, and bikini tops in one motion and running, fathers were grabbing children. The beaches became a scene of tumult and confusion as bathers raced out of the water and up dunes toward the parking lots where the cars were.

There was a curiosity almost too great to bear, the urge to stay near the beach, perhaps on the terrace of a house, and watch a tidal wave rise from the ocean like a huge wall and come hurtling at them. But fear, and the knowledge that the Hamptons were flat potatoland over which radioactive water would roll, drove most people into cars heading inland.

Up along the coast of New Jersey the water boiled north; the tidal wave at sea was merely a massive ripple, almost invisible to untrained eyes. But iron strength was beneath the surface; the wave's momentum when it struck shallow ground north would build it higher and higher.

In the Hamptons people found the small roads inland jammed and started abandoning their cars, running on foot through people's lawns and across sandy fields and farms and woods, all of them spurred by portable radios that kept broadcasting the news of the wave.

But on Long Island, as in the resorts to the south, there were those who did not get the word, or who—through some compulsion greater than fear—stayed to see this historic catastrophic wave. Among those who did were three young men on the roof of the Don Marino house on Further Lane in East Hampton baking in the sun, their bodies clad only in dungaree shorts, healthy, strong, feeling good—and also safe. The roof of the house on the dune was at least thirty-five feet high—and experts had already called in to radio stations to state that the wave would expend much of its strength by the time it reached Long Island. Still, experts had been wrong before. The three young men were a hundred feet from the water's edge. They had binoculars to spot the wave when it first started rising and a jeep to take them the hell out of range in case the experts were wrong.

Plenty of time to escape.

And so the three young men, Princeton sophomores, drank beer in the sun, talked in low tones, and prepared to take this risk to witness history being made. But the binoculars showed nothing. Then slowly, then swiftly before their eyes, they saw the sea start to rise, out beyond the breakers, a hump rising so that the breakers in front of it now lessened to white frothy ripples, then became nothing but green water as the wave towered higher and higher. And, oh my God, the wave wasn't stopping! It came across that beach, as high as the roof they stood on, and the boys made it to the door, but too late—the tidal wave with its millions of tons of water crashed on the house and they were hurled through sharp, splintered wood to the sand, swept across fields . . .

And everywhere on Long Island, cars were afloat and people struggling in neck-deep water. Kennedy airport was a lake, Jones Beach was a shambles, Fire Island's villages driftwood.

In the elapsed time of one minute the southern shore of Long Island and the entire coast of New Jersey to the south were poisoned.

22

ABOVE ATLANTIC CITY THE CONCUSSIVE WAVE THAT had struck Williams' helicopter and flipped it upside-down had passed—but the pilot could not right the chopper. Then suddenly, the controls worked. The chopper started to turn right side up. The pilot managed to reach the roof of an office building in Atlantic City and set the helicopter down.

"Oh sweet Jesus Christ," the pilot said. He was slouched back in his seat, trembling violently. The co-pilot said to Williams, "He saved our lives."

Williams agreed. If he had turned back toward the sub as Williams wanted, they would have been shattered by the blast. As it was, the shock wave had traveled in the same direction they were flying and had violently buffeted but not destroyed them.

But the sub crew out there had died because of Williams.

Williams went to the side of the roof facing the ocean and saw a view he would never forget—a city under racing water, with a mass of tumbled wreckage, chairs, tables, beds, even pianos, along with rooftops, afloat in the water. But most unforgettable were the faces bobbing here and there, victims of the wave who stared with sightless eyes, their bodies drifting. And far beneath the churning water Williams could hear the haunting sound of submerged horns and alarms sounding like wails of pain from the deep.

People who had believed they were safe in the upper floors of office buildings were now stranded, leaning out of windows. Williams heard the sound of a helicopter coming toward them. The copilot said, "I radioed for it. Thank God, the airport is far enough inland to be still in business."

23

LATE IN THE AFTERNOON GENERAL HORTON DIRECTED his rescue operations from the busy airport, as Army rescue battalions conducted what the Pentagon called "ABC Warfare."

The Army had been ready for nuclear attack since the inception of the cold war, and now the procedures were initiated. ABC warfare—A for Atomic, B for Bacterial, C for Chemical attack. This was emergency A— tents, portable showers, Geiger counters, and lead disposal containers for contaminated clothes were coming in, while helicopters and jeep patrols went into the city with men in leadlined suits and masks carrying Geiger counters and stretchers.

Soon an emergency hospital rose. Victims of the tidal wave were first moved through the decontamination tent, stripped of their clothes, checked with a Geiger counter and—if not bleeding—placed into showers with steaming hot water and scrubbed with a special soap.

Only when a Geiger counter stopped clicking were they sent to the Red Cross tent for medical attention.

But many would not be allowed in that tent because the Geiger counter *kept* registering. They were the victims who had been so close to the blast that the radioactive water had drenched them. These people were the most pitiful of all. One was a young mother with a child. Both were poisoned, and nothing science had discovered could cancel radioactive poisoning once it had penetrated the blood.

Doctors in lead-lined coveralls came into the tent for whatever comfort they could administer. But the young mother knew at once when she and her child were not sent with the others to the sterilization tent that something was wrong. "Oh, God," she cried, "What does it mean? Is my baby all right? Tell me!"

The doctors tried to calm her, but they couldn't take her into that tent either. She herself had become a radioactive time bomb. She might live for years, like the Japanese at Hiroshima and Nagasaki, with leukemia or bone cancer, but always sick and suffering. And her baby would not survive.

Williams passed the medical tent, heard a despairing scream, looked inside. He saw a pretty young mother clutching a baby to her chest, rocking in horror, and others around her staring in shock or crying, death in their blood, and no cure—and felt an overwhelming anger at Leonard Chew, the man who had exploded that bomb.

But inside the terminal General Horton said something strange. "Chew gave us a break."

"What do you mean?"

"He must have cut down the bomb. The wave was somewhere around fifty feet, not a hundred. That fifty feet less made a lot of difference. The goddam wave might still be rolling inland."

An AEC scientist arrived, heavy horn-rimmed

glasses on a bony nose. "Incredible." The scientist looked shaken. "I never thought I'd see this. I told myself it couldn't happen."

Williams asked him why the bomb had popped to the surface, and the AEC expert told him that Chew's primary initiator was the radio transmitter, so he must have used an inflatable bag. "He wanted it on the surface so he could tie in with the weather vane and explode it only when the wind was blowing offshore."

General Horton had taken off his cap and was staring at the scientist. "But the backup timer was set for only ten minutes."

The AEC expert replied, "I guess that's all he thought he could afford. Couldn't let the bomb float around on the surface all day while your birds were looking for it."

"Jesus!" the General said. "I'd like to have that bastard in my hands for ten minutes. Screw the weather vane."

BOOK IV

The Explosion in New York

1

LEONARD CHEW, IN A NAVY CAPTAIN'S UNIFORM, carrying a Geiger counter, exited from a cab in front of the Waldorf-Astoria Hotel in New York.

He wore a red beard and moustache and tinted aviator's glasses, but in reality the uniform and the Geiger counter were his disguises. People looked at image first, then particulars.

Still Chew didn't want to remain in public view for long. His picture was all over the nation. But this afternoon people didn't seem to notice anything. They stood in groups and talked, clutched transistor radios to their ears, or gathered in front of shop windows where television sets showed pictures of the ruin created by the wave. The wave had rolled safely by the protected New York harbor but it had devastated neighboring Long Island.

Chew had reserved a room at the Waldorf a month ago. Now he mounted a wide, deep-carpeted stairway that led to the lobby of the hotel, awed by its elegance, the small plaster statues, discreet bars opening off the lounge, a fleet of great couches stretching across the huge high-vaulted room, and to the right the reservations desk.

Chew avoided the desk, went to a house phone, and called Room 1703, which was supposed to be empty.

No answer. He went to the bank of elevators, watched the doors open and a crowd pour out, then got in. No one else was going up. The elevator moved soundlessly, and he was alone on his way to a room that was his, would always be his, would never belong to anyone other than the man who had brought his young wife to New York for the first time so long ago and shared an emotion that was still fresh, and would never die.

But her body had died. And the children she had borne breathed no longer. And who was to know *that* on a bright spring day in 1963 when the world seemed so open and good, people were so kind, and everyone loved the shy sweet blonde and her quiet young husband, who could see only each other, notice no other object, place, or human as they rode up in this same elevator to begin a honeymoon.

And oh God, when he entered that room again, it was wrenching for Chew because there, through that window on the right, was the city as they had first seen it. Nothing had changed, the view north across apartment buildings with the East River curling alongside, and how Hope had loved it.

2

February, 1963. Hope Ryden Chew said, "It's so . . . marvelous!" She was staring out of the window, an expression of delight on her face. Chew said, "Would you like to live here? We could, you know. I could find a job."

Hope turned. "It's the strangest thing. I think I might

like to—and I've only been in the city for thirty minutes. It's so . . . exciting, isn't it?" She went to the bureau where a bucket of ice cooled a champagne bottle. Chew was the typical honeymooner. He had even bought new pajamas. And, of course, champagne was the first room-service order.

So he opened the bottle. The cork smashed into the ceiling, and Hope laughed as bubbles cascaded down the sides and Chew desperately tilted the bottle to his lips to stop the flood. The bubbles seemed to erupt in Chew's veins, filling him with warmth.

They had a sweet honeymoon, the highlight of their life, a week Hope referred to over and over again in their marriage. They saw *Oliver!* on Broadway, wandered through art museums, tried to look "natural" in restaurants with haughty waiters, and rode through Central Park in a horse-drawn carriage.

And if that was square, as Chew had read, then it was square on target, too, in a week of love, which is what a honeymoon should be all about. And the pleasure in Hope's eyes when she saw the bent old carriage driver and listened to the quiet clop-clopping of the horses' hooves as they wheeled through a fresh green park where cyclists rode, students sprawled on grass, and softballs flew through the air—that look in Hope's eyes was unforgettable.

The man from Naughton Aircraft who had hired Chew, and paid for the expensive Waldorf hotel room as part of the deal, visited them just once. He was a pleasant man, tall, with a bland face, named Fred Harlingen. The visit occurred on the last day of their honeymoon, and what Harlingen said was that the company wanted Chew to go to North Carolina for some sort of briefing and preparation before embarking for the Middle East.

In a four-story brick building a spare, bespectacled man met Chew and shook his hand warmly. He led him to an office where Chew found himself listening to the history of weapons sales in the Middle East. A fascinating story with one great central theme: bribery.

Chew wondered what all this had to do with his background in nuclear science and finally asked the question. The response startled him.

"Oh, now that's simple. We heard you're through with nukes. At the same time we were told by our friends at Alamos that you were one of the most creative engineers ever to come to the base. Now, we have a need for that talent. We have all kinds of concepts that an inventive mind can go to town with—"

Two days later Chew found that the man was talking about weapons, that Chew, in fact, had been enrolled in an elite intelligence group representing "American industry in the Middle East" and at that point, hell, he should have pulled out.

But he was too naive then. He found he was *interested* in the idea. For the first time his life of equations on blackboards, and thick engineering books would change dramatically. In this group he would be not just a scientist in a lab, but a man of action.

And that was how ill he was at the time, sick from his revulsion at himself because of what he believed was his "cowardly" nervous breakdown. He thought only of how his father would have welcomed the opportunity and how his new wife would want him to be a hero. She looked forward to such great things from him. So he signed on and really never knew what he was signing into, never realized the operation's scope, never met the men behind this project to analyze their motives—as his father, a much more down-to-earth man, might have done—but, my God, it had been exhilarating for a while, and at the time he had never looked back, so whom could he blame? Certainly not Hope. She caught on fast that something was not right, that tragedy of some sort was coming. One night in Beirut after they had made love, the children asleep in the next room, Hope kept saying, "Let's get out, Leonard. Let's go home. I'm frightened."

Oh Christ!

Now, in a hotel room where it had all begun, he was crying; he was still a weakling. He had to stop. He went over to the fireplace on one side of the room, crouched down, then reached up inside it. Rough bricks scraped his hand. But there it was. That ledge Hope had found when she was seeking someplace to hide her "valuables"—a modest amount of jewelry—when they were absent from the room.

Chew had placed the Geiger counter on the floor. Now he opened its lid. The second nuclear bomb was there. He picked it up in one hand—one hand for New York!—crouched down again, and thrust the bomb onto the shelf.

This was where he wanted that second nuclear bomb to explode. In honor of Fred Harlingen, who paid for their room, and made their delight a bent finger beckoning them into vileness and self-hatred and death. This one is for you, Fred, Chew thought.

And for the man who ordered you to kill my family, Gustavus.

LEONARD CHEW DIALED 202 456-1414. A VOICE AN-
swered "THE WHITE HOUSE."

Chew said, "I want to speak to the President. This is
Leonard Chew. I will identify myself with the serial
number of one of the stolen nuclear weapons. Have you
a pencil?"

The woman on the White House switchboard answered yes in a trembling voice. Chew said, "AF
7-54362. Please bring that information to the President."

A minute later the President of the United States was
on the telephone. Chew said, "Mr. President, you will
try to trace this telephone connection. It will do you no
good. I am speaking to you through a connection two
miles away from the telephone."

While Chew talked, the President nodded to an aide,
Bill Conway, who rushed out the door to alert the New
York Telephone Company. Chew said, "I want to tell
you my conditions for turning in the remaining two
bombs."

The President said, "Mr. Chew, I was just about to
meet with my National Security Council and George
Williams in the Cabinet room. I'll switch this call to that
room where it will be relayed over a speaker so that all
of them can hear, if that is agreeable to you."

"It is," Chew said.

The President took his time going to the Cabinet
room so that the telephone company in New York

would have more minutes to track Chew's location. But he didn't want to make Chew so irritated that he broke off the call. In less than two minutes the members of the Council were listening to Chew's voice coming over the speaker.

"Mr. President. It was not my idea to steal the nuclear bombs. The Deep Men in Washington and Switzerland are responsible in every way for what is happening."

"You're exploding the bombs, Mr. Chew."

"Because I have no other recourse, Mr. President. Because your government refuses to move against the Deep Men. Because your government permits ex-CIA officers and German right-wingers to run this country, even at the risk of a nuclear war."

The President said, *"I'm* running the country, Mr. Chew."

In New York, Chew smiled. "You want to halt the weapons race, Mr. President. Would it surprise you that the Deep Men know the exact date and place you intend to sign the SALT III arms limitation agreement with the Soviets? August sixth, Mannerheim Palace, Helsinki, Finland. Now I believe only a few of your top advisers know that date and place because you wanted to address the American people first to prepare them. You were going to tell Americans that the weapons race is escalating until it is almost uncontrollable, with newer and more terrifying weapons being invented every day. For the sake of humanity you want to do all in your power to stop the 'insanity' before it's too late. But you will never sign that nuclear arms limitation agreement, Mr. President."

The President *was* surprised that Chew knew the exact date and place. It was true he had only told a few of his high-ranking advisers. But how many? The Secretary of State, the CIA Director, the AEC Director. The Secretary of Defense and the heads of all branches of the armed services. And an Undersecretary at State who was directly responsible for all SALT negotiations. He said, "Why won't I sign it?"

Chew said, "The Deep Men are superpatriots, who believe they are faced with a dove-ish President, who is committing national suicide. To stop you, they're willing to risk nuclear war. The nuclear bombs I stole were to be planted in three capitals of Soviet satellite nations, East Germany, Czechoslovakia, and Rumania. The bombs would be exploded one by one without warning to the population if you proceeded to enter any arms agreement with the Soviets. Under the threat of an action that could escalate in minutes into a total nuclear war, your government would be paralyzed."

He stopped, then went on. "And that's not all, Mr. President. As long as you are in office the Deep Men won't rest. The nuclear theft was only the first of their overt operations—they'll steal other nuclear bombs if necessary; they'll commit assassinations to control your actions. The Deep Men are breaking into the open from now on. They've been running your government without you even knowing it for years."

But the President scoffed, "My people have never even heard of the Deep Men. There can't be such a conspiracy as you say without someone knowing about them."

"What some of your advisers know and what you're told are two different things, Mr. President. I risked my life to testify about the Deep Men in Congress. I told a Congressional committee about their bribery, blackmail, and political assassinations in this country and abroad. I was mocked. My testimony was disbelieved. I was sent away and nothing was done about the Deep Men. And I realized then that nothing can be done in an open, legitimate way because the Deep Men are too deep undercover, too entrenched—and they control too many people in high places in your government."

Silence, then Chew said, "But I can stop them, Mr. President. I have a wedge. The Deep Men in this country are led by a traitor at the very highest level of your government. I believe he is sitting in that room with you now."

In the Cabinet room the members of the National Security Council looked at one another. The President stared straight ahead as Chew continued, "But the traitor has a weakness. He can be unmasked through that weakness. I will call your investigator, George Williams, on a secure line to give him clues to this traitor."

He stopped, then seemed to be reading a statement: "Please inform the American people of these facts. I testified about a conspiracy called the Deep Men in Congress, at the risk of my life. Nothing happened. The government didn't move. Now drastic measures are necessary to prevent this conspiracy of misled superpatriots from plunging the world into nuclear war. I am giving the government clues to the traitor who heads the Deep Men. If the government once again refuses to act on my information, if the Deep Men once again show that they control the American government, Mr. President, I will explode the second nuclear bomb, in modified form, in an area of Manhattan at eight A.M. July fourth.

The call ended with Chew hanging up. Abruptly, the President flung open the door to the hallway where his aid, Bill Conway, stood. Conway said, "They have it, Mr. President. 495 E. 46th Street in New York. The FBI is on its way."

In New York, FBI agents burst into an apartment

and found two telephones side by side. The phones were taped together so that the speaker of one was flush against the receiver of the other. The line was dead.

The President called his press secretary and arranged a broadcast from the Oval Office in thirty minutes. Chew had said the bomb was set for 8 A.M. July 4. That was only thirty-six hours away, and an entire city must be evacuated—the most densely populated city in America.

4

AMERICA REELED; THE TIDAL WAVE CRASHING UPON the coast had spread shock as far as California. Now this one-man protector of America's morality was going to destroy New York, too?

Anger at Chew spilled out in telegrams to the White House—but the anger carried a chilling undertone for politicians. Many of the senders were equally as furious at a government that had heard testimony about a secret group of assassins and nuclear thieves and had done nothing about it. Telegram after telegram recalled the Senate CIA assassination hearings that had produced no real limitations to that agency's power. Now Americans were told that before that same Congress the facts about the Deep Men had been revealed and no action was taken, not even any notice to Americans, because the hearings were secret.

The President dispatched General Maxwell to the Palisades, across from New York, where the Army would begin its evacuation of the city immediately.

Someone had once said that if one million New Yorkers simultaneously came down to the streets from their skyscraper apartment and office buildings, they wouldn't have room to stand. Now that theory was going to be tested—hour after hour. The President convened his National Security Council in the Oval Office to talk over options. "Whatever happens, you have to stall Chew," the President told Williams. "Tell him anything he wants to hear when he calls you. Lie. Prevaricate. Beg. I don't care. The man was insane enough to explode a bomb off New Jersey today, and I think he'll do it in New York, too."

Oliver Taylor, the Secreatry of State, said, "I'm amazed that he knew the date when you were going to sign the SALT III agreement." He turned to Winthrop, the CIA Director. "And I'm even more surprised at his statement about that conspiracy. How could there be some rogue agents operating in this country without your people knowing it?"

But Winthrop shrugged the question off wearily. "I went over all this with Williams and the President, Oliver. We knew about EIC—but thought it was just another covert bribery outfit run by a multinational. I personally never heard the name Deep Men before George came to me with it."

But the President was anxious to concentrate on Chew's impending telephone call to Williams. "Detente will take care of itself. I've already had a call on the red phone. The Soviet Premier wanted to know what was going on with these stolen nuclear bombs—and would it have any effect on detente? Then he said, 'If your country can't control terrorists who can steal nuclear weapons, then perhaps it's futile to sign any agreement to cut down the number.' " He stopped and played with a pen, which bore the Presidential seal. Then threw it on the desk. "But as I say, we'll worry about detente and the Deep Men later. The first thing we have to do is stop a maniac from exploding a bomb in New York." He looked at George. "Now, how do we do that?"

"We listen to what he tells me," Williams said. "And we *do* what he says."

"But suppose he asks us to do something impossible?"

"He said he had clues to a traitor. I believe him. He didn't come this far without a plan. He exploded that bomb today to let us know he means business. And now he's giving us clues to the traitor—and I'm looking forward to getting those clues, myself."

All the members of the President's National Security Council looked at one another. Williams said, "I have a feeling Chew wants that man so badly he'll do anything—he'll even return the bombs if he thinks we're going to hand over the man he wants."

The President nodded. "But if he doesn't get his man. If the traitor—whoever he is—proves too clever or is so well hidden we can't reach him in time—"

"Chew will keep escalating the pressure," Williams said. And all of them knew what that meant. A fireball consuming Manhattan.

5

SEPTEMBER, 1975. LEONARD CHEW AND HIS BEST friend, Fred Harlingen, sat in the sun on the terrace of Chew's villa in Beirut, playing a game called "Nuclear Strategy." NATO forces in Europe, in this game, had fifty atomic cannon, one hundred medium-range missiles, and thirty B-52s armed with cruise missiles. The Soviet forces had two hundred atomic cannon, one hundred missiles, and ten Tupolev bombers armed with air-to-ground missiles.

Advantage: the Soviets.

Ground forces were even more disproportionate, with a million front-line Soviet troops facing less than five hundred thousand NATO soldiers. And the Soviets could throw in more millions, in reserve.

Because of the Soviet advantage, the NATO player had "First strike." Chew rolled the dice. He was NATO. Five. His decision to strike south toward Rumania came up as result five. "Budapest annihilated. Rumanian leaders fly to Moscow to protest war. Rumanian leaders imprisoned in Moscow, NATO tank forces stopped at Tirgului River, and decimated by Soviet atomic cannon. (6 shells expended)."

"Your roll," Chew said to Fred Harlingen, and handed him the dice.

Harlingen said, "This is an antiwar game. But why is it so much fun?"

Leonard's blond wife, Hope, came out on the terrace with iced tea for the two nuclear "Generals." Fred Harlingen never took his eyes off the board. "I can't bring myself to destroy Paris," he said, "even on a game board. OK, I know, I know. It's wrong, anyway. Always attack the enemy's missile and air bases first. But then why did you hit Budapest?"

"Could be a feint," Chew said.

"You're both sadists, playing that game," Hope said with a smile.

They concentrated on the game for one more hour— longer than a real nuclear war would last, Harlingen observed—then called it a draw. Afterward they retired to a cool room with bamboo shades and wicker furniture that Hope had purchased in street bazaars. "Tonight we celebrate," Harlingen said.

The next day the Chews were to fly back to America for good. Chew was retiring from the Deep Men. His wife had insisted. The children were growing, and she wanted them in America. Harlingen was staying on.

They went to a French restaurant and over *le bifteck,* Leonard asked Fred if he could drive "Hope and the kids" to the airport tomorrow. Fred caught on right away.

"Don't tell me they want you to do something the last minute you're leaving."

Harlingen, like Chew, was a Deep Man. His cover was a professor of mathematics at a UN school and what work he did was in recruiting and bribery—never violence. He had obviously not been informed of Chew's final mission. He said to Chew, "Look, tell them no. You've had enough risks for ten lives, and now you're practically home, and suppose something happens." He paused, then said, "So far you've been lucky but—"

Leonard assured him nothing would go wrong, but he appreciated Harlingen's concern. And, really, Harlingen was a good friend, perhaps the best friend Leonard ever had—and the next day Harlingen did take his wife and children to the airport but stopped first at the art gallery opening . . .

. . . and sun blinding white in the streets after the explosion, and no more life for Chew, no more life without mental torture.

The Deep Men did what they could to help Chew. They hid him from the authorities and managed to get him out of the country and back to America. Chew remembered none of it; his mind was a blur. Even now it was merely images, impressions of doctors and a hospital room overlooking the East River and talk of clinical depression and one time a man he had never met sitting in his room telling him that Fred Harlingen, his best friend, had also died in the explosion trying to shield his family.

Another of these men whom he had never seen before showed up to take him to Haddonfield, New Jersey, where they had rented a home in his name and placed a $50,000 bonus in a bank account. All part of the Deep Men's solicitude for a loyal operative who had suffered a tragedy.

Months later Chew stood in a garden of yellow tulips behind his home when a man he knew came around the house and called to him. Kurt Edwards, vigorous, tanned, and enthusiastic. He had news for Chew. The Deep Men wanted him to do one more job—and this time the financial payoff would be immense. Chew just shook his head. A twig he was swinging idly scooped off the head of a tulip. Edwards asked him to hear him out at least, and they went into a den in the house and in front of a blank television set Edwards told him of the nuclear theft. "We're in a bind, Leonard, or we wouldn't come to you. But there's no one in the organization except you who can pull this off." He stopped, regarding Chew closely. "But it's a quick in-and-out job. Steal the MIRVs, take out the security devices inside, and your part's finished. You collect your money and go home."

Chew just smiled. It was impossible, he said. His nerves were still shot. And nuclear bombs made the condition worse. He had a breakdown over those nuclear monsters years ago. But Edwards was not to be refused. He reminded Chew of what the Deep Men had done for him. They had saved him from possible legal prosecution in Beirut; one of their top men, Fred Harlingen, had even died trying to save his family. And if he wasn't grateful, they could get tougher. They could inform Hope's parents—that Chew himself killed their daughter and his children.

Emotional blackmail. Chew was furious. But what could he do. He knew the Deep Men well enough to know that they carried out threats, not just voiced them. Two days later he and Edwards were at Los Alamos, then at Minot, making preparations. Then back to Washington for more preparation: transportation, safe houses, operatives, weapons, tools. But as the day of the theft came closer Chew realized he could not go through with the operation, no matter what the Deep Men might do. By then he had learned from Edwards the Deep Men's plans for the bombs, and he couldn't have that responsibility on his conscience, too. First the death of his family, and now the potential trigger for a nuclear world war.

He told Edwards he was quitting. Period. He just couldn't go through with it. Edwards didn't argue. It was as if he knew Chew had no choice but to go along. All he said was, "I'll have to talk to someone higher up in the organization and get back to you."

Chew wanted to reach Edwards' superior, himself. Perhaps he could talk sense to such a man, convince him that he was not the operative they wanted, that he would botch the job anyway. So he followed Edwards that day.

A sunny day in Maryland on the outskirts of Washington. Edwards was ahead of Chew, driving along the periphery of a golf club set in pine forest. Edwards parked, then walked into the forest. Chew stopped his car at a bend in the road, then slipped silently through the trees after Edwards.

A golfer was in the forest, looking for a lost ball. He was a tall, urbane man in a red sweater. Chew felt faint; he leaned against a tree, his hand feeling the rough bark, then pressing it so sharply pain shot through him.

The "golfer" was Fred Harlingen, Chew's best friend, the Deep Man who had "died" trying to shield Chew's family from the explosion. But there he was, very much alive, smiling as he talked to Edwards. Chew didn't hear what they had to say. The two men conversed in low tones for a while, then Edwards left, and Harlingen walked through the woods toward the clubhouse. He never reached it because Chew was suddenly behind him.

The man in the red sweater looked dazed. He was sitting on a tree stump in the woods, not fifty feet from links where golfers swung at small white golf balls and sent them soaring. And Chew's whole life was emptying into a black void of pain that would never end. Harlingen said, "They made me do it, Leonard. Honest to God, I pleaded with them not to . . ."

"Do what?"

"Set up that . . . accident to your family. Look, it was a personal order from Gustavus. None of us had any choice—not even Edwards."

Chew listened through pain in his mind that almost blotted out the words as Harlingen told him what happened. Harlingen himself delivered Chew's family to the scene of the explosion. The Deep Men had known the Vice-President would park in front of the art gallery, and Harlingen made certain Chew's wife and children were next to the car mined by Chew when it exploded.

Harlingen said that the Deep Men needed Chew desperately for the forthcoming nuclear theft—but Chew, at his wife's insistence, was determined to retire. "Gustavus needed a hold on you, and he ordered the accident." Harlingen stopped, as if remembering. "Even though I hated the idea, I could see how clever it was. Because it worked. You went along with the nuclear theft later out of obligation to the Deep Men, who took care of you when the tragedy happened—and because one of the Deep Men had died trying to save your family. Me. That was Gustavus' idea, too, Leonard. I had no choice."

Gustavus. Chew had heard the code name before, an Olympian figure in Washington far removed from the Deep Men's day-to-day operations. This faceless, anonymous man sitting at a desk in Washington had single-handedly decreed that his family be murdered? To further a political right-wing plot? His lovely young wife, two brilliant young children, wiped out for that?

Harlingen would die—but Chew *must* have Gustavus, too. He lied to Harlingen. "Tell me how I can find Gustavus and you'll live."

Harlingen said, "I never saw him."

But Chew persisted. "Show me how to find someone who does know him."

Harlingen thought. "There's one man he deals with personally. The custodian of his Arnold collection. The custodian operates out of a hideaway office in Towson, Maryland. Look—" Harlingen was talking fast, tension showing in his eyes "—I don't know the address. Honest to God. It's so secret they took me out there at night in a blindfold. But once inside they took the blindfold off, and I saw the hideaway office on the third floor. Room 301."

"Describe the office," Chew said, and Harlingen did. Chew listened intently. The office *was* unique in design and decoration—and Towson was a small town. If he

could locate that office, he could find the custodian inside it—and have a direct line to Gustavus. Harlingen
was going on, "Gustavus' weakness is that Arnold connection. He's daffy about Arnold—even corresponds
with the custodian in the same code Arnold used."

Chew placed Harlingen's golf ball in a sand trap and
told him to play away. Harlingen was frightened, but he
could not afford to enrage Chew even more. And the
golf ball was his own; he recognized it. If he hit it just
right what could injure him? The club swung too deep,
smashing into plastique beneath the ball, which exploded, tearing into his body—and Fred Harlingen died
bleeding in the sand.

But Chew wasn't satisfied. He still must find Gustavus, the real murderer of his family. He left the course,
where golfers were starting to appear from distant fair-
ways—they would later call it a million-to-one chance
that Harlingen struck the one spot in a sand trap where
a cruel practical joker had planted death.

Chew had set out to trace Gustavus through the Arnold connection and eventually stole the map from Edwards.

Now he had a map with a code on the plastic enclos-
ing it written by Gustavus—and a lead to a custodian
who could pinpoint the man who ordered the death of
his family. But he couldn't find that office hideaway
alone. He needed the help of the government to locate
it, to search every house in Towson if necessary. But he
knew the government wouldn't move on the word of an
ordinary citizen with a vague story about a traitor.

After a tidal wave, they would.

6

1 A.M., JULY 3. THE WHITE HOUSE. A PHONE CALL for George Williams. Williams heard a low voice order him to drive to a public telephone booth at Connecticut Avenue and Eighteenth Street. "The White House phones may still be tapped," Chew said.

The President was watching as Williams hung up and told him where he was going. He showed Williams to the door, stood there nervously. "See if you can delay him . . . that's the mission. Tell him we're on his *side—but he has to give us time*. My God, we're still trying to dig out from under the tidal wave!"

Williams wanted to take Fred Jarvis along in case Chew asked some questions that might involve the FBI. He stopped in the Situation Room and saw the FBI man sitting with Peggy.

When Peggy heard where Williams was going, she said, "Maybe you can use me, too. He might have some questions about Benedict Arnold's descendents, or about Malcolm Bennett."

Or anything that could persuade Williams to allow her to go with him. Williams remembered the Arnold code in the first threat. An Arnold descendent *might* be of help. Williams agreed, but Jarvis grumbled, "The most important call in the century, and you're bringing Peggy?"

"She helped us identify Leonard Chew," Williams said, "which puts her ahead of ten thousand FBI men and one Justice Department lawyer."

And so, an FBI agent drove them to the booth, Jarvis sitting up front, Peggy and Williams in the back. Peggy touched Williams' hand. Ever since his escape from the tidal wave she had been, in her words, on a "personal high." The near loss of Williams had affected her more than she would have believed. Williams smiled at her.

7

MINUS 30:45 HOURS. JULY 3, WASHINGTON.

The gray Chrysler following them was driven by Kurt Edwards, who had been waiting and watching nearby. Now he couldn't believe his luck. Williams had come out into the open!

The FBI men in the car didn't worry the Deep Man, who tailed them with the quiet, intense concentration he applied to every "hit." He followed the FBI vehicle up Connecticut Avenue, carefully remaining a few cars behind. A grenade on the floor beside him would do the job most efficiently. The Deep Men had told him to make the hit look like an accident, but screw them. He couldn't pass up this chance.

Then Williams surprised Edwards. The FBI car pulled over to the curb at Eighteenth Street. Edwards slowed, found a parking space, and saw Williams enter a phone booth on the sidewalk.

Edwards waited in the car.

8

Two stout men in rumpled linen suits walked by the telephone booth talking loudly and angrily about the tidal wave. "Goddam disgrace," one man said. "I knew as soon as the Democrats were in, something like this would happen." The telephone rang. It was Leonard Chew. Williams grasped the phone, pressing his body against one wall of the booth. Chew gave the serial number of the second bomb in his low sibilant voice, and then said, "The traitor who sits next to the President calls himself Gustavus, Mr. Williams."

Williams said, "So what? If he's a traitor, we're not going to find the name in any files."

"Not so fast, Williams. Gustavus is the name Benedict Arnold used when he wrote to the British about treason. Our traitor leads two lives, Mr. Williams. He's a member of the Benedict Arnold cult. He's one of the leading collectors of Arnold memorabilia. Somewhere, some other member must have heard of a high government official who is in that cult."

Williams thought it would be wise to get in the President's words right now. "The President is on your side, Leonard. He wants to root out the Deep Men just as you do."

"I'll give him his chance to prove it, Williams, but we'll do it my way."

Williams said, "What's your lead to Gustavus?"

"He has a hideaway office in a safe house in Towson, Maryland. I don't have the exact address, but I have the room number of the office—301—and a complete description of it."

"Why didn't you find the office yourself?"

"I'm not the FBI, Williams. There are thousands of houses in Towson. One man can't go into every house looking for a specific room. That's why I need the government to help." Chew added, "The FBI can find that office even without the address, Williams."

"How?"

"Towson isn't that big; the office is unique. It has a vaulted ceiling, parquet floor, brick fireplace on the right as you enter, four French windows, and a safe built into the wall on the left. Now, unless Gustavus burns down the building, he can't disguise that office."

Williams asked Chew what was in the hideaway office. Chew said, "The office is where Gustavus keeps his Arnold mementos. But, most important, he has a custodian there, and the custodian knows how to reach him personally. I'm told Gustavus and the custodian correspond with each other in Benedict Arnold's code, either for security or just a hobby, I don't know."

"Is that it for the clues?"

"Yes."

"It's not enough, Leonard."

"Why?"

"The office is going to be rented through innocent cutouts who are impossible to trace. And as for inspecting every three-story building in Towson, the office can be disguised in some way, by, say, a false ceiling."

But Chew persisted. "Gustavus has no idea that I have knowledge of that hideaway office. He won't even try to disguise it."

Williams said, "We want to stop the Deep Men, Leonard. But you can't base a decision to explode a nuclear bomb on a squad of FBI men poking around offices looking for fireplaces and safes. You're a scientist. You know you're not blowing up a 747 or an abandoned building. You're threatening to explode a nuclear bomb in Manhattan. Now this is too important—"

Chew's voice reflected growing impatience. "You don't get the point, Williams. They won't tear up the parquet floor; they won't rip out a fireplace. Most likely the custodian will just abandon the office if Gustavus knows we're onto it. But even if the office is empty, the building will give you a clue. Who owns it? Who paid rent? Who was seen coming and going?" He stopped. "And if you keep the secret, if Gustavus thinks that hideaway office is completely unknown to me, then his Arnold collection and his custodian will lead us right to him. This is important, Williams. Finding that office can bring us Gustavus."

"Suppose we find the custodian, and he points out the wrong man?"

"There's a code on the back of the plastic around the Arnold map, written by Gustavus. I have that map in my possession, minus the fragment I left at the missile site. But I can't break the code, so it must be special." Williams waited for Chew to continue, and when the scientist did he said, "Just leave me alone in a room with the man we think is Gustavus and I'll make him break that code. And if he can break it, we'll know he *is* Gustavus."

Williams made his point once more. "Whatever you think, it will take days, not hours, to search every three-story building in Towson and miles around. We'll need a lot more time—"

"Damn it, Williams. You have the whole FBI to go through Towson, and it's a suburb, not a large city. I'll call you at the White House and direct you to a secure

phone tomorrow at five P.M. and I want news that
you've made real progress. Don't try to fool me, Williams."

Chew paused, then said quietly, "Find that custodian,
Williams. Give me a lead to Gustavus. That's all I want.
And if you think I'm just bluffing, I remind you of the
tidal wave. I'll set off that bomb in Manhattan, and, as
Mr. Truman said a generation ago, I won't lose a minute's sleep over it. *If you people sit back, that bomb
explodes!*"

He hung up. Williams was left holding a dead receiver in a booth on Connecticut Avenue in Washington. He was convinced at that moment that Leonard
Chew was insane. How else to explain an obsession with
"one man" who called himself Gustavus.

For it was obvious to Williams that it was an obsession. Chew had been so anxious to talk about his clues
to Gustavus he had brushed aside the President's offer
to find the Deep Men. There was another motive working; and the ominous words in his first threat spelled it
out: "What you did in the Middle East is known."

Through Sarah Bennett, Williams had found out that
Chew's family had been killed in the Middle East in an
accident. Williams believed he knew what must have
happened in the Middle East that was "known." No accident to Chew's family. Murder. And if Chew was obsessed by one man, it could be the one man responsible
for that murder. Gustavus.

Which meant, in the twentieth century in a civilized
country, the government had to deal with a man who
had stolen nuclear bombs and would explode them for
what appeared to be personal motives.

9

Kurt Edwards watched the Buick ease into traffic and followed it cautiously, waiting for any indications of a trap or ambush resulting from that phone call. But the car turned left on Eighteenth Street, slowed down as it approached Pennsylvania Avenue, and Edwards made his move.

Williams had told Jarvis and Peggy the content of Chew's call. He wondered if he should inform the President of the clue to Gustavus' office because, "If there *is* a traitor in the White House, he'll hear of it." Jarvis said that in this emergency you had to inform the President of everything and Williams said he wasn't so sure, when a Chrysler roared up alongside them.

The man in the Chrysler looked familiar to Williams; then he remembered that FBI composite from Sarah Bennett's description of Kurt Edwards. But before he could warn his own driver something metallic flew through the air and landed on the floor in the back. A grenade! Peggy screamed. Williams threw himself across her lap, picked up the grenade in one hand and shoveled it out of the window. Too late! The fragmentation bomb exploded just after it passed through the rear window, blasting ragged metal fragments through the back of the car.

Jarvis ducked as the driver jammed the foot brake. The car skidded, then crashed into a parked truck. Jarvis sat up, realizing he was unhurt. Smoke obscured the back seat. People were running toward them, shock on their faces.

Peggy DuPont had a dead weight covering her. She screamed. Blood was coming from George Williams' back, spreading over her. She heard a door open, then hands tugged at Williams' unconscious body. She was free. Someone said, "Hurry!" and pulled her outside of the car. She stood on unsteady feet in the middle of a Washington street for a moment, her mind still dazed, then she saw people crouching around the body of George Williams. She pushed her way through the gathering crowd and bent over him, crying. Jarvis said, "He's alive, Peggy." To the onlookers he said, "Call an ambulance, quick."

A woman who seemed to know what she was doing appeared and started to loosen Williams' shirt. Blood dripped from the back of his head. Peggy suddenly felt dizzy.

10

MINUS 29:15 HOURS. JULY 3, WASHINGTON.

Peggy DuPont sat on a small white chair in Williams' hospital room. The bed was empty. Williams was elsewhere in the hospital for x-rays. Jarvis came in. He sat on the bed, looking angry and frustrated. "The bastards."

But all Peggy wanted to know was whether Williams would live. "How is he?" she asked.

"Mild concussion, cracked rib, shrapnel wounds," Jarvis said. "But it could have been worse if he hadn't thrown the grenade out of the car. He saved all our lives."

Peggy asked him what they were going to do now, and Jarvis said he would have to take over for George. He was going to report to the White House, then take a fleet of FBI men to Towson and see whether he could find that office himself.

Jarvis left, and ten minutes later Peggy wandered into the great corridor of this hospital in Bethesda. Along the corridor an elevator door opened and nurses wheeled out a stretcher with a body in white sheets. George was still unconscious, a pressure bandage around his head, his face pale. Peggy asked the orderlies how Williams was doing, and they shrugged. "You'll have to ask the doctor, ma'am."

Ten minutes later the surgeon arrived with a brisk-looking nurse. "We gave him a sedative. X-rays show no brain damage. If he takes it easy a few days, he'll be out of here. You his wife?"

Peggy said no. But she wanted to stay near him throughout the night. The surgeon said perhaps they could arrange it. He turned and spoke to the nurse, who answered in low tones, a response that caused the doctor to look at Peggy with surprise. "I didn't make the connection. You're Peggy DuPont, and this is George Williams of the Justice Department? He's on the nuclear bomb case?"

Peggy said that was right. The surgeon said, "An hour ago I heard the news about a conspiracy. And this man is attacked." He paused angrily, then burst out, "What the hell's happening in this country. A terrorist exploding nuclear bombs, people getting killed on the street."

The man who stood at the door was polite. He waited

until the doctor finished before interrupting. "FBI, Doctor. I've been sent here to guard Mr. Williams."

They placed Peggy in a room next to Williams, who was drugged and unconscious. The FBI agent sat on a straight-backed wooden chair between their rooms. At four A.M. he was relieved by another agent; Peggy heard their low voices in the hall. Then the shuffling of a chair; the next agent had taken over, and all was quiet. Finally she drifted off to sleep.

11

MINUS 23:00 HOURS. JULY 3, NEW YORK.

Leonard Chew crossed Lexington Avenue. A Cadillac convertible filled with furniture careened by him; its driver shouted angrily at Chew as he passed. Chew said nothing. He went back to the Waldorf-Astoria Hotel, a building in the last throes of evacuation, with mountains of baggage in the lobby and only two bellboys still on the job. The others were evacuating their own apartments.

Room 1703. Chew crouched beside the fireplace and reached up inside it. His hand touched cold metal. The bomb was still there. He stood up, brushing off soot that had dusted his shoulders, then went downstairs and walked to the brownstone apartment he had rented on East Twenty-ninth Street, where all of his weapons were stored.

He was an angry, depressed man. The attack on Williams last night had shown him again how powerful the Deep Men were. Williams was in a hospital; put there by the Deep Men, who had struck before Williams could even begin an investigation. And with that attack Chew had realized that time was running out for himself. He had been lucky so far, staying clear of the faceless men. But they would kill him if he gave them time.

He was not afraid for himself. What worried him was that the attempt on Williams' life was a clear message to other government investigators to back off or die.

Chew wouldn't let them quit. He would explode that second bomb if necessary. Somehow the Deep Men had to be stopped.

Nevertheless, he was depressed. He had hoped that Gustavus would be found at once by those clues through George Williams—and the Deep Men had moved cruelly and efficiently as they always did.

He walked quietly through the city he had turned into chaos. All day and night since the news of the threat followed the tidal wave, a million New Yorkers had been frantically evacuating their homes and apartments in Manhattan. The Army had done all it could to help; from command headquarters established on the Palisades across the Hudson they sent MPs to control traffic, cargo helicopters containing trucks to move stalled cars that might block tunnels and bridges. The Army commandeered every train in the East for evacuation and rolled in fleets of buses. And still it wasn't enough. The Army couldn't begin to stem the panic enveloping the city.

For one thing, escape routes were being used only north to Connecticut and west to New Jersey. Nuclear experts had told New Yorkers that Long Island would be endangered by a radioactive cloud because of prevailing winds. The second problem was that New Yorkers wanted to save their possessions—and they were ignoring trains and buses to pack cars to the roofs and launch them into the flood of traffic.

MPs had worked heroically throughout the previous night; tow trucks had scurried alongside stalled lines; sweating men had pushed wrecked cars off to the side. New York had been lucky so far—not one major accident, but at 9:05 A.M., as Leonard Chew walked down Lexington Avenue, the first great catastrophe occurred.

12

MINUS 22:55 HOURS. JULY 3, NEW YORK.

The Amoco fuel truck that entered the Lincoln Tunnel did so slowly, in a crowded line.

The truck moved into the tunnel beneath the Hudson River. Ahead the line crawled fitfully, but steadily. Half an hour later the truck was almost dead center in the tunnel when the line halted completely. The driver saw people getting out of their cars. A policeman jumped over the railing of the small footpath along the tunnel to the roadway below. The driver left his truck as the driver of the car ahead of him told him, "Dumb-o up front crashed into the car in front of him, and their bumpers are locked." A commotion made them both look toward the scene of the accident. A fight had broken out. A heavy man in shirt sleeves was swinging wildly. He hit the police officer in the nose; blood gushed as the officer went over on his back. The shirt-sleeved man turned and ran toward them between the lines of cars. The truck driver flattened himself against the car to let the running man pass. Then he saw the

policeman get to his feet, holding his gun. The policeman shouted for the man who had hit him to stop. Instead, the man kept running, and the officer fired over
his head.

The shot plowed through the side of the tank of the
fuel truck. The truck exploded.

The Lincoln Tunnel is a tube within a tube of reinforced concrete. It is vented so it can withstand almost
any pressure. But this explosion opened a crack in its
ceiling.

Drivers in the tunnel far enough from the blast not to
be hurt saw flame, then felt a terrific concussion. Immediately car doors opened; people got out to stare at
the accident. Smoke obscured the scene at first, but
when it lifted they saw an incredibly ominous sight. Water trickled from a crack in the ceiling of the tunnel.
"Holy Christ!" Tom Rich, the driver of a blue Cadillac,
said. He left his car and started running in the space
between cars toward the exit, but people jammed the
aisle. Then he felt water at his feet! He looked back,
and the crack in the ceiling was now gushing water in a
flood into the tunnel. Rich was scrambling onto the roof
of a car when he heard behind him a frightening cracking sound. The goddam tunnel was caving in! Rich
made his way to another car nearer the exit, but people
were climbing off the road, getting in his way, some of
them screaming. Jesus, he'd never make it.

Then a wrenching roar, and the whole ceiling in the
middle of the tunnel collapsed! The Hudson River fell
in, with thousands of tons of water. People between the
cars were up to their necks in water. Rich ran to the
roof of another car. A man hauled himself out of the
water between cars and grabbed Rich's legs. Rich
tripped and skidded off onto the heads of the people in
the aisle. He felt water on his back. Hands grabbed

him, he saw terrified faces—then he managed to fight his way back onto a car. Now the water was almost six feet high; people were drowning down there in the aisle; others tried to tread water that rose higher by the instant. A woman screamed at Rich; he leaned over and dragged her to safety on the car roof. But the water was rising there, too. "Hurry!" he shouted. But she was paralyzed with fear. He started to pull her along, scrambling down to hoods where the water was waist deep, then clambering onto the next roof. Rich was carrying the frightened woman right with him, when a wave of water surged along the tunnel. The woman was torn from him—he had one last look at her eyes open in terror—and then he was swept under, tumbling over and over, crashing into other bodies. And what the drivers of cars waiting in line up the hill from the mouth of the tunnel saw was a fantastic wave of green water suddenly spout from the exit, showering corpses onto cars and on the highway, rolling them over and over on the street.

One hundred and ten people died in the Lincoln Tunnel cave-in, including Tom Rich.

13

MINUS 22:10 HOURS. JULY 3, WASHINGTON.

Peggy DuPont leaned over George Williams, who had just awakened. Williams looked up into her sparkling blue eyes, which were smiling in delight. The sheet had drifted off his shoulders, exposing a totally bandaged chest. Peggy's first words were, "You look like

Rameses II." Then she kissed him on the forehead. "You frightened me, George. I thought you'd never wake up."

Williams had been dreaming of a man behind a curtain in a red velvet room, a man who wanted to kill him, and he had been reaching out, ready to defend himself, when he awoke and noticed, first the eyes, and then the beautiful face of Peggy DuPont. His chest felt like concrete, the bandage taped around his body constricted his breathing. He tried to smile at Peggy. "I *feel* like a two-thousand-year-old man."

Peggy saw that every breath must hurt, and despite her bravado, she was moved. "You're going to be OK, George. I've given the doctor an ultimatum. Your body—or his head."

Williams smiled. "I have to get out of here."

Jarvis came in, pleased to see Williams awake. He stood beside Peggy, looking down at Williams. "Ole blue eyes is back," he said. "I just saw the doctor who put your arteries together, George. You're OK. But no circus tricks, right? Like trying to get out of bed and be a hero."

Williams touched the pressure bandage on his head. "What's the damage?" he asked.

"You have a slight concussion, a cracked rib, and a back that has little flesh left. Other than that you could go out and fight Muhammad Ali today."

But Williams felt his mind clear. The pain came only from that cracked rib, and the effort to breathe with a body bandage pressing tight. Jarvis pulled up a chair next to Williams and told him that he and his FBI men had swept through Towson during the night. "We must have made fifty surreptitious entries. Broke every rule in the book. But no mansion with a third-floor room fitting Chew's description."

Williams told him they had been looking for the wrong type of building. Jarvis asked why.

"Private houses don't number the rooms like that."

Jarvis said, "Then I wasted the whole night. What in hell kind of house would have a fancy office with a number?"

"A club of some sort? A lodge? I just have a feeling this is no ordinary safe house, Fred. Maybe I'm making too much of the number."

"No," Jarvis said, "you're right. No private house we went into last night had any numbered rooms. I inspected dozens of houses myself."

A broad-hipped nurse bustled in, all smiles and good cheer, "Crank her up, Mr. Williams?"

Williams didn't understand until she gestured toward a crank that lifted the end of the bed so he could sit up. Williams said he wanted a phone, but the doctor was adamant. "You're not to use this room as an office. Your job is to rest."

But Williams informed him that he was alive, there was a nuclear bomb scheduled to explode in New York in twenty-two hours, and that telephone just might be useful. He got the phone, and Peggy asked permission to go with Jarvis. "I might bring him good luck, George. And if I keep hanging around, you might make a sudden move."

Jarvis said he'd be glad to have her and they left. Williams called the President, who congratulated him on his narrow escape.

14

FBI cars fanned out through Maryland hunt country. Green hedges and lovely wood fences climbed rolling hills, and from Peggy's car, a solitary red-jacketed rider was seen crossing a fence, horse's legs reaching for space and then landing softly on the other side and springing into the darkness of a forest.

"Tallyho," Peggy said, but her eyes moved forward to a Holiday Inn, which would be the third motel she and Jarvis had visited. Jarvis said, "I don't see a motel room with a vaulted ceiling or vaulted roof, but anything's possible."

But not at this motel. In ten minutes they were out again, riding on a two-lane asphalt road toward a country club ten miles away. "Yes, now hold it," Peggy said to Jarvis. Jarvis slowed the car. They were passing through a hilly, wooded section of Maryland, and Jarvis had seen nothing. "Was that a dirt road on the left?" Peggy asked.

Jarvis said he did not see a road, but Peggy insisted. Jarvis made a U-turn and went back and hell, Jarvis was furious with himself. He should have been tipped off by a small rusted box nailed to a tree. They left the car and saw it was a postbox. Small faded letters on the box read: MARYLAND PARK FOUNDATION.

They drove a mile before the little dirt road suddenly widened, then they saw a chain fence with barbed wire on its top and a closed gate facing them. Cars were parked in front of the fence. As they got out of the car Peggy heard dogs barking, and two Doberman pinschers bounded toward the gate.

Across a soft green lawn was a lovely Tudor mansion. It was three stories high. A security man appeared with his hand on a holster. He relaxed when he saw Jarvis and Peggy, shushed the dogs, then said through the gate. "You people lost?"

Jarvis opened his wallet and showed him the FBI card. The guard was startled. "What's this all about?" he asked, opening the gate.

Peggy and Jarvis came through the gate as one dog made a run on them, red tongue flecking saliva across sharp white teeth. Peggy shrank against Jarvis as the guard caught the dog by its brass-studded choker, and held it as it snarled. "They're good watchdogs, but you can see we'll have to talk inside."

They went into the foyer of the mansion and Jarvis asked what the Maryland Park Foundation did. "It's used for seminars. Business executives pay a fee to come here for a week, rest up, play some tennis, and meanwhile brainstorm each other."

"Who runs the place?"

"Mrs. Amanda Jones. She's down to the store. But sit down and I'll get you a cool drink if you want it."

Peggy looked around at a living room with an oak-beamed ceiling, a huge stone fireplace at one end, couches with red linen covers, and Indian blankets for rugs. The guard returned with two Cokes. Then they heard the dogs bark, a car arrive at the gate, and in five minutes Mrs. Amanda Jones was with them, a tidy little woman in a colorful bandanna, holding a sack of groceries.

She couldn't have been more helpful. "I'm the caretaker, Mr. Jarvis. This used to be my home but when my husband died, I had to sell. Well, the Foundation was nice enough to let me stay here and look after things between seminars."

Jarvis stood up. "These seminars are regularly scheduled?"

"Oh no, Mr. Jarvis. We just get a call from headquarters telling us to lay in some provisions whenever a seminar is contracted for."

Jarvis had difficulty believing her. He knew she was lying when he found Room 301, a beautifully appointed office with a vaulted ceiling, parquet floor, brick fireplace, French windows—and a safe. Something else was in the room too. A man behind the desk who must be the custodian, and two quietly dressed men with guns, standing behind the door. One of them cracked a gun butt viciously across Jarvis' temple. Jarvis sagged in Peggy's arms, his forehead bleeding.

15

Minus 20:00 hours. July 3, Towson, Maryland.

Peggy DuPont sat on a couch in a second-floor study of the safe house, under guard. Her dress had slipped just far enough up her curving thighs for one of the guards, a man named Johnson, to wish he were meeting her under different circumstances. Jarvis was unconscious on a second couch across the room. Amanda Jones held a towel to his bleeding forehead.

Amanda was with the organization, too. She said to Johnson, angrily, "That was smart."

Johnson was the man who had struck Jarvis. Amanda said, "All you had to do was play dumb—"

"He was on to you, for Christ's sake," Johnson said. "And he had his eye on the safe."

Peggy had managed to wriggle enough to show an inch or two more of thigh. She had seen Johnson's appreciative glance. The other man was a tall muscular fellow with the head of a Prussian, but he never looked at Peggy. A robot or a fag, Peggy thought. What could she do? A nuclear explosion in New York—and she, Peggy DuPont, had to be the one to make wise decisions. Williams was in a hospital, Fred Jarvis was unconscious. She said, "I'm a descendent of Benedict Arnold."

Johnson looked at her, puzzled. "You're what?"

"A descendent of Benedict Arnold. My picture was in all the papers yesterday. I was with Malcolm Bennett when he was killed. He was another descendent."

Johnson looked as if he wanted her to shut up because each word she spoke made her own death warrant more certain. But Peggy went on brightly. "So they're hauling me around trying to identify the man who killed Bennett. Neither of you is the one."

Amanda Jones was smart. She looked carefully at Peggy, whose artless chatter might be fooling the men but not her. She said to Johnson, "Watch this one carefully, and don't fall for anything," and went into Room 301 across the hall, gesturing for the second man to follow. Amanda and the custodian were obviously going to empty the safe of any evidence and clear out. Peggy asked Johnson to sit beside her. He smiled and carefully sat down at the farthest end of the couch. He must be what they call a "pro," Peggy thought. She decided to talk about the code book; anything, just keep talking.

She said, "I want that code book. Mr.—what's your name?"

Johnson smiled again and told her. Then he said, "You want that code book. We want it, too. And we own it."

But Peggy knew she had him. Three inches of skin above the knee and he was hooked. He wanted to come on like the macho moron he was, but his friends in the other room room would kill him—the word *kill* froze her mind for a second. She had to *do* something. So she did something unconscionable. It certainly showed very bad breeding. She kicked off her shoes, leaned back against the arm of the couch, and tucked her legs under her demurely. But not *that* demurely. She said, "If you let me have the book, you and I can get together."

Johnson was bemused. The girl was putting him on so naively and obviously, but why? Maybe she went to movies where that kind of thing worked. Johnson knew they weren't in a movie. On the other hand she was obviously intelligent and could be acting this way for another reason. He knew, too, the girl was one minute from death. They had called headquarters and at any time the phone might ring and the orders come through to eliminate her. Johnson would hate to do that.

The girl was a stunner, with curves that Johnson couldn't help admire, despite himself. Peggy smiled and said, "You think I'm kidding but I'm not. I don't care *why you* people want the book, I don't care why the *FBI* wants it, I want it because it used to belong to my family. I can prove it."

But Johnson had ceased to listen to her prattle, had realized this was just a frightened kid trying to think of *anything* to get her out of certain death—for headquarters would surely say die—so he just leaned back, and enjoyed the leg show, and had to wish again that he had

met her somewhere else in another time and place,
maybe the Bahamas. She would have gone for him then.
He knew it. Johnson was great down there. He made it
big with girls on those tropical islands when the Deep
Men gave him leave, and he could think of marvelous
things to do with those legs, imagine them pressing
softly around his body, then urgently, and the girl
would be in ecstasy, he knew that, and Jarvis grabbed
him around the throat from behind and pulled his gun
from his shoulder holster, and Johnson yelled and wres-
tled free. Peggy fell on him while the other man
pounded in with a gun from Room 301. Jarvis shot the
man in the doorway and he went over backward, dropping the gun. Johnson pulled free from Peggy and dove
across the room for the gun the other man dropped.
Jarvis shouted, "Hold it right there!" but Johnson
grabbed the gun and fired, just missing Jarvis. Jarvis
shot him in the chest as Johnson careened against the
wall, bleeding.

The custodian and Amanda Jones were pounding
down the stairway to the first floor below with a suitcase. Jarvis fired down the stairs and the custodian
dropped the suitcase as he jumped aside. Then both of
them disappeared into the interior of the house, heading
for the back door and the forest beyond. Jarvis would
have followed but at that point the two fierce Doberman pinschers came lunging from the living room, let in
by the security guard, tore up the stairs and leaped at
Jarvis, knocking him over. Teeth dug for his throat.
Peggy found a chair and swung at them, while Jarvis
smashed at the dogs' jaws. They were back, tearing at
his arm, when he managed to squeeze off three shots.
Bodies heaved; the giant dogs collapsed on him. Peggy
pulled at Jarvis' shoulders; then pushed at the Dober-
mans' carcasses. Together they managed to work him

free. Jarvis' left arm was bleeding badly. He was trembling.

The custodian's suitcase contained the material kept in the safe: several original Arnold letters, a medal presented to Arnold by Washington, artifacts from the home in Philadelphia from which Arnold had wooed and won his wife, Peggy Shippen, two flintlock pistols, even Arnold's tricorn hat.

In addition there were letters in a three-digit code from Gustavus to a man named Karl, whom Jarvis presumed was the custodian. A copy of *Blackstone's Commentaries,* Second Edition, on which the three-digit code was based, page, line, and word.

And, most interesting to Jarvis, a thin file on Leonard Chew, the man who stole the Arnold map.

16

MINUS 18:00 HOURS. JULY 3, WASHINGTON.

Williams looked at the material from the safe and called the Maryland Park Foundation. He was told that the Foundation was established by the Economic Improvement Corporation, based in Switzerland. Naughton Aircraft's company. He called the Chairman of the Board of Naughton, who told him he never heard of the Lodge. "We cut all our ties to EIC after the Senate got on us," Gordon Hall said. "The trouble is, how can we convince people? We thought they were salesmen, not a bunch of ex-CIA lone rangers who would steal bombs."

The real trouble, Williams thought, was how you

could prove differently. The Swiss corporation, EIC, had been set up as a blind by legal experts who made all those multinational corporations so complex that no investigator could ever wend his way through a maze of interlocking companies in different countries all over the world.

Angry John called to say he was solving all the codes in short order. All the correspondence was from Gustavus to "Karl," who was obviously Gustavus' custodian. They referred to purchasing missions and discussions of various Arnold memorabilia for sale.

Thirty minutes later Angry John came over in person to discuss a certain letter from Gustavus to the custodian that mentioned the Arnold map.

> "Dear Karl,
>   Because our people are embarked on the most crucial project in the history of our organization, this will be the last communication from me to you concerning my Arnold collection. Kurt Edwards is bringing a map to you that I purchased in Canada. It has a handwritten note by Arnold in invisible ink which I developed myself. Because of that note, the map is priceless. Accordingly, I wish you to handle it via instructions in code on the back of the plastic enclosing the map. Then erase the coded message."

Williams was intrigued. They had recovered the actual code book the custodian used, and they even knew the specific subject of the coded message on the back of the map. It referred to the procedures for "handling" the priceless Arnold relic.

But the file intrigued him more. Not the statistical information on Chew, which was sparse and riddled with code names of projects in which Chew had been involved in the Middle East. There was a pay voucher for the nuclear theft, which showed a substantial advance. But what fascinated Williams the most were the individual pictures of Chew, his wife and two children and, specifically, his son, Leonard, Jr. The photograph showed the boy in a baseball uniform, swinging a bat. Peaceful enough, but a letter clipped to the picture was baffling. It read: "Show to Chew if he refuses all other arguments to go on operation MINOT."

17

MINUS 15:30 HOURS. JULY 3. NEW YORK.

Leonard Chew heard about the discovery of the Deep Men's hideaway over a transistor radio held at the ear of a black who had just shouldered him aside on the street. Chew had made a foray to get some food and found Fred and Heinz' delicatessen at Fifty-fourth and First still open. He bought some canned food, then walked down First Avenue, and bounced right into the young black, whose transistor radio said: ". . . found the Arnold book in Towson." That was all he heard, but when he entered his apartment on East Twenty-ninth Street, the television was alive with the story.

Could they be lying? Scenes of the Towson hunting lodge came on the screen, pictures of the safe, and even Chew knew it was most likely true. And then an FBI agent showed the Arnold memorabilia, including the military tricorn hat and the code book. The mound of materials and papers on the FBI desk reminded Chew that Gustavus was human, a man of flesh and blood.

The newscasters relayed requests from Williams for Chew to call him at once, give the serial number of one of the bombs to identify himself, and he would be put through to Williams' hospital room. He did so.

Williams once again heard the quiet voice of the nuclear scientist. Chew said, "I thought you were dying, Williams."

"I'm all right."

"Who threw the grenade?"

"Edwards. I recognized him from the FBI composite."

There was a pause. "Then you might as well be dead. When they reach that high for a hit man, you're top priority on the contract list."

Williams said that they had caught the Deep Men by surprise, but the custodian and the Deep Men inside had gotten away. Nevertheless, the discovery of the safe house would open up other leads. The safe in the hideaway office had yielded the actual code book Gustavus' custodian used, plus a letter that referred to the code on the Arnold map.

"Is the book *Blackstone's Commentaries,* Second Edition?"

"Yes."

"I used a copy from the same edition, and it doesn't work. Only Gustavus can solve that code." There was a silence on Chew's end of the phone and then he continued. "It seems funny all those people got away, Williams. You surprised them—and still not one of them was caught?"

Williams said, "There was something else in that safe, Leonard. A file on you. With pictures of you and your children."

Silence. Then Chew said. "I got into this whole nuclear theft through blackmail, Williams. Involving my family. That's why they have the pictures. But what's that have to do with finding Gustavus?"

Williams said, "There's a letter attached to the picture of your son, and *no* letters attached to the *other* pictures."

The response came sharply, "What does the letter say?"

"I'll show it to you, Leonard. And I also want you to see the picture."

And now the answer was slow in coming. "My son is . . . dead, Williams. Listen, the Deep Men put me on the rack enough over my family. Don't you start in."

"When they talked you into joining the nuclear theft did they show you a picture of your son in a baseball uniform?"

"No."

"The letter with the picture says, 'Show to Chew if he refuses all other arguments to go on operation MINOT.' It sounds like a threat held in reserve. And they didn't *make* the threat, because you didn't see the picture. *They could still be holding it!*"

"But my son is dead. So what's the threat?"

"I want you to see the picture, Leonard."

Chew's mind was whirling. What he had hoped for had not materialized. The capture of some Deep Men or the discovery of evidence that would point straight to Gustavus. What Williams had to offer was a code book that was useless, some indirect leads, and a picture of his dead son with a note that *was* mysterious. What could it mean? Williams didn't know the extent of the arguments that had convinced Chew to go on the mission. The picture could just have been held in reserve to twist the knife a little more if he refused. The letter with it might have been intended for all three pictures of his wife and two children.

Still, he knew he wanted to see that picture. My God, how they all used his family to torture him. Not just the Deep Men; now the government, too.

And he had firmly decided to use that second bomb after hearing television announcers drone on about "needless horror." "Needless horror" was exactly what Americans required, in his opinion. Last night, on this same television set, he had seen protest rallies on college campuses, not only against Chew but against the government that had allowed a conspiracy allied with American business to grow to a point where it was hiring men to steal nuclear bombs. The people were beginning to speak out.

A meeting was risky. Williams was desperate to prevent that nuclear bomb from exploding; he was pursuing Gustavus only for a chance to get at Chew and somehow convince Chew he was wrong. Chew couldn't walk into a trap after all he had undergone.

And yet he must actually see that picture of his son. He had to be certain there was not more to the letter accompanying it.

He said, "Come to New York. Go to the public telephone in the basement of the RCA Building at eight o'clock. I'll call you there, and tell you where to go. But alone."

"Not alone, Leonard."

"Why not?"

"The Deep Men will kill me."

Chew hesitated. If it was a trap, would Williams tell him ahead of time that he was bringing someone along? No. And Chew could make sure his companion never saw him. He agreed to let an FBI guard accompany

Williams and hung up. Williams turned to Jarvis and
Peggy. *"He's agreed to see me!"*

Peggy and Jarvis smiled broadly, and Williams realized they felt a great victory had been won. But the fact
was that nothing had been settled, and Chew had been
wary, and to make it worse, Williams would have to go
to New York in bandages. But he felt all right when he
sat up. He could do it. He had to.

Williams called the President to tell him the news.

18

Minus 12:05 hours. July 3, New York.

Clouds scudded across the darkening sky. A woman
handed her baby to a black man standing in a rowboat
on the shore of West Thirty-seventh Street. The black
man said, "Got him, lady. Jump in now—that's a good
girl—hold on." He helped her into a green wooden
rowboat crowded with refugees. The boat sank deeper,
barely two inches of freeboard above the river surface.

Other people on the beach were beseeching the
black, but he shook his head. "No room."

A thin, bald-headed man thrust a crumpled roll of
bills at him. "Just take my son. That's all."

But the black man said, "I'll be back," and turned to
make his way to the gunwales through the sitting people. Muscles glistening with sweat, he rowed his top-
heavy boat through the swift river current.

And now, as the night went on, up and down the
length of Manhattan more and more people stood in
dense crowds as small boats pulled in and departed to

cross the Hudson River to safety in New Jersey. Arguments flared, bribes were exchanged, small acts of heroism performed; the flotilla grew. Still, thousands on the piers under the West Side Highway were sure they would make it—and avoid that long and frightening walk north. With fewer and fewer police on duty, vandals and criminals and muggers were having a field day up north.

Subways were considered unsafe. By eight o'clock breakdowns caused by mobs of thousands started to occur on most lines, stranding frightened people beneath the city. And at 8:01 P.M. the second major accident in the evacuation occurred. A Lexington Avenue train lost power and stopped at Seventy-first Street, between stations. People piled out of the stifling cars into the darkness of the tunnel, avoiding the third rail, picking their way carefully toward the station they had just passed. Suddenly, a headlight blinded them; ten cars thundered toward them, wheels locked, sparks flying from the tracks, as the engineer fought to brake the train. He didn't make it. The subway slammed into a crowd of people on the track, smashing bodies aside and under the wheels, then crashed into the rear car of the stalled train, lifting it ten feet in the air.

And so, many people decided to walk north or try to make it across the Hudson River. The Army commandeered Staten Island ferries, Shore Line boats, and two Bahamas cruise liners docked in Hoboken. Soon the West Side piers groaned under the weight of thousands of feet, and MPs struggled to control the crowds. Other people went to the shore beneath the West Side Highway to find room on the small boats piloted by men who would make a fortune that night in bribes or risk their boats and their lives for brotherhood alone.

By 8:05 P.M., as Williams passed the Waldorf-
Astoria Hotel, the center of the city was almost empty
of people and cars except for stragglers, looters, and that
strange breed of men who haunt the fringes of catas-
trophes—arsonists.

The Waldorf-Astoria was silent. Luxury suites, some
strewn with clothes left by hasty decampers, others im-
maculate, were all vacant. Room 1703 was quiet. The
nuclear bomb in its fireplace was alive. Its timer, a
small cylinder one inch long, moved up one minute.

19

MINUS 12:00 HOURS. JULY 3, NEW YORK.

The RCA Building towered above a small private avenue separating it from the ice rink, which now, in summer, was a café with brightly colored umbrellas. The
tables in the café below were empty; the umbrellas
flapped in the slight breeze above a vacant patio. Williams and Jarvis crossed the street, entered the building,
and took an escalator to the basement. They saw the
telephone booth right away, an island on the rim of a
crowd that flooded the basement on its way to the trains
below ground.

A man in a wheelchair, chubby, jovial, was being
pushed by a small woman. A briefcase rested on the
man's lap. The girl pushing him wore a mink coat, no
doubt her most valuable possession. Watching her, Jarvis thought of the women without minks; the widows,
the old women in New York who "took the sun" in

small walks, hobbling on canes. Who had taken care of their escape? Or were they staying in the city, trapped, while younger relatives couldn't reach them or didn't care? The telephone rang. The words were brief. Williams recognized Chew's voice. "Fifty-fifth and Sutton Place South. Public telephone booth. I'll be watching."

Williams got out of a car on Sutton Place South, a broad avenue along the East River lined with luxury apartment houses, none less than twenty stories high. A good place for a monitor, thought Williams. Hundreds of apartments overlooked the booth on the street.

Leonard Chew had slipped into empty 52 Sutton Place South across the street from the booth an hour ago. The elevators were unattended, baggage was strewn here and there in the lobby, left by people departing in haste, or unable to pack these objects in a car. An overturned lamp with a Princeton label on its shade, a suitcase with filmy lingerie on top that must have been opened by looters, a large stuffed panda, and a small exquisite antique bureau. Chew threaded his way through the debris to the elevators, and pushed five. He needed a corner apartment overlooking the street and chose 5-A at random. The door was open.

From there he had called Williams at the RCA Building. Now he watched from the window as the Justic Department man arrived on the street below and stood by the phone booth. The man in the car must be the FBI guard Williams wanted along. Chew had brought binoculars to the apartment: he trained them on Williams and got his first live look at the man who had been his opponent so long.

The first thing he saw was a gray hat covering what appeared to be a white bandage around Williams' forehead. For the rest, Williams wore a conservative blue suit, red and blue striped tie, buttondown shirt, polished black shoes; a conventional Justice Department lawyer. Chew concentrated on the face and saw penetrating blue eyes beneath craggy eyebrows.

Chew swept Sutton Place north and south with the binoculars. Nothing. No tails. No suspicious cars. Williams had kept his word. Chew went to the side of the apartment and looked in the direction of Fifty-fifth Street. Nothing. Williams was playing it straight. He dialed the number of the public telephone.

"Send your friend away," he told Williams. "You won't need him now."

"Why not?"

"Because there won't be a third call. I'll meet you alone—without an FBI man to give me extra problems. OK?"

Williams told him to hold, went to the car, and spoke to Jarvis. Jarvis drove off, and Williams came back to the phone. "OK. Where are you?"

"Right up the street. Forty-seven Sutton Place South. Apartment Fourteen-E."

Chew was actually in 52 Sutton, not 47. After he hung up, he went to the window and saw Williams disappear under the canopy on the other side of the avenue. He would wait a few minutes to see if Williams was following his instructions before he crossed the street to join him.

Chew took the binoculars and panned up and down the avenue. No headlights. All clear. He was about to put the glasses on a table when a movement caught his eye. A car roared around the turn from Fifty-sixth Street and raced toward the building. From Fifty-fourth Street on the other side two more cars appeared. They skidded to a stop in front of the apartment house and

Chew saw it was a trap, the government had lured him into a corner. Chew was sick with anger. He went out of the door and down the stairs, passing floor after floor until he came to the street level.

20

MINUS 11:15 HOURS. JULY 3, NEW YORK.

Fred Jarvis had been told not to return to the location under any circumstances. But he couldn't help worrying. This whole scheme bothered him since Chew had asked to meet Williams alone. The telephone in his car rang. He picked it up and Williams said quietly, "The Deep Men are here, Fred. Forty-seven Sutton Place South. Get back quick—and use the siren."

Jarvis almost froze. The *Deep Men* were there? They had a murder contract out on Williams. Jarvis was furious with himself. Why had he agreed to Williams' plan? He picked up the phone, called FBI headquarters for reinforcements, and raced back toward Sutton Place.

21

MINUS 11:14 HOURS. JULY 3, NEW YORK.

The apartment house Chew was in sat on the west side of Sutton Place, with a side door that led to Fifty-fifth Street. The cars were converging on 47 Sutton

across the avenue, far enough from the side door that
Chew had a chance to escape. He pushed the door
open, looked up and down the street as he heard police
sirens. He ran up the street toward First Avenue, then
ducked inside the empty lobby of an apartment house.
Cars with FBI licenses raced by, confirming Chew's
suspicions.

Williams had used that story about the picture of his
son only to try to trap him. Williams was a goddam liar.
The government had betrayed him once again. This was
the last time. A nuclear MIRV would do the talking
now.

22

MINUS 9:00 HOURS. JULY 3, NEW YORK.

A deserted city except for a hubbub of activity
around the FBI Building on Sixty-ninth Street, which
was staying open until the last possible moment in case
the bomb was found. Helicopters would transfer the last
remaining agents from East Sixty-ninth Street at seven.

Jarvis' arrival at 47 Sutton had caused the Deep Men
to flee in the cars on Fifty-fifth Street. The Deep Men
hadn't yet located Williams' apartment. That was the
only secret they hadn't discovered. "I checked my car,"
Jarvis said. "A goddam beeper on its bottom. They
were following us all the way."

"How did they get to your car? Wasn't it in the FBI
garage?"

"Since the evacuation started I parked it on the
street," Jarvis said.

Williams made no reply. The Deep Men had sabotaged the meeting in an effort to kill both him and Chew. No doubt as soon as the President knew of the meeting, Gustavus had known—and alerted his operatives in New York. And they were efficient, all right.

Williams could imagine what Chew was thinking—betrayal again. The image in his mind ended in a mushroom cloud climbing out of Manhattan.

23

MINUS 08:00 HOURS. JULY 3, NEW YORK.

Midnight. Peggy DuPont had flown to New York through the good graces of General Maxwell, who complimented her on her work uncovering the Towson hideaway. But Maxwell argued with her when she said she wanted to be taken into Manhattan, until Peggy patted his cheek. "George is there. He'll take care of me," she said.

Williams and Jarvis were at the FBI Building on East Sixty-ninth Street in Manhattan. The two men and ten FBI agents who had volunteered, would remain in the target city until seven A.M. The street in front of the FBI Building was cordoned off for helicopters, which stood silent, rotor blades drooping.

Maxwell finally allowed Peggy to take a helicopter to the FBI Building, and from the air Peggy saw a vast rim of solid light around the city, headlights of cars making last-minute escapes. Inside the center of Manhattan, lights in office buildings still beamed, but there was one new element. Fire. With fire departments gone, spontaneous conflagrations were starting. The helicopter passed over Central Park, deserted Fifth Avenue, then put down in the street outside the FBI's headquarters.

Peggy found Williams on the tenth floor in a room where a television set was on. Jarvis and the other agents were there, too, watching the evacuation.

Both Williams and Jarvis were distracted. The Deep Men's surprise attack had been a masterpiece of deception. If Chew knew the attackers were Deep Men, he would think that Williams was in league with them.

If Chew thought the attackers were FBI, then he would believe Williams set it up as a government trap.

Williams had authorized a statement over television telling Chew that he had survived; that he, like Chew, was a victim of the ambush, but no answer had come.

And now, because Williams had failed, a nuclear bomb somewhere on this island would mushroom into an explosion that could devour the city. And Williams had almost stopped it. He had been *right there!* Across the street on Sutton Place from a man willing to *talk.* He showed no emotion as he spoke to Jarvis, but he was seething inside.

At 2:30 A.M. Peggy lay on an old leather couch in the hallway, feeling so numb from the day's excitement that she didn't care if FBI agents who passed her stopped to stare when they saw her curled up there.

In a semi-daze, half sleeping, she heard voices through the door. She could see Williams in the office across the way. An Army doctor had removed the pressure bandage, and there was now only a modest white bandage near the base of his skull. He seemed in good shape. Very good. George was so strong . . . Peggy's eyes closed. She thought of the first night she had ever spent with George, "Nice, George, nice," and then murky figures rose in her mind like clouds, swirling images of Presidents, and a man skulking across the ground somewhere, a dangerous man bent so close to the earth that his knees almost struck his chest as he scurried into a tenement somewhere—where?—with an object in his hands, smooth, shining, cylindrical, what was it? It had to be the bomb—and then he was gone in a fire so high she could not see its tip—

And Peggy was asleep. Williams came out into the hallway to talk to an agent and saw her, huddled on the couch like a child, breathing deeply. He smiled.

24

MINUS 02:30 HOURS. JULY 4, NEW YORK.

Leonard Chew sipped coffee, waiting. He had rented the apartment on East Twenty-ninth Street a month ago because he knew he couldn't stay in a room in a hotel where questions might be asked. His original plan had been to join the flood of refugees and slip out of the city by midnight.

But the ambush had changed that. Everyone now knew that he was still in the city, and so much of his description was also known; his height, build, shape of head. MPs might be posted at exit points outside of Manhattan.

But Chew had an edge. He knew the limits of destruction of the bomb he had planted. It would destroy a twenty-square-block area of midtown Manhattan around the Waldorf; the rest of the city would remain untouched.

So he decided to go to the abandoned Wall Street

area, find an empty room, and wait there until after the explosion occurred. In the chaos after that blast it would be easy to get lost in the confusion.

At 5:30 A.M. he made his move. He walked toward the place where he had parked his car, still dressed in his Navy captain's uniform and carrying the Geiger counter along with his briefcase. But he was more cautious now, alert to any military jeep or patrol car. By this time, only two and a half hours before the explosion, the streets in the interior of the city were almost empty.

Then on Park Avenue he saw a jeep. He was abreast of a large brick building. Quickly he entered its foyer and waited. The jeep passed; Chew was about to leave when a voice from behind startled him. "What are you doing here?"

Chew turned to see a boy about seventeen years old in a blue T-shirt that said, "N.Y. Giants." Chew held up the Geiger counter. "I'm inspecting buildings." He saw for the first time the bronze plaque on the wall of the foyer that said GRAMERCY CLUB. He said, "People can hide bombs in clubs as well as anywhere else. What are you doing in the city two and a half hours before it's going to explode?"

The boy said, "My father works for the city and the Mayor asked for volunteers to help with the evacuation until six. They're taking us all out in a special train."

"Your father lives in the club?"

"Yes. My mother and he are divorced. Just when I come to visit him, some maniac decides to blow up the whole city."

But all the time the boy was speaking, Chew thought he seemed suspicious. He had seen Chew standing in the foyer, looking outside at a jeep instead of entering the building for an inspection. Chew had to justify his

Navy uniform and the Geiger counter and his entrance to the building at least for a few minutes or the boy would alert his father and the whole Army would be looking for a fake Navy captain. He walked up stone steps into the lobby, which was furnished with green leather chairs and old mahogany tables under a crystal chandelier. In a small room on the right was a pool table with balls scattered around and two cues lying on it. Chew moved the Geiger counter over the couches, then along the walls as the boy watched.

Then he went into the poolroom and started passing the counter around the walls. The boy picked up a cue and tried a shot. Two balls went into different pockets. Chew watched them roll. Pool had always fascinated him; the vivid color of the balls against the brilliant green was hypnotic. "Nice shot," he said.

"Want to play?" the boy asked.

"It's against regulations, but if you won't tell your father, I'll try one shot."

The boy smiled, Chew's first small victory. Chew leaned over, steadying the cue against his raised left index finger, and sighted the seven ball nestled in the far corner, a few inches from the pocket. It would be nice to drop it *not* in that hole, but in the opposite corner. And the eleven ball, if touched just so, might make it to the middle pocket on his side of the table.

The cue stung the white ball; it shot on a long diagonal across the table and rapped the seven ball sharply on the nose. The ball seemed to spring of its own volition across the table, charging into the side of the eleven ball, which rolled majestically for two feet straight into the middle pocket. The seven ball then changed course and softly rolled into the corner hole.

"Jesus!" the boy said. "Did you mean to do that?"

"No. I was aiming for the nearest corner hole," Chew

said. He put the cue down and resumed checking the room with the Geiger counter as the boy's father walked in. He was a small man with a high balding forehead, dressed in a lightweight blue blazer and gray slacks. He said, "Isn't it a little late for that, Captain?"

"Not if one of us finds the bomb," Chew said. "We're going to stay right with it till seven."

"Brave men," the father said. "Come on, Jim. The train leaves in twenty minutes." He said good-bye to Chew, and they left. Chew relaxed. He would go quietly to his car in ten minutes and drive down to the empty Wall Street area. Everyone had fled north and west when the bomb threat came, not wanting to be trapped on the southern tip of the island.

But he stayed a moment in the poolroom to take one more shot. My God, when he leaned over a pool table and focused his mind on round colored balls and possible angles he was momentarily rid of his torment. He took the cue again in the empty Gramercy Club Building and tapped that white ball one more time. An easy one. Eight ball on a carom shot into the corner.

But as soon as he straightened up, the torment was back. He picked up the Geiger counter and his briefcase and walked out of the Gramercy Club. The first thing he noticed was a public telephone booth across the street. The father he had just met was on the phone, and his son beside him impulsively nudged his father and pointed to Chew.

Chew started running toward his car. He was blown!

25

The phone rang on the desk in front of Williams. He answered it and an excited voice said, "FBI!" Williams said yes, and a man said, "Herb Randolph here. I'm with the Mayor's office. My boy thinks he spotted a man in disguise." He paused to catch his breath and Williams told him to calm down and state his information.

Randolph said, "My boy was in the Gramercy Club when this Navy captain came in. He said he was inspecting the building, but when my son saw him first he was standing in the foyer hiding out from an MP jeep. At least, it looked that way."

"What makes your boy think he was in disguise?"

"Because my son is in the dramatics club in high school, and he knows all about false beards and wigs. And when the Navy captain leaned over a pool table in the club, my kid saw under the bright light that the beard was fake. He could see its edges."

"Is he sure?"

"He says yes. But you could only see it if someone stuck his head right under a high-powered lamp—which is what the man did when he took the pool shot."

A fake beard—and a fake inspector, too! Williams knew the military had called off inspections as a futile endeavor seven hours ago.

He heard Randolph say, "What's that? Oh . . ."

"What's happening?"

"He's running to a car."

"Right now? You can see him?"

"Yes, sir. Now hold it—he's getting into a black Plymouth."

"Stop him, somehow," Williams said. "Risk your life. He must be the man."

"Oh Jesus," Randolph said, "that's just what we thought, too," and the line went dead.

Three minutes later he was back, breathless. "Too late. He took off. Turned south on Lexington Avenue. License number OLL-275, New York."

Williams thanked him, hung up, and told Jarvis, "A man in disguise pretending to be a Navy inspector—at six in the morning! Stay by the phone." He started for the door.

"If he's Leonard Chew, put the whole Army on him," Jarvis said.

"Let me try it first," Williams replied. "If I can get to him, he might talk to me. He'll never talk to the Army."

Peggy said, "You can't chase him alone—" but Williams was already out of the door.

Jarvis said, "We have a chance to stop a nuclear bomb from exploding, and we have a whole Army to do it. I'm calling General Maxwell."

He made the telephone call and soon helicopters rose from the Palisades in the west, red and green lights blinking, as they swept across the dark rolling Hudson.

26

George Williams drove down Lexington Avenue. It was a nightmare. Periodically there were jam-ups as abandoned cars completely clogged the avenue. In those instances Williams turned onto the pavement, stopping now and then when trash or abandoned supplies or pedestrians loomed ahead. But Chew must be having the same difficulty.

Then Williams saw, three blocks ahead, another car on the sidewalk heading south. Closer. It was a black Plymouth. Williams stepped on the accelerator and shot through an intersection, nearly killing two people, who emerged suddenly on foot in the middle of the cross street. "Goddamn you!" they screamed.

Williams couldn't see the Plymouth anymore but that meant the driver must have found free space in the street again. Williams turned onto the street himself until he reached a place where it was blocked solid and turned right to get back on the pavement. That avenue was blocked, too, by a black Plymouth, license number OLL-275. Leonard Chew was waiting in a doorway for the man following him. With a gun.

Minus 01:30 hours. July 4, New York.

A helicopter's engine was heard. The chopper passed them and started to return. It landed, and a soldier appeared in its doorway. "Mr. Williams. Are you all right?"

Chew stepped out from behind a car with his gun trained on Williams. To the soldier he said, "Get out and tell the pilot not to use the radio."

The soldier spoke over his shoulder to the pilot. "He has Williams. No radio." Then he carefully stepped onto the street.

Chew told him to throw his gun on the pavement, and when he did, Chew kicked it far away. Then he urged Williams into the helicopter. The pilot was young and frightened. Chew said, "Take off, and turn off all your lights. Now!"

He slammed the door and the chopper started to lift. The soldier below ran for his gun and squeezed a few shots at the departing helicopter. No one inside was hit. Helicopters were coming in from all corners of the island, alerted by the pilot's first report. The whirlybird rose into the clouds before they arrived.

Inside the cabin Williams asked Chew, "Where are we going?"

"South and then east to Jersey. I know a place to land."

"What happens then?"

"To you, Williams? I'm afraid you have to die. You tried to kill *me* today."

MINUS 01:15 HOURS. JULY 4, NEW YORK.

Dark oil seeped over the canopy of the chopper and poured heavily down its side. The engine coughed.

Chew saw the fuel gauge drop. The pilot said, "He must have hit the fuel line with one of those shots." The engine made a hacking sound again as the pilot looked nervously at Chew. "A chopper doesn't glide, mister. We better set her down quick."

They were high above the bay of New York, silent and black beneath them. Ships had fled to safety up the Hudson or out to sea. Abruptly the motor cut out and the chopper dropped sickeningly toward the water.

The pilot jammed full power and the engine caught again; the limp blades once more jerked into a horizontal pattern by centrifugal force. But only briefly. Williams saw a sensation of green rising above him like a curtain as the chopper dropped toward the water and pitched nose first into the bay.

Darkness in the cabin. Williams was stuck in the back seat, and water was flooding the cabin as the helicopter sank. He pulled himself loose from the wrecked seat in front of him. The pilot's head lolled limply. Chew reached in from outside the open door and pulled his arms. Williams ducked out of the opening just as the helicopter sank with the unconscious pilot inside.

When Williams came to the surface he saw he was close to the island from which the green Statue of Liberty rose hundreds of feet into the sky. He tried to swim, but a searing pain from his fractured rib enveloped him. Chew swam out from the island, put his arm around Williams, and hauled him to shore. Williams lay on the rocky beach for a minute, catching his breath, but Chew was in a hurry. "Come on, Williams." Williams saw Chew's briefcase: the scientist had swum to shore to make certain it was safe before returning to Williams. But why had he saved Williams? Williams was being prodded quickly toward the Statue of Liberty when Chew told him the reason. "I may need a hostage."

They moved up in an elevator through the pedestal of the Statue, which was three stories high. Chew's face showed no emotion, even though he must know that the crash on an isolated island, from which there was no escape, was the end for him. The elevator opened, and they faced a narrow, curving stairway that spiraled three hundred feet high through the hollow Statue. "Move it, Williams," Chew said. They climbed and climbed, and at 7 A.M. arrived in the small observation room through whose windows you could look toward Manhattan from the Statue's crown.

29

MINUS 01:00 HOURS. JULY 4, NEW YORK.

Williams watched Chew remove weapons and a gas mask from his briefcase. "You won't make it, Leonard. You'll never get off this island."

"We'll see," Chew said, and went to a window from which he could look toward Manhattan. Helicopters flew above the skyscrapers. None was heading in this direction. Williams turned to Chew. "We didn't trap you today. The Deep Men did. They put a beeper on our car."

"So you're innocent," Chew said. "So what? You don't count anymore, Williams."

He was taking a weird-looking weapon out of his briefcase. It seemed to be a shotgun muzzle on a pistol grip. Williams said, "I told you I was bringing you the picture of your son and a letter, and I did." He reached inside his coat pocket. The letter was soggy. He withdrew it carefully and flattened it out. Then he took the wet picture from his pocket and handed them both to Chew. Chew read the letter, looked down at the picture, then up at Williams. For the first time he seemed shaken. "They are such *bastards,* Williams."

Williams said, "What does the letter mean?"

"They set it up so that I killed my own family, Williams. And this picture was to shove the knife in deeper, that's all. My kid loved baseball. Here"—he thrust the letter and picture back to Williams—"I don't want it now."

Williams was disappointed. Chew went to the window. Many skyscraper offices in Manhattan had been abandoned with their lights still burning. Red-tipped flames rose from burning blocks uptown but not in the Wall Street area, whose skyscrapers remained untouched. Williams wanted Chew to keep thinking of that picture. At least it had shaken him. He said, "When I was his age I had a uniform myself. I was a New York Giants fan. Willie Mays. Leo Durocher. Dusty Rhodes."

But all Chew said was, "Get off it, Williams. I know what you're trying to do." He turned and glanced at Williams. "For the record I was a Phillies fan. My son was, too. But my son never even got a chance to see them play. All he could do was wear their uniform in some godforsaken desert." He turned back to the window. "Reminding me of my son isn't going to help you. *I don't want to hear about him again!*"

Chew added, "If the helicopter sank—and the tides are strong—there'll be no trace of us."

Williams said, "So answer one question about you that puzzles me, Leonard. You loved your family. You're human. And that's what's so confusing."

Chew turned on him. "What's confusing?"

"You're *not* a terrorist. And yet you're bringing the worst suffering to the country it's ever had." Williams paused. "I saw a young mother and her baby today, Leonard. They had been drenched in radiated water, and I watched them realize that they were going to die and nothing could save them. Not just the mother. The baby, too. Because of you, Leonard."

The scientist came to the wall and sat down beside Williams. He said, more to himself than Williams, "I'm trying to shut them out of my mind, Williams. But I've already been spread on that rack. I've had a breakdown over nuclear bombs."

He continued in a low voice. "Years ago in Los Alamos I had a hero, Williams. Enrico Fermi. He designed and supervised the first nuclear reaction in the history of the world on that squash court at the University of Chicago. Then he built the first nuclear bomb that worked—the Hiroshima bomb—and you know something? Think of this in the light of that young mother and baby you saw—*I worshiped that man.* He was—" Chew searched for the right word, "dapper. Jaunty. My God, he even had a sense of humor! And he started this whole nuclear misery. Crazy—right, Williams? You expect him to look and act like Mephistopheles—and here was a marvelous little guy making jokes, while doing everything better than everyone else.

"I loved that guy back then. I wanted to be like him, Williams."

Williams said, "Then why did you get sick at Alamos if Fermi was your hero?"

And Chew said, "Because I didn't have the intelligence—or the stupidity—or the courage; whatever it takes for a man to enjoy himself while perfecting these eighteen-inch bombs."

The sun rose higher in the east, sending orange rays across Manhattan Island. Chew went back to the window. From the Statue's head he looked down at the gray waters of the bay. Its shimmering surface was empty. Only the helicopters patrolling ceaselessly over the doomed city showed movement and life. In the observation room it was silent until Chew said softly to Williams, "You think I'm crazy, don't you, Williams? Unbalanced. What's the legal definition of temporary insanity? Unable to distinguish between right and wrong at the moment of the explosion."

But Williams only said, "If you do this thing, the entire country will turn against you. The Deep Men will dance on your grave."

"I'll take that chance, Williams. Somebody has to. You've got people stealing nuclear bombs to plant in Soviet satellite countries and where's that going to end, Williams? In someone pushing a button in Moscow or Washington. And no more people. And suppose it all happened because a few hotshots want to sell more aircraft and weapons and oil, and go around the world saying, 'We're Number One!'—It's not a game, Williams. Eisenhower warned everyone a generation ago. Eisenhower! One of theirs! Even *he* saw it coming. The military-industrial complex growing so large it's uncontrollable." Chew glanced out of the window, then turned to Williams again. "I started out as a high school boy in a small town, Williams. I ended up a sadist killing people all over the world. Why? Because I believed in America, Williams. And that what I was doing was *for* America. Jesus." He dropped his head. When he raised it again he said softly, "It turned out it wasn't for America, Williams. But what the hell did I know? Naughton Aircraft? Who hadn't heard of it? What could be wrong in helping an American company in the Middle East? And who could know when they hired you that it wasn't really Naughton Aircraft but a political offshoot?"

He stopped again, then said, "The politicians in Washington are going to cover this up the minute I'm dead. But that pit in the middle of Manhattan will keep the pressure on them, Williams. The people won't rest."

Williams said softly, "You're a liar, Leonard."

"What do you mean?"

"You're doing this for *personal* reasons. So don't make yourself out to be some kind of an idealist trying to stop a conspiracy that steals nuclear weapons. You're after one man you hate so much you don't know what you're doing. You're just cloaking it by words about unmasking the Deep Men."

Chew said nothing. Williams continued, "You want Gustavus so badly, and why? My guess is you found out he ordered the murder of your wife and children, right, Leonard? Cold, ruthless, inhuman—but for three people you're exploding nuclear bombs and killing hundreds, maybe thousands, maybe tens of thousands, if a cloud blows the wrong way? You can't do it, Leonard!"

Chew stood up, walked to the window to look outside. No helicopters. He returned and stood over Wil-

liams. "I asked you before—but tell me the truth now."
He was trembling. "Am I insane?"

"You're obsessed," Williams said. "So what's the difference?"

Chew crouched down and stared into Williams' eyes.
"OK, Williams, I am obsessed. I admit it. But last night
I saw protest rallies around the country, not just aimed
at me, the nuclear terrorist, but at a government that
would let those bastards operate so long, and grow so
big, and never let the public know what was really going
on. To this day they don't know."

Then Chew's voice hardened again. "But I'm going
to break them, Williams. And if it gives me a chance to
meet Gustavus face to face in a lonely room along with
it, so what? I'v done something none of you Justice Department
people could have done. I've stopped a war,
with a few lives instead of millions.

"But I'm going to do more than that, Williams. I
won't quit. The Deep Men destroyed my life from beginning
to end. And I'm staying the course until I see
them *hung.*"

7:15 A.M. Forty-five minutes to go. Williams had
lost. New York was gone. The two men looked at each
other. Williams was remembering a beach near 2872
Central Avenue in Ocean City, looking out to sea, with
a puzzled colonel beside him, talking of Hiroshima.
Weren't all of them, this tortured man before him now,
the people in New York, yes, even the Deep Men, all
helpless prisoners of a weapons race that had begun so
long ago on a squash court with scientists cheering?

And yet the Deep Men were so arrogant they would
steal these terrible nuclear bombs and risk their own
private war.

Whatever happened to New York, the Deep Men
must be stopped before they tried again. Williams stood

up. Chew had walked to the window. He turned to Williams and said, "Sooner or later after the bomb explodes, the boats will come back in the harbor. I'll flag one down and get off here."

"Not until I see the map, Leonard. And I need whatever clue you have to a traitor in the government. I want the Deep Men, too."

At that moment an Army helicopter flew by the face of the Statue of Liberty. It came so close to the observation room that Chew and Williams could see the pilot look down toward the sea.

30

Minus 00:43 minutes. July 4, New York.

Peggy DuPont sat on a desk in the FBI Building on East Sixty-ninth Street. For the last hour they had been listening to the radio chatter of pilots who were searching for the missing Army helicopter, which they believed Chew had hijacked. Because Williams had not called, Fred Jarvis said, he was either dead or held by Chew as a hostage.

Jarvis had three FBI helicopters at his disposal. They had planned to remain in the city until seven in the hope that Chew might change his mind at the last minute and reveal where the nuclear bomb was planted.

But since Williams had disappeared, all agents were staying past the deadline for departure. If Williams were alive and could somehow break free and call for help they wanted to be there. Peggy saw Jarvis fire a match above the old gnarled bowl of a pipe, then suck in the smoke. He had been pacing up and down the office in front of her.

Suddenly the excited voice of an Army helicopter pilot filled the radio. "Wreckage, sir. It looks like a helicopter rotor blade. And a panel. On the beach."

The heavy voice of radio control at Maxwell's headquarters was heard: "Firefly One, this is Academy. Observe radio procedure. What beach? What position? Over." But the pilot was too excited for procedure. "Bedloe's Island, sir. Statue of Liberty." And in minutes the controller was excited himself, ordering a fleet of helicopters into the air to converge on the Statue of Liberty.

Listening to their voices, Peggy DuPont was tense. Wreckage? Chew had crashed in that helicopter—with George? Peggy grabbed Jarvis' arm but didn't have to say anything. Jarvis saw the expression on her face and said, "It could be another helicopter, or they could have gotten out alive and holed up on the island."

He turned to order an FBI pilot to fly to the Statue and report back what was happening. Peggy said that if George was in trouble she wanted to go—but this time Jarvis said absolutely no and turned to confer with his FBI agents. Peggy tugged at his shoulder. "Why not?"

"Because if it *is* Chew there'll be shooting."

On East Sixty-ninth Street the FBI pilot went to his helicopter in the middle of the street. Shoes clacked behind him. Peggy DuPont said she was flying with him. The pilot called Jarvis over the helicopter radio and heard curses before he nodded to Peggy and she climbed aboard. "He said he gives up," the pilot said. The pilot was smiling. He didn't mind having a woman like Peggy along. Even old J. Edgar might have turned straight for her. Then, his eye on the instrument panel, he guided the helicopter straight up between skyscrapers in the swirling treacherous winds of Manhattan.

The FBI helicopter, bobbing in the sky, flew south across the center of the island. Peggy saw destruction below; fire had devastated whole city blocks. Caved-in blackened wreckage pitted Manhattan. But her attention was on the Statue of Liberty far ahead in the harbor. As they flew closer and closer the Statue grew until it became an enormous, green maiden thrusting a torch toward the sky.

And now Peggy saw helicopters hovering above her pointed crown, lowering teams of paratroopers on dangling ropes. Higher in the sky, above the torch, another helicopter attempted to place a soldier near one of the Statue's huge eyes, but the wind swung the man back and forth until he finally found a foothold. Other helicopters orbited the head while helicopter crewmen peered inside the crown. On the island around the great base helicopters landed and spewed out soldiers to begin the climb up the Statue's body toward Leonard Chew.

31

MINUS 00:40 MINUTES. JULY 4, NEW YORK.

As Williams watched Chew he momentarily forgot the terror that awaited them all and was totally absorbed in what the quiet nondescript scientist suddenly became. Chew was now a one-man killing machine. The helicopters disgorging soldiers below were the greatest danger. The soldiers from the ground could come up in force. Chew took some buttons out of his briefcase, went to the stairway curving down into darkness, and dropped the buttons. Explosions thundered; they heard men on the stairway below scream as the whole bottom of the stairway blew away.

For the moment Chew and Williams were now cut off from pursuit from the ground. Chew had breathing space. But the helicopters above were landing men on the crown, and the choppers orbiting the head prepared to launch tear gas rockets. The orders were to take Chew alive.

A helicopter moved in, fired a tear gas rocket toward the crown. It missed the window, hit a point of the crown, and exploded harmlessly outside. "Duck, Williams!" Chew said. He took the odd-looking gun with the shotgun muzzle and dropped a metallic egg into it. Then he broke a window with the butt of the gun just as a second helicopter launched two tear gas rockets in a row. Both hit the points and exploded outside. Chew aimed his gun at the helicopter and fired.

A magnetic grenade shot toward the chopper and stuck on its brown hull. A roaring red explosion erupted in front of the Statue's face. The chopper disintegrated, hurling bodies in great loops into space. One of them struck the face of the Statue and careened down the length of her green gown, leaving a bloody trail.

The remaining helicopters moved away, but Chew must have realized that all his defensive powers and weapons were not enough because he suddenly said over his shoulder, "See the intercom, Williams? On the wall?"

Williams nodded.

"It connects to the ground floor. See if you can contact the soldiers down there."

"Why?"

"I'm going to make a deal."

7:30 A.M. Thirty minutes to go. New York might be saved! Williams spoke into the intercom. A far-off voice answered. Williams said, "Chew wants to make a deal. Contact General Maxwell and tell him."

But even as he said it paratrooper boots smashed a window. A soldier appeared, dangling on a rope from the crown. The rope was tied around his waist. He dropped swiftly in front of the window, planted his feet on the casement. Chew threw away the grenade gun and reached for the pistol he had placed on the floor. The soldier was a heavy man with one muscled arm on the rope and the other pointing a gun at Chew. Chew shot him. The soldier let go of the rope and clutched his throat. His momentum carried him away from the window; he dangled upside-down in front of the Statue's face.

Now Maxwell's orders were radioed to the helicopter pilots: "Cease fire. Chew will make a deal. Await further instructions."

In the battered observation room shattered glass was all over the floor. Chew said to Williams, "Tell them to clear out all helicopters but one."

Williams asked him how he was going to be picked up on the ground when the staircase was blown up. Chew said, "Tell them to lift me from the torch, take me wherever I tell the pilot. No one is to follow. If that's done, I'll radio back the location of the bomb."

Williams spoke into the intercom, and minutes later the fleet of Army helicopters began to lift away into the sky. "Hang up, Williams," Chew said. Williams did and Chew asked him if he was strong enough to climb to the torch.

Williams said yes.

"Good, Williams. It's important."

Williams was surprised once again by Chew. "Why?" he asked.

"I believe you didn't set that trap today," Chew said. "So if anything goes wrong, I want you to have the map in the briefcase."

Williams wondered what he meant by saying "if anything goes wrong," as Chew led him down the curving stairway as far as a gate fifty feet below. This gate prevented the public from climbing the long tortuous ladder up to the torch, high in the sky. Chew opened the gate with a pick and nudged Williams through it. Williams was halfway up the ladder when he understood what Chew behind him might have meant. He said to Chew, "You lied to them, didn't you? You're not going to tell us where the bomb is planted."

"You'll see, Williams."

32

MINUS 00:25 MINUTES. JULY 4, NEW YORK.

From the FBI helicopter orbiting beyond the battle around the Statue of Liberty, Peggy DuPont had alternately winced and cheered. The cheers came when she saw George, through binoculars, alive. The fear came whenever gunfire exploded.

Now, as the soldiers on the torch and crown were lifted into the sky an angry voice from an Army pilot crackled over the FBI pilot's radio. "You in the civilian chopper. Clear out."

The FBI pilot moved his control rod and the helicopter banked; Peggy had one last glimpse of the green statue.

One Army helicopter flew toward the torch. Williams and Chew stepped out on the high windblown platform that surrounded the torch. The island of Manhattan in the distance was laid out like an architect's scale model lined by gray waters. Smoke rose in a haze around most of the skyscrapers. Only a few thrust clear, the twin towers of the World Trade Center, and One Chase Manhattan Plaza, which reflected the sun. A seat was lowered from the helicopter, swinging wildly. Chew caught at it. Holding the seat steady, he turned to Williams and said, "I'm sorry, Williams."

And at that point Williams knew his fears were real. Chew was going to let that nuclear bomb explode. He had lied. Chew slid into the seat, his feet on the ground, and closed the restraining rod around him. The briefcase was in his lap, the gun in his hand pointed at Williams. But Williams couldn't let him go. He would grab that precious briefcase with its map and Chew wouldn't leave without it. He reached into his pocket and withdrew the picture of Chew's son. "Take this with you, Leonard. I won't be needing it." He was planning to go for the briefcase the moment Chew's hand reached forward, but something in the picture stopped him. An insignia on the boy's chest. A picture of a cub. The uniform was the Chicago Cubs. He said to Chew, "Your son's alive, Leonard."

Chew was about to signal the helicopter to lift him. Now he stopped and looked at Williams. *"I told you to get off—"*

"You said he was a Phillies fan. He's wearing a Chicago Cubs uniform. You didn't buy *that* for him, did you?"

The picture was roughly pulled from his hand. Chew held it up to the light to examine it closely and noticed for the first time the small insignia on the uniform shirt.

Then he looked up at Williams, his eyes blank. "My God, Williams. He never owned a Chicago uniform in his life. He wore the Phillies uniform in every game he played."

"Your son survived the explosion, Leonard. And the Deep Men held him in the Middle East as a hostage if you refused to go along with the nuclear theft. They took the picture to show you he was alive and in their hands. If you balked at the job they would have said, 'Sign on or your son will be killed.' But you went along anyway, so they held the picture in reserve, just like the letter said."

Chew unbuckled the restraining rod and lurched out of the seat, which swung wildly behind him. Williams thought for a moment Chew was going to be sick. He stood on unsteady legs, one hand on the wall of the torch, looking out to sea, then turned to Williams. "Oh my God, Williams. He's alive. *Alive!* I've got to see him."

"The Deep Men won't let you live to see him, Leonard. Give *me* your help. Help me track down the clues. If we find Gustavus, we'll have a wedge to get your son back. But don't keep fighting the Deep Men alone. You can't win that way, Leonard."

Leonard looked over the railing of the torch, his eyes wet. "You think there's a chance, Williams?"

"Yes. Just a chance. No more. But together, who knows?"

Chew hesitated, then handed him the briefcase. "It's all in there, Williams. You take over because I . . . just . . . can't . . . do . . . it."

At that moment machine-gun fire erupted. Williams was flung backward, holding the briefcase in front of him. He looked up and saw the "colonel" in the helicopter door above was Kurt Edwards. Edwards! Chew was the quickest man Williams had ever seen: he actually got off two shots at Edwards while throwing himself to the side.

But Chew couldn't avoid the hail of bullets from above that poured into his body.

33

ENRICO FERMI IN A WHITE SUIT, WHITE SHOES, AND white cane walked jauntily down a desert lane. From time to time he twirled the cane and seemed to be singing some sort of tune. But Chew could not distinguish the words. Then, as Fermi came closer, Chew heard them.

> "You are my sunshine,
> My only sunshine.
> You make me happy
> When skies are gray.
> You'll never know, dear,
> How much I love you.
> Please don't take my sunshine away."

Fermi had a red carnation in the lapel of his white suit and below it a badge that read, "Peace." When he finished singing, he was just abreast of Chew and turned to him with a look of recognition. "You," he said—and then his face faded there in the desert, and the desert was gone, and a very strange thing occurred, a crowd of Lebanese college students was singing, "You are my sunshine." They were seated in the grandstand

of a small baseball park run by the U.S. Army. A Little
League game was in progress, and Leonard, Jr., age
ten, was at bat. He could hit. The pitcher hurled the
ball. It was a curve. Chew could see that, and his little
son—what a ballplayer he was going to make!—swung
that bat, and the ball disappeared high and higher and
higher, and never really came down at all. Chew remembered that home run so clearly. If his own father
had only seen it—it was all there, genetics transmitted
through himself into the muscular little body of
Lenny—and Hope was jumping up and down, laughing
and clapping her hands as their boy came around the
bases and touched home plate . . .

   . . . and afterward what a celebration they had.
Dinner in a posh restaurant overlooking the Mediterranean, and the proprietor, with much help from Hope,
producing a cake on which was written:

> "WHO
> NEEDS
> JOHNNY
> BENCH?"

   . . . and really it was so American, and that's what
Chew was, after all, and his children, too, despite the
fact they had spent all their young years in the Middle
East, and Chew knew that day it was really time to go
back home, time to quit the Deep Men; he had paid his
dues over and over again.

   But what was that? Dead people on a pavement. The
little girl on the street a policeman was turning over beside an exploded car, was that his daughter? And, Oh
God, why wouldn't they quit singing that song, he could
endure it no longer, but the singing grew louder and
louder, "Please don't take my sunshine away."

. . . and then, thank God, Hope was with him again, the children were alive beside her—that scene had been a bad dream, and what little Lenny was doing was offering his father a soda. Chew crouched over to sip it; his daughter took the opportunity to hug him, then kiss him on the ear. And if Chew had led a life of death on the edge of nuclear catastrophe, what did it all mean as long as you had a moment like this, with children who loved you and a wife who made your life so sweet?

"What did it all mean? We beat the Nazis, didn't we?" A chorus was shouting the words somewhere, unseen. "We beat the Japs. And now we'll beat the Commies!" A carnival barker was shouting while his family watched in the crowd, "Yes, sir, gentlemen, step right this way and you'll see the eighth, ninth, and tenth wonder of the world. Looks like a firecracker, doesn't it, gentlemen? You know what it is? A smile on a general's face, gentlemen? Did I hear someone say, 'A smile on a general's face?' Well, how did you guess? I thought the metal might fool you . . ."

And then the faces started to dwindle as if they were being sucked back into a huge black void, and Hope was saying, "No, Leonard, no," and Leonard Chew tried to reach out to her and his son and his daughter but they were pulled away, and suddenly it was dark, and he was alone, shivering, trying to wake up. He had to wake up, someone was trying to hurt him . . .

. . . and Leonard Chew died face down on the rusty floor of a torch, above New York harbor.

34

Peggy said, "They're shooting, and George is in there," But the FBI pilot was already on his way. The Army helicopter flew away as they approached.

Suspended in space over the torch they saw a body sprawled on the platform. George was on his knees, holding the side of the torch. He did something strange when he saw them; he reached for a gun on the floor. But then he saw Peggy and waved them in, urgently.

35

Williams. held the briefcase as he was lifted into the FBI helicopter. The briefcase had saved his life. Peggy was hugging him, but Williams was busy finding out what had stopped those bullets. He pulled out a thick diary. The map in a plastic casing was inside the diary, but that was not what caught his attention, nor the bullet holes in the book. It was a date on the first entry. His fingers trembled as they ripped through the pages of Chew's diary until he reached an entry: "July 3. Planted nuclear device in Waldorf, Room 1703. In memory of honeymoon. Inside fireplace."

Williams grabbed the mike and said, "Jarvis. Room 1703. Waldorf Hotel. Inside fireplace. Cut the timer!"

And then thought of a fireball at Egg Harbor and a man hacking at a wire.

36

MINUS 00:08 MINUTES. JULY 4, NEW YORK.

A helicopter took off from East Sixty-ninth Street with Jarvis and two FBI men. If only Williams had got to them sooner! Eight minutes was not time enough to fly to the Waldorf, land the helicopter, ascend to the seventeenth floor, then find the nuclear bomb and disarm it. One of the men said to Jarvis, "We'll never get close."

Jarvis agreed, but he couldn't tell them that. He was sending them to certain death, along with himself. He was no hero, never had been. And yet, somehow, in some way there might still be a chance to stop the monumental horror from happening.

The chopper sped directly down Park Avenue, low, and it was 7:54 A.M. when they landed. The three men boiled out of the helicopter and rushed through revolving doors and up the great carpeted staircase to the lobby—and it was 7:55, and they were still seventeen floors away. But getting closer. An elevator beckoned with open doors. They piled inside, pressed the 17 button, and it lifted swiftly, up, up, up.

7:57 and three men running down a hallway and the door was locked. Jarvis fumbled with keys he had brought. He dropped them on the carpet. Goddamn it, he said. 7:58 and still outside. He picked up the keys, slid one into the lock and the door opened and there was the fireplace across the room—the bomb was inside, where? Jarvis was the first one to reach it, he thrust his arm up inside and felt around. A ledge. What was that? The bomb!

7:58:30. He pulled a smooth football-sized bomb onto the carpet, and there was a tiny timer attached to it, a sophisticated, almost elegant cylinder, and someone handed him a knife, and he started cutting the wire. But it wouldn't give. What kind of wire was this? The bastard had used some sort of reinforced cord shielded by brass. It couldn't be cut. "Jesus Christ, hurry!" one of the men shouted. The timer was moving. Jarvis sawed and sawed. Nothing. The wire wouldn't give. Too late. They had lost. One of the agents panicked. "Christ! It's going!" He shoved Jarvis aside, picked up the nuclear bomb with two hands, and hurled it through the glass window above Park Avenue. All three of them threw themselves face down on the carpet, for no reason that made sense in the cauldron of a fireball that would rise a mile wide.

The bomb glinted in the sun as it fell toward Park Avenue. The helicopter pilot waiting on the street had been talking to himself. Why was he staying here to die? What was the reason? How much money could the FBI pay a man— A metal object smashed on the pavement in front of him, bounced, then rolled to the steps. He jumped. What was that? For Christ's sake it looked like—it was—the fucking bomb! He started to run, but what was he doing? How far could he go before he was killed? He stopped, heart beating wildly, and turned to look at the bomb. It wasn't shattered. Why wasn't it exploding?

He ran to the bomb and found it dented, but otherwise in perfect condition except for a timer whose face was smashed, and whose bent hands stood permanently and irrevocably at 7:59.

37

RELIEF AND JOY ESCALATED INTO CELEBRATIONS along the whole East Coast. New Yorkers cheered in tent cities where medical units had been waiting for patients, and helicopters and jeeps with rescue teams had prepared to go into a destroyed city. The city stood whole. There was no great pit in the ground where the proud Waldorf-Astoria stood; no mountain of broken steel and stone where Rockefeller Center glittered untouched; no rubble-strewn path where Fifth Avenue promenaded among fashionable stores. The city had survived; the danger was over.

Within minutes the bridges came alive with cars. The tunnels, except for the damaged Lincoln tube, filled with traffic, and trains roared in Pennsylvania and Grand Central stations with people whose relief was so great that many of them just sat in silence, while others paraded up and down aisles, talking and laughing, as the tension of the last two days drained from them.

The "21" Club reopened at twelve; P. J. Clarke's was already jammed by one; Maxwell's Plum and Daly's Dandelion and Charley O's and Michael's Pub welcomed crowds whose celebrations would last all day.

And only in small snatches of conversation could one hear the name Deep Men, and the anger that had been building against Washington politicians and the conspiracy was already being forgotten as iced martinis were poured and people contemplated their own lives, which would now go on as if nothing had happened.

"Chew was right when he said people would forget about the Deep Men if his bomb didn't explode in New York," Williams remarked to Peggy as they emerged from a doctor's office in Manhattan where Williams had been x-rayed. The physical examination showed that Williams was fine, except for his earlier injuries, which were healing. Now on Fifth Avenue, among people smiling on the streets, Williams said, "But he was wrong if he thought I would forget."

They took a taxi to the FBI Building, in which Peggy had waited so nervously just hours ago. Now they saw that the FBI, maligned in the past, suspected in the present, was receiving a spontaneous accolade. People stood on the street in front of the agency's offices, holding a small enthusiastic rally. Williams' role was as yet unknown, but his photograph had been in the newspapers and on television, and he was recognized and cheered when he and Peggy emerged from a taxi in front of the building.

General Maxwell was waiting for them with an Army colonel. Williams knew that Maxwell had conducted a furious investigation of the shooting incident on the torch. Maxwell had found that Edwards and another Deep Man had presented themselves at the Palisades as a reserve crew "from Andrews" and in the confusion at the field had been assigned one of the extra helicopters. Now Maxwell shook Williams' hand. "I'm sorry, George. It was my fault." He indicated the colonel. "I sent Colonel Martin to pick up Chew, and I should have made sure it *was* Martin who did it."

The colonel said, "It wasn't the General's fault, Mr.

Williams. I got my orders from him and started right over to the Statue. But out of nowhere this other chopper appears above the torch, and he's dangling a seat down to you, so I figured communications got messed up. While I was checking headquarters, they started shooting."

But at least, the General told Williams, Edwards had paid the price. Maxwell had immediately sent "every helicopter that could fly" after the two Deep Men, and when they landed in a field in New Jersey and attempted to make their escape on foot, they had been killed in the exchange of fire with the Army. "So at least we got the bastards," General Maxwell said.

Williams said, "We needed Edwards alive so he could talk."

But the General responded, "You're dealing with strange people, George. We found that both of them had cyanide pills in their pockets."

And at that point Fred Jarvis entered the office, looking happy. "We found the third bomb, gentlemen." He walked to a desk and half sat on it, looking pleased. "If this keeps up, people are going to start liking the FBI again. They'll call us G-Men like they used to and start collecting bubble-gum cards with our exploits."

Maxwell smiled at Jarvis. "Where did you find it?"

"Staten Island. Chew's briefcase had the rental agreements of all the safe houses he used. We sent agents to every one, and in a wooden two-story house in the middle of a crowded block on the island, we found the bomb in the attic." He smiled. "It's over."

With nothing accomplished, Williams thought. No traitor exposed. No conspiracy destroyed. But he remained silent. Jarvis was pouring champagne taken from an illegal wholesaler, saying, "We have recovery missions whenever we need more supplies," and why dampen the joy of the moment? A city was intact. Lives had been saved. That was something to celebrate. Williams sipped the champagne, too, wondering if Gustavus was enjoying the same wine in Washington, while he toasted the President.

BOOK V

Gustavus
Lives

1

WILLIAMS STUDIED THE CODE ON THE BACK OF THE Arnold map. Leonard Chew had thought he could prove who Gustavus was by that code. The letter the FBI had found in Gustavus' effects in Towson, Maryland, said that this code contained special instructions to the custodian of the map on how to handle this priceless map. But Chew also said he was unable to break the code, using Arnold's code book.

A bullet hole had punctured the upper right-hand corner of the map, but the number in the middle was intact. It read:

94869353746473818303227324521

Chew had attempted to decipher the code, breaking it down into three-digit numbers. Immediately there was a problem because there were two digits left over, so the code didn't fit a three-digit pattern. Nevertheless, Chew had begun, and the first words must have thrilled him. They were translatable.

TO CUSTODIAN CONFIRM RECEIPT

But then the message became gibberish: AGRICULTURE DEFENDANT NIGHT ROCK ORANGE YES ORGANIC FORWARD COSMIC SUNDAY 2 1.

Williams told Peggy he was going to take the message to the National Security Agency. But Peggy said she had something more important for him to decode. Williams asked what, and Peggy said, "My feelings for you."

"If you fly to Washington with me, we'll spend some time on that decoding, too," he said.

Late at night in Williams' bed, a kiss here, caress there. Peggy said, "How can we make love? Every place I touch, you hurt."

"Just don't be your usual blundering self," Williams said, echoing a remark she had once made to him. Peggy laughed, and made some magic below, and then eased herself delicately upon him. She leaned above his body, barely touching his bandaged chest, her hair swirling over his face. And he looked into blue eyes and felt no pain at all, only an emotion that built into ecstasy that was almost unbearable, flesh upon flesh, until Peggy tensed and then cried out, sharply, and Williams could hold back no longer.

Afterward Peggy kissed him deeply, then rolled over, holding his hand, and smiled. Her only comment on the tender performance was, "You're sick, and *I* got the injection," and then she leaned on one elbow, looking at him and saying, "I'm never going to get married."

"Why not?"

"I can't stop making jokes at the worst possible times. Men can never stand it."

"I like it," Williams said. "Without jokes you're just another DuPont."

"What's that mean? How many DuPonts have you met?"

"One is enough for a lifetime."

Peggy smiled. "You're sweet, George. I mean you're not as stiff as you were—I mean, you're not as tense. Oh hell, forget it. You're still close to . . . great."

"Do you want to marry me?"

"Why do you ask?"

"To see whether you'd laugh."

Peggy said, "Will you go to Saint-Tropez with me and Gstaad and Sun Valley and—"

"No."

"I could break a leg skiing, George. I could catch pneumonia running around naked on the beach at Saint-Tropez." She kissed him on the cheek and smiled. "Maybe you're saving my life by this proposal."

"It wasn't a proposal, it was a question."

"What's the difference?"

"I would have *meant* a proposal—"

Peggy laughed. "Then I'll answer your question. Yes and no." She paused. "But I'd like to move in with you for an interrogation in depth."

"We can still take the vow," Williams said, "until depth do us part," and Peggy couldn't have been more surprised. She clapped her palm to her forehead. "My God, I've ruined him."

And so they laughed and made love again, gently, and Williams slept, and the next morning went to the National Security Agency to try to unearth a traitor in the memory of Leonard Chew.

But how was he to fathom a code that must have a second code overlaid upon it? Williams took the map and the copy of *Blackstone's Commentaries* to a shirt-sleeved man in NSA, who looked at the code and said, "You told me Arnold's code is a three-digit system. This can't be based on that code because it has extra digits."

Williams said that, nevertheless, the custodian's copy of Arnold's code book, *Blackstone's Commentaries,* had been found in the safe of a house belonging to the Deep Men, and he was certain this code was based on that book. "The first four words can be translated from it."

"OK. But you better leave," the NSA man said.

"Why?"

"Because if you're right, this is the toughest code to crack. There's a random number inside the message that throws off the progression. I'll have to isolate that random number, and that's a complex process."

Williams didn't know what he was talking about, but he said, "Do it fast."

The NSA expert nodded. Williams descended to the cafeteria, escorted by a blue uniformed security guard, a big tag on Williams' lapel that read: VISITOR. BLUE AREAS ONLY. He sipped a cup of coffee at a table lined with employees eating off trays, before going back to the gray computers, electronic listening devices, satellite receivers, and microwave interceptors of this most secret agency in the U.S.A., which would someday make CIA obsolute. Then he went back to the cryptanalyst, accompanied by the guard who had waited by the door. A visitor in NSA was as rare and welcome as a typhus germ.

The cryptanalyst was looking at lines of gibberish. "Tell you what, Mr. Williams. Take a seat over there. I'll break this code if it's possible, don't you worry."

Williams sat in a brown leather chair and read a copy of *Air Force Digest* retrieved from a nearby desk. Naughton Aircraft had a full-page ad for its F-20. The fighter-interceptor-bomber a Middle East country couldn't do without. A bargain at $2 million per plane. Lighter, more firepower, more maneuverable than its competitors. *"And can pack nuclear air-to-ground missiles, too."* Williams heard the analyst say, "I have it, Mr. Williams!"

Williams read:

TO CUSTODIAN CONFIRM RECEIPT 18303227324521
FILE IN SAFE UNTIL FURTHER INSTRUCTIONS.

Williams said, "Can you decode the number?"

"No, Mr. Williams, because the number is in the
clear. It's not in code." The analyst stared at it, accus-
ingly. "It could be a file number," he said.

Williams thanked him, went to his office at the Justice Department, and checked the other messages that
had been found in the safe and decoded so easily by
Angry John. No numbers in those messages. No help.
He studied the number in the message, trying to draw
out its secret. It couldn't be a file number. It was too
long. But what did it mean?

He placed the map back into his briefcase, more depressed than he had ever been. Gustavus' secret was
hidden forever, locked into a string of digits that no one
could decipher. And Chew was dead, and everything
that had begun in Minot with a man leaving a map fragment at a missile base where empty silo doors stood
open—Williams stopped. Those open doors. That sergeant who had provided the keys. Williams had an idea.

2

THE OVAL OFFICE LATE THAT EVENING. A PRESIDENT
in blue jeans with the muted sound of Brahms from
somewhere down the corridor. The President apologized
for the late meeting. "The details involved in repairing
the damage caused by the tidal wave are incredible. We
won't be back to normal for months." Williams told the
President that he believed, as Chew did, that Gustavus

was most likely a member of the National Security Council.

"Why the NSC?" asked the President.

"Because every move I've made has been known to the Deep Men before I made it. So it's one of the few people at the top who have been in on the decisions." The President nodded, and Williams said, "If that's true, I might have an idea how to expose Gustavus."

The President sat up straight. "You do? How?"

"This time I'm not telling anyone in the White House, Mr. President, because Gustavus could find out. But I need your help. I have to get all four of the NSC members in an airport or a railroad station, preferably an airport."

"An airport?" The President was puzzled. "Well, let me think. I'm going to Brussels next week to open the preliminary negotiations on SALT III. I moved up the date just to show the people as quickly as possible that the SALT talks are going on despite the Deep Men. The President is running the country, not some right-wing conspirators." He paused, then said, "I was planning to take only the Secretary of State and his staff. But I could tell the other members of the National Security Council that I want them to come along to show the Russians that the entire Council is behind this."

Williams stood up. "Do that, Mr. President. And tell them also that Fred Jarvis and I are flying with you for extra security in case the Deep Men make some attempt to sabotage the talks in Brussels. I'll need Peggy DuPont along, too. She can help me on the flight."

The President was more mystified than ever. "Help on the *flight*? How will she do that?"

"I remembered something about a sergeant," Williams said.

A Deep Man crouched in front of a fireplace in a Chevy Chase home stuffing documents into crackling flames. The Deep Man was an aide to Gustavus. Gustavus had sent him to this great white stone mansion in Maryland to destroy certain papers.

The papers seemed harmless enough to the staffer; but Gustavus, as always, was being extra cautious even though the crisis was over. The Deep Men already knew that Williams couldn't break the code on the back of the Arnold map. Gustavus was safe. He was in business. Things were about to happen.

The Deep Man took a bronze poker and stirred the black curling ashes to powder, then went to the den in Gustavus' home to use the phone. Gustavus had good news for him. "You're accompanying me to Brussels in *Air Force One*. The President's going to launch the SALT talks with a speech over there."

The Deep Man said, "And we do nothing to stop him?"

Gustavus said, "Our people in Brussels have something in mind."

3

JULY 20, ANDREWS AIR FORCE BASE. A DRUM AND bugle corps formed on the field in front of *Air Force One*. In the lobby of the air terminal Fred Jarvis said to Williams, "Even if your idea works, it will give us just a clue. Not proof." Jarvis, Williams, and Peggy were standing in the midst of military men, civilian government chiefs, and newsmen. Peggy suddenly brightened. "Oh, there's Bob!"

Williams and Jarvis turned and saw that she was referring to General Robert Maxwell, who was approaching with his aides. Jarvis said to Peggy, "Bob? When did you two get so chummy?"

Peggy smiled. "While you and George were chasing Chew in New York, the General and I spent a lot of time together. I think he's kind of cute."

"You call him Bob?"

"Not to his face. I don't want to see him drop dead of a heart attack."

Maxwell smiled as he stopped to say hello to Peggy, and Jarvis was amused by his shy expression as Peggy kissed him on the cheek. Maxwell said to Williams, "If we put Peggy into a room with Gromyko for an hour, we'd have the SALT agreement."

"My body in exchange for five hundred less missiles? Not enough," Peggy said. But Maxwell's mind was on another subject. He said to Williams, "You think we'll have any trouble on the trip?"

Williams said that people who would explode nuclear bombs would think nothing of sending a plane into the sea.

"Comforting," Maxwell said. Jarvis looked over Maxwell's shoulder, then whispered into Peggy's ear. "Here comes the target." Peggy quickly excused herself and went toward Winthrop, the CIA Director, who had just entered the terminal. Jarvis followed at some distance and then groaned when he saw Peggy trip and sprawl headlong on the floor. "Beautiful!" the FBI man said to himself. "Give her a job and she falls on her face." A startled Winthrop was helping Peggy up, and by this time Jarvis was close enough to hear Peggy's ladylike reaction to the subject: "Shit!" Winthrop winced, and Jarvis turned away. Peggy had blown it. Williams and he would have to do it themselves, some way.

The P.A. system announced that the takeoff would be delayed thirty minutes because of "maintenance problems." Jarvis knew this announcement was made at Williams' suggestion. He and Williams circulated through the airport, then all passengers on this maximum-security flight were led through a control area where the security men patted them up and down, looking for weapons. Only guards and Secret Service men were allowed onto *Air Force One* with weapons.

They sat aboard watching the last passenger, the President, walk toward *Air Force One* as the drum and bugle corps played a modest fanfare. On the gangway he turned and waved to the people in the terminal, who clapped.

Air Force One reached the end of the runway, turned, and began roaring along the airstrip. By the time it lifted from the ground Williams was examining a clue. He believed he knew who Gustavus was. He was on this aircraft right now.

4

ABOARD *Air Force One,* EN ROUTE TO BRUSSELS.

"When do you tell the President about Gustavus?" Jarvis asked Williams. Jarvis, Williams, and Peggy were in the President's spacious compartment in the front of the aircraft, separated from him by only a few seats, so Jarvis was talking in a soft voice. The President was

chatting with an aide and seemed absorbed in the conversation.

Directly behind them was a compartment filled with
Secret Service men, and behind that another compart-
ment for the President's press secretary and other aides.
The rest of the huge aircraft had been partitioned into
three areas, one each for the Secretaries of State and
Defense and General Maxwell, with their staffs.

Williams had drawn the Arnold map from his briefcase. In answer to Jarvis' question he said, "I'll tell him
just before we land at Brussels. That will give me five
more hours to try to break this code." Jarvis was exas-
perated. "Will you never give *up?* If NSA couldn't solve
it, you can't."

But Williams said, "As you said before, we need
proof, not just a clue that he can explain away. You and
I believe the clue is proof—but will a jury?" He looked
down at the map. "I still believe the real proof is right
in this number. And I'm not quitting until I find it."

Peggy placed her hand on Williams' arm and said to
Jarvis, "Let George have his way, Fred. He was right
about the airport, wasn't he? We found what he said we
would."

"That kind of detective work made sense," Jarvis
said. "But this is a code. It's for little people with shiny
bald heads and thick lenses who spend years decipher-
ing one page of numbers."

The speaker above them came alive with the captain's droning voice. "This is your captain speaking.
We're at thirty thousand feet. Weather clear. No turbu-
lence expected. Estimated time of arrival in Brussels
seventeen thirty."

Jarvis said, "Seventeen thirty, not five thirty. You
can tell it's a government pilot."

Something triggered in Williams' head. He looked at

the unbreakable number in the code that was on the back of the Arnold map. The first four digits were 1830. He read the words in front of the number, TO CUSTODIAN CONFIRM RECEIPT, then touched Jarvis' elbow. "It could be a *time*, Fred."

"What?"

"TO CUSTODIAN CONFIRM RECEIPT. Maybe this code number is telling the custodian what *time* to confirm receipt. 1830. Everyone in the government uses 1830 in messages instead of 6:30—and Gustavus was in the government, according to Chew."

Jarvis became interested. "Let's pretend you're right. But then what?" He snapped his fingers. "If he gives a time he might give the day. Right?"

The next numbers in the code were 3227324521. Peggy looked over Williams' shoulder. She said, "322 could be 3/22. March 22. Are we on to something?"

"Possibly," Williams said, but the next digits baffled him. If they were right about a time and date, *how* would the custodian confirm receipt at 1830 on March 22. A note? A message? A telephone call?

A telephone call. Williams looked at the last remaining digits again. 7324521. 732 was a Washington telephone exchange. Could the message mean CONFIRM RECEIPT at 1830, 3/22, at 732 4521? Williams went forward and spoke to the President. "Are we too far from land to call a Washington telephone number, Mr. President?"

"Never too far under satellites," the President said. "What have you got, George?"

"A possible decode that may mean nothing. It involves a phone number." He explained to the President how they had arrived at the decode. "But if we trace the number and it belongs to a certain member of your Security Council, it's the proof we need."

The President started. "A *certain* member? You
mean you have a clue to Gustavus? You got what you
wanted at the airport?" Williams said he believed they
did, and the President was so excited he was trembling.
He said, "What do we do, George? I want him arrested
right away."

"We can't do it right now, Mr. President, because the
clue isn't enough proof. But what we will do is get the
NSC members to come up to this compartment right
now. I want them here while we trace that telephone
number in the code."

Gustavus felt his shoulder touched by an Air Force
steward. The President wanted to see him and the other
NSC members in his forward compartment. What did
that mean? Gustavus had been edgy all during that wait
in the airport, had watched as Williams and Jarvis circulated around the airport talking to the NSC members.
Something was wrong, or Williams wouldn't even be on
this flight.

Gustavus hated Williams. A softheaded liberal who
shouldn't even be in the government of this great country. He walked forward into the large Presidential compartment along with the other NSC members. Gustavus
saw Williams with headphones standing by an open
door in the front of the compartment. Beyond him a
military radio/telephone operator sat before a gray
metal phalanx of transmitters. What was Williams doing? Gustavus heard the Justice Department man ask for
a certain telephone number in Washington and almost
tensed, then controlled himself. The telephone was illegal, cut into the electronic lines without the telephone
company's knowledge. The Deep Man technician who
had installed it had told Gustavus that it was absolutely
untraceable.

And even if the technician was wrong, even if they did somehow trace the phone and uncover his identity, Gustavus had a final weapon in reserve.

The President saw perspiration on the forehead of the Secretary of State. The CIA Director, General Maxwell, and the Secretary of Defense looked calm enough. He asked them to take seats, pointed to three armed Secret Service men and apologized. "I'm sorry for this, gentlemen, but it's necessary. We think we have the answer to the code." He explained the possible breakthrough on the telephone number. Winthrop, the CIA Director, nodded and sat down, adjusting his dazzling white shirt cuffs. Secretary of Defense Flanders took the seat next to him, casually crossing one tweed-clad leg over the other. Only Maxwell sat erect, angry. He said to the President, "Am *I* a suspect, too?"

The President said, "Everyone in the NSC, General. You may all be innocent, but you must—"

A telephone operator's voice from Washington crackled across the loudspeakers. Williams had turned up the sound. "We've traced that illegal telephone, Mr. Williams. It's in a private residence rented by"—Williams turned up the speaker even more—"a general."

Silence. General Maxwell seemed almost unable to comprehend the words he had heard. He stood straight up, looking horrified. "Is this a trick?" he said in an icy voice. Williams asked the operator, "What is the general's name?" The operator's voice, tinny and crackling, said, "General Robert M. Maxwell, sir."

"That's a lie!" Maxwell shouted.

"Computer age, General," Williams said to him. "They called the telephone number, left the line open, and the computer traced the location in minutes. That number is in the code." He took off the headphones.

"Talk to the operator yourself, General. I didn't know it was your number."

Maxwell stared at him. The telephone number was right. Williams knew who he was. He *knew!* Suddenly he reached into his chest pocket. Flanders saw what he was doing and shouted "NO!" Too late. Flanders grabbed his arm. The arm broke free, and General Maxwell swallowed a small white pill. "You bastard," he said to Williams.

He began to turn pale. The cyanide pill worked in seconds. Everyone in the compartment looked in shock at the man who had been a poised and powerful general minutes ago.

Three "military" aides of Maxwell broke through the door with guns drawn. But the Secret Service men were ready. They grappled with the Deep Men as other Secret Service agents poured into the compartment to help subdue them. But the President saw none of this. He couldn't keep his eyes off General Maxwell as death began to contort his features. Maxwell said his last words, "You'll never find out about the Deep Men from me, Williams. And my people will . . . revenge me." Then he sagged, his face changing color, and it was over, the President knew. The code of the Deep Men extended into death, from a sergeant in Minot to a four-star general in Washington. You couldn't defeat these fanatics, the President thought. Even Williams had failed in the end. Williams looked somewhat pale himself as he said, "It was sugar, General."

Maxwell's hands gripped the sides of the seats along the aisle. His head was lowered as he stared at the floor, waiting for the agony to come. He had shown that bastard Williams. What was Williams saying? "It was sugar, General. Not cyanide. We switched the pill. You're going to live."

And now Maxwell's brown eyes lifted as he stared at Williams with contempt turning to horror, seeing again this man he should have broken long ago—

—and, oh God, the Justice Department man was right. No pain. No dizziness. No blackness. The God-damned pill *was* sugar. They *had* him. Alive. He'd have to talk. They'd *make* him.

5

THE CHAIRMAN OF THE JOINT CHIEFS OF STAFF WAS handcuffed in the Secret Service compartment, along with his "military" aides. The President sat beside Williams, still in shock. "Maxwell. My God, of all my aides, Maxwell. I can't believe it. He worked so hard for me."

But Williams was remembering a military helicopter over the Statue of Liberty; Leonard Chew dying, face on the floor. And then the news that Edwards, who might talk, had been killed. He said, "Maxwell was the logical one. He was in on everything."

The President said, "How did you know that cyanide pill was sugar?"

Williams said, "Peggy found which pocket it was in when she kissed Maxwell in the airport. She did the same to Winthrop later when he picked her up off the floor. Then when the passengers went through control at the airport and were searched for weapons, we had specially trained FBI men do the frisking. And they made the switch." He stopped. "We found both Winthrop and Maxwell carried pills, but only Winthrop was in a secret agency. So why was an Army general carrying a cyanide pill? I believed the pill meant Maxwell must be Gustavus, but it wasn't proof that would stand up in court. Maxwell could say he always carried pills on sensitive missions because of all the classified knowledge he had, and who was to tell the Army commander he was lying?"

The President considered, then said, "So if you hadn't broken the code and traced the telephone number—"

Williams said, "We *didn't* trace the number. The Washington operator told me it would take *days* to trace it. So I told her what to say over the loudspeaker after I turned up the sound."

The President turned to stare at Williams. He said, "You mean Maxwell *wasn't caught?* He didn't have to take that pill?"

Williams shrugged. "He wouldn't have *taken* the pill if he didn't know the number was right." He placed the Arnold map neatly into his briefcase, remembering a sunlit windy day in Minot, a fragment of a map glittering in the grass with a code that could be the key. They would break the Deep Men now. Williams was sure of it. In the end Chew had won. An Air Force steward tapped his shoulder. "General Maxwell wants to see you, sir."

Williams glanced at the President, who nodded. Williams went back to the Secret Service compartment where General Maxwell sat with hands cuffed. "I did what I thought was right, George." His face was flushed. The price of living as a known traitor was the one price a traitor couldn't bear, Williams thought. Maxwell would remember what had happened to Arnold in exile.

Williams said, "The people elected the *President* to run the country, not you, General."

The General said, "I want my men removed from this compartment so I can talk to you alone." Williams gave the orders and the aides were led back into the next compartment. Maxwell said, "I just want dignity, George. If it's to be death, I want a military firing squad. Give me that honor, and I'll tell you what you want to know about the Deep Men."

There was a silence before Williams said, softly, "If you cooperate, it will be done. But there's a procedure. You have to be tried in open court." He looked into Maxwell's bloodshot eyes. "It's the American way, General."

Dell Bestsellers

At your local bookstore or use this handy coupon for ordering: